VIRTUOSO

Also by Aseem Kumar Giri

Imposters at the Gate: A Novel about Private Equity
A Permanent Exile

VIRTUOSO

Aseem Kumar Giri
Tusk Publishing Inc.

Publisher's Note

You will notice on the front inside flap of the cover a BIN™. This is the work's *Book Identification Number*. Please use it to register on our website www.tuskpublishing.com to receive additional benefits and services. We hope you enjoy this work.

To Gerda and Manfred Ziemer.
My beloved "Mutter" and "Vater".

Part I: 1949 – 1953

CHAPTER I

Manfred Ziemer woke up with the intensity of a cannonball exploding out of its barrel. He found it was always that way the day of a concert of the Berlin Philharmonic. As he got up from the three cushions that served as his makeshift bed, he already had a song going through his mind. It was one of his favorite songs, a *Lied* by Schubert. The semester prior he had passed one of his singing classes at the Berlin Conservatory using that song. Within minutes he realized he was actually singing aloud. He worried that he would wake up his two roommates; one of them, Torsten Meltzer, also a singer, slept on the other side of a bed sheet that hung from the ceiling.

He stepped outside his unit and walked down the creaking staircase to retrieve the newspaper from the front of the building, adjusting his stride by habit for the third and sixth steps that were missing from the first flight of stairs. The buildings on either side of his had not survived the bombings of the past few years. The top floors of the missing townhomes were replaced with open sky, and the bottom floors were piles of concrete, wood and glass.

Picking up the *Berliner Morgenpost*, he noted the date: May 31, 1949. He read the article about this evening's concert. The reporter had asked Sergei Celibidache—Celi to his friends—the principal conductor of the Berlin Philharmonic, "Beethoven's Ninth Symphony is usually reserved for celebratory occasions—in the aftermath of the war, what are you celebrating this evening here in Berlin?" Manfred marveled at Celi's taut response. "Music."

Light from a cracked window radiated the staircase. As it bounced off the dust particles in the air it made the yellowish glow almost palpable. As if brightness, somehow, could be touched and held. Manfred thought of pocketing it or bottling it for the future.

He sighed with relief before he began singing the chorus again as he realized it would be many months before the cold air would necessitate a replacement of that window.   As he entered the apartment, he saw that Torsten was now awake.   His roommate greedily swiped the newspaper from his hands.

"Oh, thank you," said Manfred.   "I didn't know what I was going to do with it now. I read the whole thing on the way up the stairs."

Torsten was too engrossed in reading the article about Celi that Manfred had already scanned to react to his friend's banter. "It's incredible," said Torsten.

"Oh I know," declared Manfred. "There is such controversy, not to mention risk, for Celi in performing this piece."

"Ever since he announced he would play Beethoven, all of our visitors have cast a wary eye on musicians," said Torsten.

"Yeah, visitors," said Manfred shaking his head remorsefully. He made a mental note that his roommate was not speaking in rhyme, which he had a tendency to do. Manfred took this as a sign of duress. "Berlin does not belong to Berliners," Manfred added. He lamented how the Allied forces from America, Britain, France and the Soviet Union were in control of the city.   "We don't question the importance of their presence," commented Manfred, "but, with the Allies in the midst of their de-Nazification of Germany, any activity considered pro-German stands the chance of being perceived as sympathetic to the Nazis."   Manfred was especially concerned because Celi was not just performing Beethoven, but specifically, the Orchestra would play Beethoven's Ninth Symphony. This had caused even greater alarm. It had yet to be played after the surrender. For that matter, Celi had heretofore steered clear of performing German composers. He, like much of the rest of the country, had become suddenly shy of doing anything or saying anything that might be perceived as pro-German.   Not only would Celi have the talent of Beethoven on display, but the last movement of the Ninth Symphony was a choral movement set to the words of a poem by a celebrated German scholar, Friedrich Schiller. Nationalism of any kind was considered taboo.

"Celi had been considered a prudent choice when he had taken the helm just three years earlier," remarked Torsten.

"I wonder if the Orchestra know questions whether that was wise or not," mused Manfred aloud. As Manfred went to the bathroom to get dressed he saw that his cellist roommate, Juergen Mueller, had fallen asleep on the floor with his cello underneath his arm. He usually didn't do that. Manfred picked up his roommate's arm, pulled out the cello and placed it back in its case. He noticed there was a scratch on it, likely from the impact of the floor. Manfred took the end of his shirt and tried to rub it out. He was pleased that he was able to make most of it disappear. As he draped a sheet over his roommate to give him some warmth, Manfred noticed the bow on the floor, by his friend's head. He picked the bow up and before he placed it in the case, he rubbed some rosin on it for him.

Manfred had heard rumors that Celi had changed the program, succumbing to pressure. Manfred certainly hoped that he would not. He wanted to hear the voice of young Thomas Stoltz sing the baritone role. It was rare for a student of Manfred's meager means to be able to attend a concert of the Berlin Philharmonic. He had saved for weeks. Manfred had heard that there would be a master class taught by Stoltz at the Conservatory. Manfred could only get in after passing an interview. He wanted to see one of Stoltz's concerts and be able to comment on it during his interview to help increase his chances of getting into the class.

As Manfred got dressed, he observed the war wound on his leg where a small portion of his upper thigh was missing, no bigger than the size of a sausage. He wished he had a mirror large enough so that he could see how the wound appeared to others. He recalled how in those days of war, all he wanted to do was sing. He was thrilled that now, finally, he could spend his days training and perfecting his voice.

● ● ●

Later that evening, on her way to the concert, Gerda Majowski muttered to herself, "Where would I be without music?" It was almost a whisper. Her audience consisted of herself, a broken sidewalk and a line of trees. *We all need something to rely on to get us through our hardships,* she reasoned. She recalled how as a child, she would enjoy talking to trees, pretending that they were all her friends. She held her sweater close to her body. It was a chilly night in Berlin. Spring had brought its blooming flowers, and Easter had already passed. Nonetheless, there was a crispness to the air uncharacteristic of this time of year. Did she shiver because of the cold air or because of the troubled thoughts on her mind? She didn't resolve the issue as she continued her brisk walk. Her brother was on her mind. Heinrich Majowski's safety was a paramount concern.

The colors from this spring's flowers seemed to lack their vibrancy compared to years past. There was a perpetual gray hue about the city that was unrelenting in its recurring daily presence. She kept her arms folded across her chest as she moved down the street, and although it wasn't windy and there were only a few other passers-by, she clutched the letter from her father in her fist tightly. With her free hand, she discovered another hole in her sweater, just under her armpit. *How many beautiful jackets I once had.* They would have come in handy now. The velvet ones had been her favorite. They had beautiful embroidery on them and were from the finest clothiers of London and Paris. They were a distant memory now. She had only one evening gown; she somehow managed to find material to be able to sew it. It would have been appropriate to wear for such a concert, but she felt as if she had already used it numerous times. As she walked she had a knee-jerk reaction to check her ears and her neck to be sure that she was wearing jewelry. She felt the earrings and the necklace. She realized she had her reaction because they were so much lighter than they had been in the past, making her feel as if she were not wearing anything at all. How inappropriate it would have been for a lady, thought Gerda, to

4

leave the house without jewelry. The pieces she had with her this evening were borrowed from someone who became a friend during the war, or more accurately, as a result of it. She felt warmth inside as she reflected on how music had brought her together with Herman Zschacher and his sister, Adelle. Both were still in East Berlin; Gerda was glad that Heinrich had gotten her out.

She slowed the pace of her walk, stopping intermittently, so that she could read the letter from her father again, taking comfort from it during the brief moments it took her to glide through each line. She found that the sensation was short-lived—a low-dose medication that would lose its effect after a while, compelling her to read it again to get her next fix.

> *My Dearest Gerda,*
>
> *Amongst the devastation, there was one unfaltering, unwavering, unyielding narrative of human experience that had withstood the calamity of war. Music. The miracle of bringing discrete sounds together in artistic order, harmony and rhythm; the chaos and cacophony giving birth to a marvel of sensation that stirs the soul. The desire to convey emotions, incidents and the phenomena of life to other beings that propels the creative faculties producing music would not succumb to the ammunition, to the bombings, to the deaths.*
>
> *Music had defiantly lived on, tangible proof that the human spirit, as torn and tattered as the city, could survive in this suddenly barren place. Music is our wellspring of hope. It is proof that perfection exists. In these years of war and war's aftermath, it can be held in one's mind and one's heart, and be relied upon even when the physical world, and its people, betray you. It feeds the belief that, once again, there can be a better time, a better place, a better world.*

"When will I get there?" Gerda asked aloud.

She suddenly looked around to see if anyone else was within earshot. Again, it was just her, the tattered sidewalk and the near darkness. The line of trees had been left behind and were no longer listening. Trees used to line all streets of Berlin, and sidewalks had once been smooth. As she surveyed her surroundings, she blinked repeatedly, trying to fight back the tears. She didn't want her brother to see her crying, again. She made her way to the municipal hall in the Zehlendorf district of Berlin. The paper that her father had written on was severely weathered. It had been folded and creased in a number of places. There were accidental pen marks, fingerprint smudges and even a coffee stain. The paper was soft to the touch. She had no idea how much longer it would last. *I've only had this for a month*, she bemoaned to herself. She had already transcribed it in her journal, under a heading "Father's Manifesto". She could have crossed out the word 'Father' and written 'Gerda' she thought. There was comfort in this paper, however. It was like the scent of cigars; it made her feel like he was there, whispering the contents of the letter in her ear.

She passed by the Dahlem church and the American consulate. There were long lines of people waiting to enter both buildings. Gerda had to look away from both scenes quickly. The collective sadness of the people in the lines was too heavy a weight on her. She didn't want her strength to be compromised. The Dahlem church had been spared in the war, although buildings around it had been razed to the ground. *Perhaps all hope had not been obliterated*, Gerda thought. The American consulate looked as if it were in makeshift quarters. The scaffolding revealed that soon a proper building would house it.

When she thought of hope, she thought of her brother. She was looking forward to seeing Heinrich perform. He was a cellist with the Berlin Philharmonic. She had yet to miss one of his concerts in Berlin.

It had been four years since the Allied forces had taken over the city. Berlin lay in ruins. Gerda felt that she was walking through a graveyard. Most forms of fine artistic human expression had taken their leave of the city. Novelists, painters, sculptors, and poets had either been killed or had escaped. Cafes, art galleries, and architectural splendor had been replaced by rubble. The Berlin Blockade, which had only just been lifted, starved the city of basic necessities—clothes, toiletries, food.

Music found its most brilliant expression with the one group that had been determined to keep it alive in Berlin. Gerda was overwhelmed with gratitude for them. She re-opened her father's letter.

They were the self-anointed guardians of the musical tradition that was not only a hallmark of the city of Berlin but of the entire country of Germany.

This, after all, was the land that had given so much to music, thought Gerda, for its glory and its development. This was the land of Beethoven, Brahms, Bach, Wagner, Liszt... the names went on.

For the Berlin Philharmonic music was the sacred holy grail; they were the defenders of the faith, the soldiers standing guard at the eternal flame, martyrs preserving its sanctity.

Gerda read on, then closed her eyes for a few seconds. *Thank God the orchestra was there,* she said to herself. She marveled at how the Berlin Philharmonic had continued to play through World War II and through the surrender of Germany. Her brother had reminded her a few days earlier that the world had not yet decided whether the Orchestra was right in continuing its performances during the Nazi era or if the Orchestra's members had been too sympathetic with the Nazi cause.

But those issues did not deter the Orchestra this evening; tonight the curtain would go up once again. Nor did it deter Gerda. She found such assaults on the Orchestra's character offensive.

"These are utterly obnoxious," she said aloud once again, in response to her thoughts, and only afterward did she look around her. Fear remained an afterthought for Gerda. There was so much she had to become used to. Heinrich would be playing his cello tonight, and she was determined to be at the concert.

"Let them question me, I don't care." She declared her stance to her brother when he suggested she might be safer staying at home. Heinrich had just joined the Orchestra and was not a member during the war. Gerda matched Heinrich's concern for her with her concern for him. Gerda was extremely worried about how Heinrich would be judged because of his affiliation. "You are not a sympathizer. Don't let them think of you as one of them."

She also had other concerns, more personal. It seemed as if the Soviet officer that had been chasing after Heinrich, Colonel Andrei Kasparov, needed only the smallest provocation to begin anew his relentless efforts to pursue Heinrich's demise. Kasparov was a faceless nemesis to Gerda; she had never seen him. She had only heard about, and experienced, his dark deeds. She was convinced he was the catalyst for destroying her marriage.

Try as she did during her walk, relying on her father's letter as her crutch, Gerda could not seem to steal away any moments of peace. She worried for her brother so much. It had only been a few weeks since he had rescued her from a harmful marriage and potential persecution herself. The idea that he himself might be in harm's way was deeply troubling for her.

She considered the debate regarding Celi's choice of performance for that evening. Normally, Gerda would have been more idealistic and insisted that the Orchestra not compromise its artistic integrity. But the matter concerned her brother. She saw the world differently when it came to him. "Playing Beethoven's Ninth could be viewed as over-the-top, in-your-face bravado," Gerda had insisted to Heinrich. "Can we afford that? Can you afford that, Heinrich?" There was a flinch in her heart as she said it. Hearing Beethoven's Ninth was an important family tradition for the

Majowskis. Without fail they would listen to it every New Year's, right after the stroke of midnight. It would mean a lot to her to hear it, but not if it compromised her brother's safety, she concluded.

As she kept re-reading her father's letter, Gerda was forced to acknowledge to herself that there was more than concern for her brother that weighed on her mind. In fact, her brother was the one who highlighted this the last time they spoke. Worry for her brother was a cover. It was easier to articulate, because she could just act; she didn't have to cope. She hated thinking about herself so much, but it was becoming hard for her to contain her emotion, her apprehension, her fear. She had survived the war, but how was she going to re-build her life? Would she find love again? The manner in which she, they, her family was raised was now a distant memory. That manner gave her life meaning, context, purpose—could she regain it? The music that permeated every aspect of their lives—could she resurrect that? How would she do it? Gerda's head began to spin. She felt dizzy and nauseated. She closed the letter and clenched it in her fist again. She tried to think of other matters. It was easier to worry about her brother.

● ● ●

Manfred thought he would feel good to be in Berlin again, the city of his birth. He had dreamed of the city during all the months and years of his absence for the war. When he came back the city wasn't recognizable. He knew he was in Berlin, but this was not the Berlin of his memories. Too many buildings had been lost, too many landmarks had been destroyed. He had to re-draw the mental map he had of the city. He was downtrodden. Around every corner he would seek something from his memory and be dismayed when it wasn't there in actuality. He felt as if the Berlin of his past and his dreams would forever be lost, relegated only to his memory, as if it were a fantasyland he had created in his own mind.

He passed by a house where a man was at the piano and a woman was singing a *Lied* that he recognized. It brought a smile to his face. "Ah yes," he mumbled to himself, "now I know I am in

9

Berlin."

It prompted him to continue singing the song as he walked away from the window and the man and woman could no longer be heard. Theirs was the only house to remain standing on the block. *How fortunate that they also still have their piano to sing their songs.* It was a typical Berliner *Lied*, with the unique Berliner dialect and idiomatic expressions of the city. *This is all I have,* Manfred thought to himself. These songs would never be played in any other part of Germany, unless a Berliner was singing them. Walking past that window reminded him of what his mother would do many an evening, teaching him the songs of Berlin. He loved each individual *Lied* and the collective whole of the *Lieder*—the vast pantheon of German songs. He recalled how while he was away serving in the military for the war, a member of his unit who had been wounded at the same time as Manfred, Gunther Steiger, would sing with him the *Lieder* of home and they would collectively fondly remember being back in Berlin.

As he made his way to the concert hall, Manfred recalled the last time he saw the Berlin Philharmonic play, several years earlier, under the direction of Wilhelm Furtwangler. Furtwangler, the prior Principal Conductor, was no longer there because of the politics of war. He had feared for his life and fled to Switzerland in January 1945. The Orchestra was not deterred, however. They had an intuitive understanding of their calling, and they heeded that call. Leo Borchard was elected by the members to take over the Berlin Philharmonic.

Manfred checked his jacket pocket to be sure he had his ticket. Juergen and Torsten had expressed a desire to go, but were not able to save enough money. Manfred had discussed with his roommates how Borchard had been considered to lead the Orchestra prior to Furtwangler's arrival, over a decade ago. Manfred supposed that because Borchard was Russian-born he had not been considered a safe choice in the mid- to late 1930s as perceived as unreliable politically as a foreigner. *That had all changed, however.* By

VIRTUOSO

January 1945, the tide of war had turned decisively against Germany. *Thankfully, the Orchestra had been clairvoyant.* By that time, the Soviets were closing in on the region and the city of Berlin. *Isn't it interesting that what had been considered an unsafe choice years ago in Borchard was now perceived as a wise choice, the best choice?* Of course, Manfred knew that this was not the driving force behind the decision; it was just convenient. In keeping with the spirit of the need for music to sustain and nurture the frail human condition, the members of the Berlin Philharmonic knew that in electing Borchard they also had a man who would uphold their ideals. *At least that is the interpretation that I like best.*

Manfred remembered Borchard conducting the Berlin Philharmonic in April 1945 when they had played their last concert prior to the surrender of the city to the Soviet Allied forces the very next month. He had read how the Orchestra voted to have a concert at the end of that May, a few weeks after the surrender. Surprisingly, there had been no loss to the Orchestra's membership. Nobody ran. Nobody escaped. *Noble musicians*, Manfred thought.

In every other part of Germany, or German-occupied territory, when the Soviets came, the Germans ran. That's what Manfred had done. Other Allies had not been so severe, but the Soviets were merciless. They raped the women and imprisoned the men. They were not liberators like the Americans, the British, or the French. They were conquerors. They came to exploit the spoils of war. To occupy, to command, to own. *Borchard knew that.*

Manfred knew that with that in mind Borchard paid homage to his Russian heritage and chose Tchaikovsky's Fourth Symphony for that first concert post-surrender. In addition to its being a politically correct choice, it was significant in another regard as Tchaikovsky had been a long-term admirer of the Berlin Philharmonic, impressed that they were government-supported and able to pursue their craft for the expression and the beauty of the art form, rather than as a means to earn money for a profiteering owner. *I think I like that interpretation better. That's the one I will hold on to.*

Borchard's leadership ended unexpectedly that August when he was accidentally killed by an American soldier. The members of the Berlin Philharmonic astonished the music world when they chose the young, relatively unknown, Celibidache fresh from finishing his studies. Manfred sensed the Orchestra must have felt he was a secure choice in that he was not German-born so there was little risk that he would be forced to flee or that an interrogation by the de-Nazification campaign of the Allies would not go in his favor and abruptly end his tenure. Also, Celibidache had studied enough in Berlin to have understood and lived the musical tradition of the city and the country.

● ● ●

Kasparov surveyed the concert hall and went through the plan once more in his mind. It would be less than an hour before the audience would fill the venue. The space seemed odd compared to the grandeur that he had anticipated for an orchestra of the caliber of the Berlin Philharmonic. He recalled with regret, how his comrades had destroyed the predecessor arena, which did, in its palatial wonder, befit the majesty of the quality of music that this orchestra performed. He remembered that as a child in St. Petersburg, his father had commended in passing the brilliance of the orchestra. He recalled the words he heard as a boy, "Even Tchaikovsky celebrates their ability!"

He had enlisted the help of four of his best men. They were also his most loyal. He intentionally wanted to keep the number small; the fewer who knew about his scheme the better. He reviewed where he had decided to locate them, before, during and after the performance. The stage was raised and the audience sat in front of it, subsequent rows declining in elevation as you moved closer to the front. It reminded him of a military concert hall. He looked up, expecting to see a larger chandelier or ornate designs. He saw only black. He had to admit to himself that the meager surrounding emboldened him and chased away whatever trepidation he had felt, as a result of the orchestra's stellar reputation.

"I will indicate the person by bumping into her. Watch for that," he had instructed his men earlier. "Other than that, mingle and fit in."

He hoped his insubordinates wouldn't ruin the preparations this time. He had carefully laid out the plan. They had to be sure to conceal the rope and the tape before the performance began. Without their overcoats it might be a challenge. Wearing them, however, would make them stand out too much. It was too hot to be wearing thick overcoats. Nonetheless, he didn't want any questions asked. Once it was dark, there wouldn't be a problem. He shifted his coat as he pondered this with his one remaining arm, on his left side.

● ● ●

Gerda knew that Celibidache had the support of the members of the Berlin Philharmonic in terms of his choice for program that evening. She had heard from Heinrich that they had practiced a few variations on the program and were prepared for whatever the final decision may be. They were true artists and hated that their choice of music would be determined by political pressure. They had a keen sense of the risks too. Gerda was not shy about sharing her concerns with Heinrich. She could tell also, that Heinrich had some concern of his own. Gerda had been agitated by all of this talk. She did not want her brother to be perceived as a supporter of the Nazi cause. Once anyone knew and understood the story of the Majowskis, however, no one would ever have accused Heinrich or Gerda of being adherents.

"I don't think it is wise to take this risk at this time. With the Soviets, Americans, and British watching our every move, is Berlin ready for this? No. It is not. This will be misunderstood as too pro-German," Gerda roared.

Heinrich responded, "It is true that the Russian composers would be a safer bet."

"Borchard understood that." Gerda's tone had lowered a few

notches and she carried the strain of an exasperated plea in her voice.

"Celi is taking a bit of a risk," Heinrich acknowledged.

Life without music was not fathomable for Heinrich and Gerda. They grew up in a musical household. Music nurtured their souls the way food provided sustenance for their bodies. Sylvester Majowski, referred to by his children as Father, was insistent on that. Heinrich had held a cello in his hands since the age of four. It wasn't even a proper cello—he was too small. Sylvester had gotten him a viola, which Heinrich played as a cello. Many years later, when he went for his audition for the Berlin Philharmonic, Gerda could see how nervous he was. He looked like he was trying his best to hold it in, but when Gerda demanded, "Hey what's the matter?" he knew he had been found out, and he immediately lost his lunch. After he was done with his audition he came to Gerda, who dutifully waited outside of the hall for him, asked for a cigarette and passed out. When Gerda finally revived him, he proclaimed, "I made it, I made it!" Nobody was more elated, nor did a better job of expressing her joy, than Gerda.

Heinrich first worked under Celi. "He rehearses with no shirt on!" he exclaimed to Gerda. "It is a blessing during these emotionally trying times to have a conductor like Celi who is so engrossed in moving the audiences' spirits."

Gerda approached the concert hall. Several Soviet soldiers milled about. *I didn't think they were so fond of music.* She immediately thought of Kasparov. *I wish I knew what he looked like.* As Gerda entered, there was a musty smell that hit her like a wall as she came through the doors.

One soldier, tall and slender, with short hair that was mostly a sea of black with sea-foam of gray, stood just past the doorway. As she tried to sidestep him, he moved the same way, and she bumped into him.

"Pardon me," she said. She gave him a careful smile; she didn't want to seem in any way inviting, but it wouldn't be wise to be impolite, either.

He scowled at her, not saying a word. The expression made his face, riddled with landmines, look sinister. He had so much scarring, all the size of pinpoints, that his cheeks almost appeared porous. They drew attention away from his large, bulbous nose.

Embarrased by her clumsiness and afraid that he might think she was staring at his scars, she looked down and continued into the auditorium. Still he said nothing, but she thought she could feel the weight of his stare on her back. That figures, she thought. *They are all so heartless.*

She made her way to her seat with its red cloth cover worn through in the center to the white cushion underneath. It was a far cry from the velvet-covered box seats of the past. *Poor Heinrich, having to perform in such a drab hall.*

Though Gerda wanted to concentrate on the upcoming performance, she was still strangely unsettled by the encounter with the Soviet soldier. She had grown accustomed to men looking at her over the years. Before the war, she would even solicit those looks, confident and empowered that they were admiring her. She had specifically used her eyes in the past to, well, play with men, she admitted to herself. But, in these times, with these Soviets, she had trained herself not to do anything that could be construed as flirting. *I have had to deal with too many such stares from Soviet soldiers lately.* It typically meant bad news. And this one... this one's stare had been odd. It was a bit eerie, the way he had seemed to focus on her eyes. His had been cold, narrow, grey. They had a melancholy intensity to them, but then they became as thin as slits as he stood there, taking on a menacing overtone.

When she looked back again, she saw him shaking hands with another Soviet officer. It wouldn't have normally struck her as odd, but he was using his left hand and didn't appear to have use of his right hand. It sent a chill down her spine; she knew Kasparov had only one arm. She strained to look closer to see if it was true that he didn't have his arm. Unfortunately, the lights dimmed for the performance to begin. She sat down nervously.

● ● ●

As the attendees entered the concert hall, Kasparov spotted his target. She looked a lot plainer than he had remembered. She was thinner, her face more gaunt. It made her five-foot-two inch frame look even more slight. There was no mistaking it was her, though. He would always remember her large blue eyes. Like Faberge eggs, they had an alluring splendor to them. He eyed his men to be sure that they saw that he was in motion.

He walked towards Heinrich's sister and intentionally collided with her. When she turned around to face him, he tried hard to contain any sense of satisfaction or gratification. She had groomed herself well this evening. Kasparov had to admit to himself, she was beautiful. Look at all of those heads that she was turning. She seemed so innocent. *Her beauty is almost an affront,* Kasparov thought. *How dare she make herself up so well— does she not know the pain I am suffering? She has no concept or idea of what my plan is.* The notion excited Kasparov, but he didn't allow any of that emotion to be displayed on his face. He touched the scar on his right cheek as he thought about this. It started mid-cheek and traversed his jaw line. The man who did that to him, even though it was an accident, had his arm broken by Kasparov as retaliation.

Kasparov looked forward to the expression on Heinrich's face would be at the instant it happened. Heinrich would be powerless to help her. *There are much easier ways to achieve the same objective,* he thought to himself. But none would be as devastating to Heinrich as doing it here, at this time, in this way.

"We won't move until the applause at the end of the performance starts," he had told his insubordinates.

● ● ●

Manfred took note of the Soviet soldiers standing about as he went to his seat. His heart beat faster as he saw them and then he realized that this was just a reaction to having had to run from them for so long. Manfred sat down and tried to think about the concert in order to calm himself. Celi was a Buddhism enthusiast, he

16

reflected, and because of his religious readings, Celi was very focused on crafting a spiritual experience of music during his live performances. He maneuvered his way through each work in a manner that would optimize the audience's experience of the music in a live format. Manfred had even heard that he would shun the practice of releasing recordings of his material, insisting that a live performance was the only way to experience the magnificence of music. *A true practitioner of the art form.*

As the curtain opened, the audience sat motionless, each individual straining to hear the initial sound, awaiting the first notes to see what the maestro had chosen to do. As the music began, some gasped and others, including Manfred, smiled knowingly. Celi had chosen Beethoven.

Manfred watched in wonder as Celi worked the tempo to adjust to his interpretation. He quickened the pace of the sprightly first movement. Manfred experienced vertigo as Celi maneuvered through it. *Wow*, Manfred thought to himself, *like being in a train going at three times the speed—you really feel every bump on the track, each rocking back and forth of the railcar—you have to hold on tightly.* The bold second movement was done with such gusto that the beating of the timpani drums reverberated like a pacemaker for Manfred, setting the palpitations of his heart rhythmically with a fierce and emphatic pounding. The slow third movement Celi elongated intentionally and purposefully. As Manfred sat there, he felt that a single draw of the bow across a violin or cello sent a deliberate shiver through his spine—and seemingly through all other spines seated around him, each note trembling in resonance with the emotions emanating from his heart. Or perhaps the emotions were being hand-plucked from within him, and with tightly held hands being cajoled out of his body. Celi quickened the pace of the fourth movement, the voices during the choral portion coursing through Manfred's body with a thunderous boom that caused his arms and legs to quiver involuntarily. Manfred had heard that Celi had instructed the singers, "When you sing '*Alle Menschen Werden*

Bruder'—all men will be brothers—I want you to sing with such force that you are lifted off the stage!"

A magician, thought Manfred. Or perhaps he was a tour director—*what other worlds are you going to open for me?*

As his circumnavigating hands spawned imaginary orbits in the air, evoking the image of two birds flying gracefully—music, and not air, supporting their wings—to bring the last seconds of the final movement to a close, Manfred knew that Celi had mastered this performance. Manfred had been moved. The way the audience sat, in earnest, leaning forward, not a single cough, sniffle or clearing of the throat could be heard, Manfred could tell that Celi had moved the audience as well. When the final note was played, Celi awaited. Manfred caught the expression on Celi's face. It was a side-profile, but Manfred still detected an expression of restrained glee—water waiting to crash through the floodgates or a child waiting for a locked door to open at a candy store. Manfred could tell that Celi was expecting deafening applause.

Celi threw down his baton emphatically as the last note was played. Manfred knew it was to create added effect. Seconds passed. Manfred watched as the expression on Celibidache's face fell to a panic. Instead of the applause he had anticipated, he was met with silence. Oh no, thought Manfred, had Celi made a grave error? Did people feel that this was too extravagant a display of German nationalism? Were people that afraid of the Allies? Manfred felt a combination of puzzlement, bewilderment and, and, in a nod to his idealism, disgust. *I can't believe it,* he thought to himself. Manfred wondered if he should start the applause. *No, no,* he chuckled to himself, he couldn't do that. He would wait to see what others did.

CHAPTER II

Manfred watched as Celi stood motionless. He continued to look down. Manfred wondered about the different degrees of death Celi might encounter in the aftermath; was it merely career death or would he be hanged for being a Nazi sympathizer? Manfred was so lost in his thoughts, he didn't register the muffled sounds coming from the people seated around him. Manfred was distracted by the sound of a door opening and closing, and then movement on the stage caught his eye, bringing his focus back. As had happened when Beethoven debuted his ninth symphony, the baritone soloist came over to Celibidache and turned the conductor around. Beethoven, who had lost his hearing, had been greeted with thunderous applause. Celibidache faced an audience in tears. Manfred looked around him. He now saw what Celi had been turned around to see. Not a single word was uttered; there was just the sound of controlled emotion emancipated. It was just the tears. This was followed by the sobbing and the deep intake of breaths, interspliced with involuntarily convulsions of the body, sighs and the sound of people rummaging for a napkin, tissue or handkerchief. *This is amazing*, Manfred thought, *a concert hall packed with the elite of a city and a world-class orchestra arrayed before us, but it is the pent-up emotions that have taken center-stage.* Every member of the audience wept.

Manfred became swept up in the collective release of emotion that began with every individual man and woman in the audience and gained force with each passing moment. All were united in their communal sorrow. Manfred knew why they cried. They cried for the lives that had been lost, the friendships and the family that would be there no more. The caliber of the artistry they had just witnessed was a painful reminder of their longing. Manfred had the same desire as the rest of them. All desired to return to what they had before the war began. A longing to have things as they were—when a performance of Beethoven was a celebration of music and not a perceived risk to one's life. The sense of loss was immense and far too much to express in words alone. It took music to break below the façade and masters like Celi and the Berlin Philharmonic to liberate years of constrained emotion.

Manfred thought about his desire from earlier in the day to approach Thomas. That seemed trivial, he now thought. Beyond that, the notion was inconsequential; he realized that he couldn't make himself get up. He first assumed it was the war wound to his leg, and then he realized that he couldn't hold back his feelings any longer. His heart had become too heavy. His emotions had overwhelmed his body and all he wanted to do was to weep.

What was that tenor's name again? Did the concert start on time, or was it delayed? Who sat around him? Manfred knew that he would never remember these details going forward. It would just be what he was feeling at that moment.

● ● ●

Gerda looked at her brother, and both cried together. Both knew that they remembered their mother and their cousin Helmut Majowski. There were also the parents of Bastian Abramowitz, the man whose surviving family had saved their lives, and countless other names. The list was too long to mention individually, thought Gerda as she tried to recall each of their names, but their faces were all freshly imprinted in her mind. Family and close friends were all that Gerda had and could rely on. Music was the bond that held them all together. That was a Majowski family convention. Gerda and Heinrich had the best intuitive understanding of this of all six of the Majowski children. Her relationship with her brother was very special—although three years younger than Gerda, he had taken great care to look out for her. She could turn to him for support at any point and she had made a pact to be there for her brother as much as she could.

● ● ●

Kasparov's men looked at each other and then at Kasparov.

VIRTUOSO

Kasparov didn't signal anything. They no longer had the cover of applause. They stood awaiting his command.

Kasparov couldn't keep his eyes dry. His mind was racing with thoughts, images and sounds. He knew he had an objective to fulfill, but he couldn't break the barrage going through his mind. The music had paralyzed him. He thought about his smashed violin. He thought about his father, the man who had gone through so much to get it for him. He thought about how much his father had to fight with his mother because he'd bought the violin. He thought about how that violin had caused his father's death. He would never forego the vendetta against the man and the family that ruined that violin for him. He touched the stub that was left of his right arm. He thought it would give him strength to proceed with the plans. He couldn't move. He felt like he had been standing in the rain, his face was so streaked with tears. He couldn't even look at his men. How could he face them like this? He quietly exited from a side entrance.

● ● ●

Manfred saw someone bring Celi a chair. He sat and joined in with the others in alleviating his grief. Manfred watched his expression in between his own tears. *He's still the conductor*, Manfred thought, *I shall see how he guides us*. Minutes passed. There was no end to the sorrow.

"Friends," Celi began. "Let us reflect on the music we have heard tonight and the Orchestra that presented it to you. As you know, the words of the choral portion are based on a poem by Schiller. Beethoven modified it to bring it into the realm of music. The first words implore people, *'Not these tones'*. The people are singing. We can appreciate Beethoven's message: *'All men will become brothers'* through music."

The crowd was transfixed on Celi, hypnotized by his words. Manfred listened in earnest.

"As we witnessed here tonight, it can happen and we should strive to make it happen. Let us end misery and allow healing to begin."

Celi, who was now standing, went to the four choral soloists. They all embraced. He turned to the crowd.

"Let us also not forget the lesson of this Orchestra. I beseech you, make your lives from this point as rich and eventful as your lives until this point have been. Do not succumb to the devastation, the loss, the emptiness. The one gift of life which will allow you to suffer through the low points and triumphantly relish the high points will always be music. Like it was for this Orchestra, music shall be the force, the energy, the passion that should propel you forward. You all, like the Berlin Philharmonic through the war, must never stop performing."

● ● ●

Gerda smiled to herself. "Just like Father," she said aloud. She didn't care who heard her.

CHAPTER III

"Hurry up in there, Ziemer!" shouted Torsten, Manfred's roommate.

This woke Manfred from his singing bliss under the shower. It was a bit of a habit for him, entering another world as he got lost in the words, intonations and delivery of his singing.

Torsten banged on the door again. "You are using up all of the hot water!" he shouted.

Manfred hated being disturbed, but he hated imposing on his roommates even more. He wondered how long he had been in the shower. When he pulled back the curtain, the bathroom was full of steam. No image was visible in the small oval mirror dangling on metal wire over the sink. The tips of his fingers and toes were white and had developed ridges on them—a telltale sign that he had been in the water too long.

"Sorry, Torsten!" shouted Manfred. He was suddenly overcome with guilt that Torsten and Juergen might have to take cold showers on account of him. He hated the idea. *I wish I didn't get so absentminded most of the time. Well, maybe it is only some of the time.* He corrected his thinking, giving himself some credit.

It was the fall of 1949 and Manfred was beginning another semester at the Conservatory. He had dreamed of attending the Conservatory as a young boy. His mother, who pursued her passion to sing but was limited to doing so as a hobby, had encouraged Manfred to pursue singing as a profession. He was thrilled to learn that the Conservatory was still operating after he had returned to Berlin. Through the US Marshall Plan, Manfred was able to receive funds for his studies. It reinforced his fondness for the US which started from stories he would hear from his aunt and uncle who were residing there.

Not a day would go by when Manfred would not think back to the Celi performance of Beethoven's Ninth. The fact that he was present at the musical event that defined that period made him a hero amongst his friends. They all envied him. He managed to get in to Thomas Stolz's master class. Manfred was so enthralled with his singing instruction not only in that class, but overall at the Conservatory. He relished every day that he had the opportunity to develop his voice. He studied the works of Schiller and Goethe and memorized the *Lieder*. He focused mostly on Schubert's *Lieder*. They were his favorites.

"There are six hundred of them to learn," Manfred joyfully told Torsten and Juergen. He had the exuberance of a toddler stumbling upon a chest full of toys. It then dawned on Manfred. "I don't think I'll ever be able to memorize all of them."

Berlin seemed to be piecing back together, Manfred observed, as he walked to class. Albeit, slowly and painstakingly, he added. First, the roads opened, then the major deposits of rubble were pushed to the side. In time, stores would re-open. It had seemed to take forever, noted Manfred, before the stores had their shelves stocked with goods. Manfred noticed the number of soldiers that were always around—much like during the war, but with different flags on their uniforms. Most often, he saw the American flag on the soldiers' uniforms.

Manfred remembered when he had to be in a uniform himself. It covered his five foot eight inch frame well, but he felt he always looked out of place in it. His eyes were too soft. They betrayed that his spirit was that of an artist and not a military man. His manner was very slight and gentle. Beggars and con men would single him out of a crowd as their target. Not because he looked naïve, he knew, but because he looked like he had a good heart.

He had dark brown hair that had miniscule curls in them. He combed it back, the curliness of his hair hugging the contour of his head from the top of his hairline to the base of his neck. He was always impeccably dressed. His favorite phrase was, "that's how it is", delivered with a movement of hands, that were they his shoulders would be called a shrug, and a slight pursing of the lips and a gentle nod of the head.

Manfred's greatest trait was that he loved being an ambassador of all things he found wonderful. He was a concierge for experience; he leapt out of his seat to share with others the experiences that had stirred something in him. Manfred's was a life of sharing—with the skill of an expert tour guide, Manfred wanted all to relish and enjoy what had moved or impacted him.

Early on in the semester, Manfred had arrived home very excited. He found both of his roommates at home. "Did you hear the one about the Viennese fellow who approached his friend that is digging a hole to build a duck pond?"

"No," Juergen and Torsten said in unison.

"He asked his friend what he was going to do with the pile of dirt he had pulled out," Manfred continued. "His friend said I dig another hole and put it in there."

Torsten and Juergen both walked away.

Manfred's roommates had also been forced to be away from Berlin for several years. Torsten had been trained as a clarinet player since his childhood, but a war injury to his wrist prevented him from continuing. Luckily for him, he had some talent as a singer. This natural ability, coupled with Manfred's encouragement and support, aided him significantly in developing as a leading singer. Torsten also had the quirky habit of conceiving impromptu lyrics in normal conversation. Manfred harassed his roommate Juergen about his seemingly compulsive cello playing; without washing up he would wake up and begin to play.

Manfred's days were full of lectures, personalized singing instruction, and hours upon hours of his own practicing and rehearsing. Sometimes he would join with other students and they would practice together. They all pursued their passion with fervor as there was hope in their hearts that the musical tradition of Germany would be maintained and that there would be opportunities for each of them to pursue their passions. They held true to this even though they had been receiving reports that some of the recent graduates had ended up in factories, in government jobs or even as waiters.

As a student at the Conservatory, Manfred was automatically granted season passes to the concerts staged at the school either by students or outside professionals. He and his two roommates reserved seats next to each other for the entire season where they watched every performance together. All of them dreamed of being the performers on the stage. At the end of a show, they would sometimes close their eyes and imagine that the audience was cheering and applauding for their own displays of musical talent.

Manfred particularly liked the monthly Friday evening performances by non-student artists. They would always choose engaging material. That evening he was looking forward to hearing some arias performed from the works of Wagner, including *Tristan und Isolde.*

It had been Gunther's birthday the night before. Gunther had been Manfred's war-time singing mate. While Manfred joined Torsten, Juergen and Heidi, Gunther's wife, for dinner, he had to excuse himself early because of an exam he had to complete Friday morning. By the time Friday evening had come around Manfred thought to himself, *Now it is my turn, I am looking forward to this concert to relax a bit and have a good time with my friends to make up for last night.* Torsten and Juergen, however, had enjoyed a long evening of drinking revelry the night before. They had stumbled in drunk after Manfred had finished his exam.

"Nice of you both to remember to come home," Manfred quipped.

Both clambered to their beds without even responding to Manfred.

Manfred shook his head as he picked up both of their coats from the floor. It was less of an admonishment and more an expression of regret that he had missed out on the fun.

Later that evening, Manfred approached Torsten and Juergen about joining him at the concert.

VIRTUOSO

"Manfred, it is with great dread,
But I must inform you thus,
We can't leave our beds,
Obliging you to go without us!" Torsten sang.

"Your penchant for talking in song amazes me," Manfred said, trying to avoid, for the time being, dealing with the disappointment that he was feeling. "Your capacity for alcohol, on the other hand, disturbs me." He attempted to scold them, but it was to no avail. "That's how it is," he concluded, throwing his hands in the air. It was a wonder thought Manfred, that Torsten had developed a jovial outlook on life, despite his tragedies.

Manfred walked to the concert hall and took his usual seat in the auditorium; he typically sat in the middle between Torsten and Juergen. The lights in the concert hall dimmed, the curtain was lifted and the music began. After two to three minutes, Manfred noticed someone approach from the corner of his eye. He could tell from the silhouette that it was a woman. She seemed petite, slender and shapely. She was able to glide through the row with minimum disruption to those seated. She was bent down so he could not get a good look at her face. She seemed to have sharp features, a pointed nose and high cheekbones. But it was her eyes that he caught a quick glimpse of that made him hold his breath. He couldn't tell the color but they were large and portrayed exuberance. He wondered what seat she was moving towards as the row, other than the two season ticket holders that belonged to Torsten and Juergen, was full. To his astonishment, and he had to admit to himself, to his excitement, she sat down next to him. He knew that seat could not have been hers; it belonged to Juergen.

At first Manfred had a feeling of injustice. He thought it was wrong. He even thought of telling the ushers. He then began to feel sympathetic and wondered that there must be some reason compelling her to take that seat. He decided not to say anything. He focused on the concert and attempted to enjoy that. He thought about what arias they might perform. Manfred was a baritone, and he always hoped that the performances he attended would display baritone singing. The only baritone voice in *Tristan und Isolde* was that of Kurwenal, Tristan's servant. Manfred was hopeful that they would perform an aria that included the servant.

At the intermission, Manfred stood to get up and the young lady sitting next to him did the same. In getting up, her purse fell to the ground from her lap. Manfred, reached down to pick it up. He called out to her, "Excuse me, you have…"

At that moment she turned around and looked at him. This was the first view that Manfred could see of her with the light. He was first awestruck by the sparkle in her blue eyes. He marveled at how those glistening wonders could be seen in the dark; it was a testament to the intensity of their glow. Her eyes had the spark of incandescent flames at the tips of long candles. Or perhaps her pupils were tiny candles, delicately resting atop leaf petals floating on the vast ocean of the blue color of her eyes. He noticed her long, curly, dirty blond hair that was perfectly set—not a strand out of place. He noted how immaculately she had groomed herself. The evening gown she was wearing was very elegant. It was maroon in color, had no sleeves and flowed freely about her ankles. It was almost as if she was dressed for a grander occasion but somehow had ended up here. Manfred let his thoughts wander about some fancy ball or gala that was currently missing her presence. The design of her dress, or maybe it was her shoes, enhanced her petite frame making her appear taller than she was. Manfred could tell, standing next to her, that she only reached his chin. Her lipstick and make-up were done with such precision and care that she looked like she had just stepped off of a movie set. Her hands and nails looked like they had been sculpted by an artist. She carried herself with all of the grace and composure of a Hollywood actress.

"…dropped your purse…" Manfred's voice trailed off as he finished his sentence. He felt a little dumbstruck.

"Oh, thank you so much," came the response, teeming with an effervescent fervor. When she smiled she betrayed her dimples.

VIRTUOSO

They were like shooting arrows that ensnared Manfred's heart as they had done to many a man before him, he was sure of it. Manfred chuckled in response to her comment. The bubbliness with which she responded sent an instant rush of warmth through him. He couldn't help but smile.

She responded to his smile with a smile back and a light chuckle of her own that she protracted for a few seconds. "I'm Gerda," she offered and extended out her hand.

"M-M-Manfred," he responded, his voice trailing off and barely audible. He held her hand close to his mouth, he had not kissed it yet, and stood still, lost in thought.

"I will see you after the break?" Gerda asked, cocking one eyebrow upward—her eyes asking the question as much as her words were—as she lifted the corners of her mouth in a broad smile.

Manfred didn't have a chance to answer. For the first time, he was a singer who could not find his voice. He gave her another smile. She pulled her hand away gently, turned and walked away.

At first he thought she was glamorous. And then he realized that glamorous could inadvertently suggest that she lacked substance. No, he decided, glamorous was a misnomer. Any beautician could take an empty canvas and make it glamorous. In a word, she exuded elegance. What she had came from within.

Once Gerda left, Manfred collected himself and walked out as well. He was searching the crowd for her. He saw her close to the bar. She was drinking a glass of champagne. She started talking with a group of people. It didn't seem as if she had come to the performance with them. And if she had, she would not have been sitting next to him, he realized. Some people just had that ability, thought Manfred, they could be the center of attention comfortably anywhere. Manfred tried to get closer. All he could overhear was a man in the center say 'regards to Heinrich', to which Gerda responded, 'Bye, Bastian!' *They must know her from somewhere*, Manfred reasoned, *and boy, there is that effervescence again.* By then the lights had flickered signaling that the performance would continue. Manfred suddenly got nervous. Before he could move away, Gerda turned around.

"Oh," she said while smiling at him. Her smile got bigger after a few seconds.

Arrows shot forth again.

"Shall we go back to our seats?" she asked. The same cocked eyebrow and broad smile greeted Manfred yet again, disarming him for the second instance.

"S-s-sure," Manfred responded.

Gerda walked in front, and Manfred followed. They took their seats. The lights went out. Manfred thought to say to her that he knew that this was not her original seat. Just as he was about to, the curtain lifted, and the music started. Manfred sat back and waited.

They began playing some of the more moving arias from *Tristan und Isolde*.

Bliss beyond bounds,
joyful delirium!
Confined to my bed,
how can I bear it!
Up then and onwards
to where hearts are beating!

What irony, Manfred thought. *What an opera to be hearing right now*. Manfred felt as if his heart was leaping from his chest. He felt like jumping out of his seat as well. It seemed as if the opera were goading him, taunting him to heed the sensations that he was experiencing. It dared him to capitalize on the opportunity. *How cunning fate is*.

with bleeding wound
I now pursue Isolde!

Manfred was so eager to look over at Gerda, but he held his concentration.

Ah! It is I! It is I!
sweetest beloved!
Up, just once more,
listen to my call!
Isolde is calling:
Isolde has come
faithfully to die with Tristan.

Manfred thought he saw Gerda stir from the corner of his eye. He took the opportunity to look over. She looked toward him. *It's true*, Manfred thought to himself. *Her eyes, two radiant stars, can be seen sparkling in the dark*. Manfred experienced their luminous glow. She turned away, and Manfred was forced back to the concert and the dark.

He waited for the show to finish. He didn't care anymore about hearing an aria from Kurwenal, the baritone. He wanted the show to be over. While the audience clapped, Manfred's applause had a quick pace and an over-zealous energy to it that seemed to be driven by a force of excitement coming from within. He suddenly realized that maybe he was showing too much enthusiasm for the performance to be over. He stopped clapping immediately.

Once the noise level died down, he turned to her. "I know that this is not your seat."

"Oh," Gerda responded, suddenly sounding very shy. Her face was turning progressively darker shades of red.

Manfred saw her reaction and suddenly felt embarrassed. When she began to look down and seemed to search for words, Manfred cut her off. "Would you like to go for a cup of coffee?" Manfred blurted out. He was even surprised at himself that he could ask the question.

Gerda was silent for a few moments. It felt like an eternity for Manfred. She was fiddling with her handbag and looked up and around several times. Manfred felt like waving his hand in front of her and saying 'Hello, I'm right here'. The thought made him laugh to himself on the inside but in reality he was growing concerned. *She's searching for a way out*, he worried.

"I won't keep you too long," Manfred added, "if you'd like to be home early." He added that last thought in time, intentionally leaving the door open for her to say she wanted to be out longer if she so decided.

"Coffee would be lovely," she responded, flashing him a quick smile before resuming her coyness by looking down.

Manfred helped her with her coat at the coat check. They walked mostly silently from the hall to the coffee shop.

Manfred pulled a chair out at the table for Gerda and then sat down next to her. He kept looking into her eyes. After seeing her repeatedly look down and away, Manfred finally spoke up. "What beautiful eyes you have." They had sparked a wildfire within him, Manfred decided. *The blue is an illusion. It tricks you into thinking it is an oasis, but I have neither peace nor relief gazing into those eyes. They delight me with an unease, torment me with a thirst and invite me to embark on a journey. But they are not barren, like the desert.* Her eyes were rife with life and emotion.

"Thank you," Gerda responded.

Manfred looked around him. He had chosen the nearest coffeehouse he could find. It was a dump of a place. There was filth piled in every corner. Broken tables, broken chairs. The others there looked disheveled, unkempt. It was clear that they were the only ones who had come from the concert.

She looks like she should be out of place, Manfred thought, *but she seems really comfortable. I bet she grew up accustomed to going to fancy balls all of the time. It doesn't feel as if her personality or disposition has been tainted by those meanderings. She seems pure of heart, unpretentious. I don't see a hidden agenda, and she has yet to put on arrogant airs with me. I can usually discern such people quickly. She seems so approachable. Equally comfortable in a poor village or dining with royalty.*

In a seeming attempt to break the uncomfortable silence, Gerda asked, "So, how are you affiliated with the Conservatory?"

This solitary question sparked a flood of dialog. *A dangerous woman,* Manfred thought, *her eyes commit arson and her lips cause a deluge.* Just thinking it made Manfred excited. He became more animated as he spoke.

They proceeded to talk for four hours. Manfred shared stories of his life, Gerda shared hers. They talked mostly about their families and about the war and the impact it had on them.

"I had to serve during the war," Manfred offered.

"My family had to move about extensively," Gerda commented.

Manfred sensed that fatigue was overcoming Gerda. In an effort to try and wrap up the evening, Manfred mentioned how late it was.

"I haven't been up this late since the Celibidache performance of Beethoven's Ninth, when I couldn't sleep," he added, deliberately trying to end the discussion on a high note by impressing her as best as he could. The technique worked well with his friends back at the Conservatory.

"You were at that concert?" a disbelieving Gerda asked.

"Yes, it was very moving," Manfred responded, his eyes looking up into empty space, his head swaying from side to side and his right hand making a motion through air as if he were conducting a few notes from the performance. All the while, he was thinking, *Fantastic—it worked, she's impressed.*

"I WAS THERE TOO!" Gerda shot up as she said this. The force of her movement was so great that her chair fell backwards. "My brother is in the Berlin Philharmonic. I always go to his concerts. I was there. I WAS THERE."

Both suddenly remembered the event and fell to a silence. Manfred got up to pick up the chair, support that Gerda seemed to need because the weight of emotion that had just come over her seemed to make her knees weak as she looked like she was going to collapse. With tears in his eyes, evoked by the sight of Gerda weeping, Manfred sat back down. This was a peculiarly intimate moment, Manfred felt, for two strangers who had just met. Manfred realized that he probably would have felt this kinship with anyone who had been at the concert. Probably, but not definitely, he decided, modifying his thinking. He took her hand in his and tried to comfort her.

Both Manfred and Gerda fought off fatigue and kept talking. The coffee shop owner began giving them cold glances which graduated to his idling about their table and eventually ended in his first asking, then insisting, that they leave.

"It's already three AM, you two!" he protested.

"I'd like to say to that guy 'thank you, but I have a watch'," Manfred said to Gerda in a hushed tone.

The coffee shop owner overheard him and did not appear amused. *At least I got a grin out of Gerda*, Manfred thought.

Manfred and Gerda then walked through the streets of Berlin. What would have otherwise been ease in strolling through the streets of their familiar Berlin several years ago was now unease. There was a sense that this was their city but they were not of it—it was controlled by outsiders. "This is like an out-of-body experience related to geography," Gerda mused. They were sure to stay close to the well-lit streets. They noticed several of the American soldiers that were patrolling the area.

After the emotional outpouring, Manfred was drained by talking of the war and his family. He could see that Gerda was strained as well. He could see the weight in her eyes. They were glimmering with a little less intensity. Manfred decided to steer the conversation toward a topic that he knew would be upbeat for both of them and represented hope.

Manfred broached the topic of music. As a result, the evening did not end soon, rather the torrent continued, unimpeded by exhaustion. They spoke an encyclopedia about music. They attempted to talk about other topics—philosophy, religion, art—but it all came back to music. It became a game to try to discuss topics other than music.

"I am reading this work by Goethe," Manfred said as they continued to walk through the streets, "However, I find it easier to digest Schiller than Goethe."

"Schiller was influenced by Goethe," Gerda responded. "Even the Ode to Joy that is a part of Beethoven's Ninth that we heard had some influence from Goethe."

"And Wagner was influenced by Shopenhauer—another contemporary of both Goethe and Schiller," added Manfred.

"Ah, back to music again."

"Yes..." Manfred chuckled.

"You know, they are deciding what to do with the Memorial Church or *Gedachtniskirche* on Kurfurstendamm. It was badly damaged by bombings during the war, but a fair amount of the structure is still there. They are debating whether to tear it down and put something else there or to try to repair the damage," Manfred said.

"You know," Gerda began, "I should be thinking about the beauty of that church or about what other buildings or monuments should be placed there, a memorial of some kind would be appropriate, but all I can think about is how I like Beethoven's Missa Solemnis so much more than Bach's Mass in B Minor." She began laughing as she spoke.

Manfred had to chuckle as well. "You know," he said, "I suppose there is no getting around it. Music is ingrained in both of us." He emphasized the last part of the sentence to be sure that Gerda understood the fact that they both had this in common. After another forty-five minutes of talking—Manfred was explaining how in fact Beethoven had written Missa Solemnis to stand alongside Bach's Mass in B Minor as Beethoven was a deep admirer of Bach's work—they reached another lull in the conversation.

Manfred tried to stay focused on the conversation, but he couldn't help but let his mind wander. *I am amazed that such a woman exists.* He became a little disheartened. *How can I get a woman like her to be interested in me? She hesitated so much earlier when I asked her out. She has had such a wealthy life in the past. Can I ever make enough as a musician to give her a life to which she has grown accustomed? Will she deliberate with me again? If I call her will she respond? Did she just get caught up in the moment after hearing those beautiful arias? Can I convince her to come out again?*

Gerda took the opportunity to say, "I had a chance to see Edward Munch's *The Scream*. I felt like that painting so many times over the last few years."

Manfred realized her mind had been wandering as well. He felt as if she were thinking more about the past and her current anxieties than about the future. Manfred then wondered whether she was trying to change the course of the conversation or if she was naturally sharing her thoughts. He decided to proceed with the very next thought that entered his mind, fully realizing that he was diverting back to the topic of music.

"Next Tuesday, the student orchestra will be playing *Pictures at an Exhibition* by Mussorgsky," he said.

Gerda said a quick, "Oh." She seemed to almost ask it as a question, Manfred felt, as if she were prompting Manfred about whether there was something more that he wanted to ask. *At least that's how it sounded to me*, Manfred thought. He was secretly delighted but remained equally concerned about the outcome.

Manfred then proceeded. "Maybe you would like to attend with me?" He didn't look up as he asked the question.

Gerda took a few seconds and then said, "That would be lovely."

Manfred stopped walking. He let out an imaginary sigh of relief. He turned to Gerda. "I know what you mean about feeling like *The Scream*. I am sure you have had some very painful experiences."

Gerda looked off into the distance, her eyes beginning to swell with tears.

Worried that he was losing her interest, Manfred quickly added, "I love talking to you. It helps forget some of the pain surrounding us."

Gerda managed a smile for Manfred.

The air around them was growing brighter and brighter. The dark night retreated, being forced aside by the burgeoning light of daybreak, its strength proving mightier. They watched a brilliant sunrise in front of them. The moment felt more like the introduction to a piece of music as opposed to a finale. *Cue the orchestra,* Manfred thought. They walked in silence as they enjoyed the moment. *Even the sunrise can't drown out the glow from Gerda's eyes,* Manfred thought. *The sun has nothing on her.*

"Let me walk you home," Manfred said, his voice a little more confident than earlier.

● ● ●

Gerda entered the apartment she shared with her brother. It was in an upscale part of Berlin that had largely been spared by the bombings. Her block of buildings had been preserved. Gerda knew that if Heinrich were on his own, he wouldn't be spending the bulk of his salary on an apartment for the two of them. Both knew that it would be some time before the luxury of comfortable living would be theirs again with ease. There would be years of hardship before getting there, if they ever got there.

Gerda smelled the flowers in the lobby and climbed up the circular staircase, her hands running along the mahogany railing. She entered the hallway to her unit, hung her coat in the closet, slipped off her shoes so as not to make noise on the hardwood floor, walked past the powder room, dining room, piano in the living room and entered the kitchen.

Heinrich was sitting at the table drinking coffee. He seemed to be wearing a distraught expression. Gerda was proud of how refined a gentleman her brother was. Her mother worked hard to make him a spitting image of their father. Heinrich had attended the best schools and lived and breathed music, just like Gerda. While he was very articulate, he was always more comfortable expressing himself with music. He epitomized their father's aphorism regarding music expressing thoughts that could not find the right words. He was a poet using a bow and his cello instead of a pen and paper. He was tall and very handsome. He had a round face, and his smile evoked an expression on his face of open invitation, almost seductively so. Gerda was always impressed with how people were drawn to him. He captivated their attention well with lively stories and engaging dialog. If people were coming to town, he would drop everything to make time to be with them. He was always a favorite among women. But Gerda, and others who knew him best, knew that there was only one true love in his life: his cello.

"Nothing to worry about," she said to him before he could say a word. Her tone was soft, sweet and uncharacteristically relaxed. She took a glass from the cupboard, filled it with water and began drinking as she walked to her bedroom. It was one of four in the apartment.

Heinrich had a confounded look on his face. Gerda glanced at him briefly from the open door. He looked as if he were about to stage his protest, but then he looked at his watch, proceeded to collect his things and left.

Gerda sat on her bed and looked at the wall. She was relieved to finally have some space to attempt to catalog her thoughts. Her luck with men had not been the best. She kept struggling with that fact when Manfred had asked her for coffee. She had promised herself that she would be far more circumspect and cautious with any new potential relationship. At the time she knew that she should have probably quietly turned down the offer. She couldn't help herself though.

"What happened to me?" she asked aloud. As she had done before, she decided to follow her heart. *Boy, he made me uncomfortable when he kept looking at my eyes*, Gerda thought. She wanted to continue to look at him, but she had been well schooled in the art of social custom and etiquette. She knew that this was not appropriate behavior for a lady. She often received compliments on her eyes. Many had told her in the past that her eyes were her best feature. She remembered once attending an art gallery opening. The featured artist stopped her and took time out of the event where he was the guest of honor to do her portrait, right there in front of everyone. His main focus, he commented, had been her eyes. And she'd never forget how the conductor Furtwangler called out to her from the stage and complimented her eyes in front of the orchestra and the audience, eventually dedicating the concert to her. Then there was the state dinner that her father had taken her to with Jozef Pilsudski, leader of Poland at the time, when she was fourteen. As she stood in line to greet him, he commented to her that her eyes were the biggest and brightest that he had ever seen.

Gerda wondered about what else may have impressed him. She thought back to the comments people had made about her in the past. With whomever she was with she could dole out so much attention that that person would feel like they were all that mattered in the world. She would express her elation for happy news that was shared with her. Her hallmark was jumping up and down on the most exciting of news. She would remember minute details about a person's life and ask about them in the future, at a time when the person had likely forgotten about them. Her jovial nature was contagious, she had been told. Merely being in her presence tended to make people automatically happy. She was a doctor who prescribed a free-flowing, intoxicating drug of happiness for everyone that interacted with her.

Gerda also held dear the art of living that had been ingrained in her since she was a child. Even when there were not ample means to support that fine art of living, Gerda would, just like her family had, make it a priority to preserve as much of the practice as possible.

Gerda thought back to Manfred. His eyes seemed so gentle. There was something about him that felt safe. *How adorable was he when he picked up my chair*? Gerda wondered how nice it would be if she had someone like him to always pick up her chair. Gerda thought to herself how nice it was that given all of their fondness for sound, both could be perfectly comfortable silent with each other.

● ● ●

When Manfred got back to his room that morning, Torsten and Juergen had become quite worried for him. "We thought you had been taken in by the Soviets!" an exasperated Juergen exclaimed.

Manfred, who normally would have jumped at the opportunity to allay his roommates' fears and be apologetic about not communicating, responded to Juergen in a muted tone with a simple, "No…nothing like that." The corners of his mouth involuntarily rose as he spoke, and Manfred tried to move them back down to preserve his composure. He then proceeded to pull out his chair, look into empty space, sit at his chair, look into empty space again, smile to himself, look into empty space again, open a notebook, look into empty space again, stare at his notebook, smile to himself, and look into empty space again.

Torsten observed his friend's aloof theatrics with interest, and got a sense of the situation, and said:

"I wouldn't have thought it true,
He is flying higher than a dove,
He benefited from the concert more than me or you,
Our Manfred's in love!"

CHAPTER IV

The courtship between Gerda and Manfred continued, and a budding love flourished. Gerda enjoyed the time she spent with Manfred. She was always thrilled to receive his phone calls, read the notes at the front of her building, and hear the songs that he would use to serenade her. For over a year and a half they spent the vast majority of their time together while Manfred finished his studies at the Conservatory. The exciting thrill of the newness of their involvement seemed to be rekindled every time they met. Gerda wondered if they would ever get tired of each other.

She worried also, as they grew closer, about how he might react to her past and to her family's current situation. She hadn't told Manfred about her earlier marriage or the time she spent in East Berlin. Gerda didn't feel as if Heinrich was completely safe from Colonel Kasparov. *Perhaps she should tell him these things?* They were having so much fun together; she worried about how he would react.

Gerda and Manfred attended countless musical events together—sometimes two or three in a week. Gerda encouraged Manfred to join her in the fine art of acquiring seats at concerts so that they could enjoy performances at the Berlin Philharmonic. Manfred was always nervous about getting caught, but he had such a fond appreciation for Gerda's boldness in the matter that he went along for the ride.

There was no stone unturned in terms of their discussion of music. They attacked and analyzed it from every angle.

"What aspect of life is not, somehow, tied to music?" Gerda wondered aloud one day.

"You know, it would seem that music is so universal, you can find it anywhere and relate it to just about anything," Manfred said philosophically.

"I suppose that is true."

41

"I think we should attempt to find something that is not related to music," Gerda suggested playfully.

"Well, we can try." As always, Manfred was willing to indulge Gerda in a whimsical exercise.

"Garbage," Gerda offered after deliberating for several minutes, "Garbage is not related to music."

"Sure it is," Manfred contested. "When you put a bunch of senseless music together or you play a piece improperly or out of key, it's garbage."

Both laughed heartily.

"So many people try to define music," Gerda said, her mood becoming more pensive. Gerda added, still absorbed in her thoughts, "My father used to say, 'When you have a thought or emotion in mind but you can't find the words to express it, you can rely on music to express it for you'."

"That's beautiful."

"So is my father," Gerda said ruefully. Gerda saw Manfred nod his head in acknowledgment. She wondered if he detected the quiver in her voice as she spoke.

● ● ●

They attended the Mussorgsky event with Torsten and Juergen.

"Mussorgsky did his first composition when he was twenty-five. Can you imagine being so young and composing a work like that?" Gerda asked.

"Sure. That doesn't surprise me. I am only twenty-four," Manfred said.

"Well, I am twenty-eight, and let me tell you, that is very young to write music. My brother Ernest is a composer, and he began producing in his late twenties, but his best work came when he was in his early thirties," Gerda responded.

"I suppose Mozart was the exception..." Manfred looked away, and his voice suddenly took a more serious weight to it.

"Hey, what's the matter?" Gerda asked, giving Manfred a

light push on his arm with both of her hands and then adopting a boxer's stance with her feet, as if she was challenging Manfred.

Manfred found her mannerisms so charming. He was not sure how to bring up what was on his mind, but her little stunt was so disarming that any fear or concern melted to laughter.

"I didn't realize we had such a difference in age," Manfred finally said. "Is that going to be a problem?"

"What, are you kidding me?" came Gerda's response.

Somehow Manfred knew it was a rhetorical question. They both laughed. *I can see this becoming her hallmark phrase,* Manfred thought to himself. He found her lack of concern for what others might think or say endearing. Bold and progressive, he characterized her to himself.

● ● ●

Manfred entered his third clothes store. It wasn't easy to come by such shops in post-war Germany. It was a struggle for him to find a shop that had enough inventory of clothes—so many were so empty—and then to find a place where he wouldn't have to spend a fortune to buy a new blazer and a tie. He had been invited by Gerda to meet Heinrich. Manfred felt that he needed to make a good impression. He could have asked Gerda's opinion on which clothes to buy. *These sartorial concerns come so easily to her.* But instead he wanted to do it on his own and impress her with his choice. It was important to him. He eventually settled on a selection, paid and left.

Manfred was looking forward to meeting Heinrich. As he was walking he recalled how in their last conversation Gerda had described her father as beautiful. Manfred understood that by beautiful she was referring to his character and not his physical appearance. *She must really adore her father,* he thought. *She is likely also missing him,* he reflected. *I'm beginning to understand this woman intuitively.* The idea excited him and made him feel warm inside. And then he vacillated; maybe everyone would have understood that about her comment. *I like my interpretation better,* he decided. *It will probably take a lot for me to be able to impress Heinrich,* Manfred worried, suddenly.

Manfred had high expectations for his meeting with Heinrich. He had heard so much about him from Gerda. Manfred also had the deepest respect for any and all who had devoted their lives to music. There was an inexplicable bond that naturally formed for Manfred with such people. Manfred felt that he could intuitively understand that person and what drove them and formed their passions.

Before leaving his apartment, he pestered Juergen and Torsten for their opinion. He wanted to be sure that he looked as good as he possibly could. Both got tired of answering his repeated questions.

As he approached the flat where Heinrich and Gerda lived, he tried to see if he could view himself in the glass window of a store or restaurant. He straightened his tie, pulled back his hair and kept walking.

Manfred arrived at the building. Although he had been there many times, he always marveled at the huge contrast in settings. He had yet to have Gerda to his place, out of fear of how she would react. *I always feel vertigo coming here—I am excited to see her, but I worry about whether we will have a future together.* She seemed so progressive in her thinking, but he couldn't help but worry. He knocked on the door of the flat and was led in to the living room by Gerda. Heinrich came out from the kitchen, arms held out wide.

"Manfred!" he shouted, a gregarious tone accenting his words.

"Hello," he said back.

"You must be Manfred."

"Yes, Heinrich. How do you do?"

"I am doing very well, my friend. How are things by you?"

Initially there was the natural awkwardness that accompanies two people meeting for the first time. Manfred soon realized that he was probably the only one who felt that awkwardness. Heinrich seemed remarkably comfortable. Manfred felt the need to defer to Heinrich and not steer the direction of the conversation. After all, this was the first member of Gerda's family that he was meeting. He wanted to be sure to give a good impression.

He was about to dive into his description of being at the Celi performance. It had been his ace in the hole with all his friends when he attempted to impress them. It always worked like a charm. He thought, *I know how to impress him.* He took a breath in to begin and had a quick flashback to the time he told Gerda, as she had just entered the room to place something on the coffee table. Thankfully he stopped himself before continuing. Heinrich had performed in the concert, Manfred realized. *Oh, how embarrassing that would have been.* Gerda paused for a moment and gave a quizzical glance towards Manfred, as if she were anticipating his saying something. He managed a smile, and she left the room continuing with what she was doing. Manfred looked up at the ceiling and exhaled that breath he was holding in as a sigh of relief. *Oh, that would have been bad. Maybe I shouldn't try so hard.* He suddenly felt lighter.

"I understand you were in the war," Heinrich enquired, snapping Manfred back to the present situation.

"Yes, I had two tours on the Soviet front."

"I see," Heinrich said. "I was there too."

Gerda piped up. "Why don't we stop talking about the war. I don't want to talk about it. The war is over. We are trying to re-build our lives."

Both men looked over at Gerda. Manfred was overcome with a sense of awe. Manfred caught a glimpse of Heinrich's expression, and it appeared to be the same with him. Perhaps they felt the same thing. They both appreciated her personality and the manner in which she could at times become combative. Manfred thought back to the boxer's stance she had taken with him when they were at the Mussorgsky concert.

Luckily, thought Manfred, music was a mutual topic of love

45

and interest. Once the conversation moved into music, there was no stopping. Once again, the floodgates were open and all levies broke—they talked for hours. Manfred felt relieved, the wet circles under his armpits notwithstanding. By the way Heinrich was talking, it seemed as if he was impressed with Manfred's deep love and respect for the art form.

"You see, Manfred, I do believe that through music, we are able to connect with anybody—even our enemies during the war, if you can imagine that," said Heinrich, his voice assuming a didactic quality.

"Oh yes. Music is very powerful. I agree with you that it can bring people together. Like all of us today," added Manfred.

Gerda came into the room and asked Heinrich several questions about where to find things in the house. He got up and went to the kitchen.

Oh, Manfred thought to himself. *He seems the outwardly intellectual type.* Manfred wondered how being more outwardly intellectual would suit him. He tilted his head back, lifted his eyebrows, made a gesture upwards with his right hand and moved his lips as if her were pontificating some great universal truth as an orator. He had this sudden sensation of being in an oversized trench coat. Drowning. *Not for me,* he thought. *I'll stick with being lucidly self-aware.* He chuckled to himself.

"I wish you wouldn't move everything around," Manfred overheard Gerda telling Heinrich from the kitchen.

Manfred was feeling really comfortable with how the night was going. He and Heinrich seemed to have a lot in common when it came to music. There didn't seem to be many other topics that made that list though. *Perhaps we have very little in common on other matters.* As the evening progressed, and Manfred consumed a few more glasses of wine, he was beginning to feel more and more at ease. Manfred knew that his repertory of jokes had gone a long way to win over Juergen and Torsten, who were also musicians. Hence, he thought he might give it a try with Heinrich. Manfred started to tell a joke.

"Did you hear about the American GI who was stopped by customs?" Manfred asked.

"No," Heinrich replied.

"They asked him if he had any pornographic material with him."

"And?"

"He replied no, I don't even own a pornograph," Manfred replied.

Gerda chuckled uncomfortably, and Heinrich looked straight at Manfred. He created a furrow with his eyebrows and started to laugh.

"Perhaps we stick to the music, yeah?" Manfred conceded.

"I think you are right, my friend," Heinrich said with levity.

● ● ●

On Gerda's birthday, which happened to be the day after Christmas, Manfred took Gerda for a nice lunch at one of her favorite restaurants, which had just begun serving again. Despite the cold, Manfred insisted that they go for a walk. They happened to bump into Heinrich sitting on a bench in the park. He had his cello out, poised to perform music.

"Since you are here, let me play something for you," exclaimed Heinrich. Heinrich started on his cello.

Suddenly, Gerda heard some higher notes. She quickly turned around towards the source of the sound. She saw an Orchestra member, Heinrich's colleague, playing the viola. As she greeted him, she was surprised yet again when she turned her head towards yet higher notes, to see two violinists approach. Gerda was elated. She felt a rapture that took her to greater heights with every movement of the bow across the instruments' strings. She thought she could fly.

Manfred then serenaded Gerda with one of the many love songs he often sang for her. She was always enamored with how Manfred would let the emotion of the song captivate him. It was as if he were acting out the parts that he was singing, his intonations expressing his emotion much the way dialog and action would do the same for an actor.

She looked lovingly at the two men who had staged the seemingly impromptu string quartet, with choral accompaniment. "What a team the two of you are!" she exclaimed in awe.

Gerda and Manfred had limited means for their pursuits, but Gerda never felt that as a burden. She once told Heinrich, "When I had all the money in the world, I didn't have a partner to share with, now I have no money but I love the time I spend with him."

Heinrich turned to Gerda and said, "I like him for you. You can be yourself." Gerda was elated. She had not sought Heinrich's approval, but she was thrilled to have his acceptance.

Gerda often invited Manfred to join Heinrich and her for dinner so they could spend time together inexpensively. They would largely be alone, as Heinrich often rehearsed until late into the night. Even though she cooked at home, at times food would be tough to come by. The shelves in many stores were seldom full, even though the blockade had been lifted and the Soviets were allowing food and supplies to enter the city. The airlift had continued for several months after the blockade ended; however, goods remained in short supply. One of the nights that Manfred came over, the meat that Gerda was hoping to get was not available. She was stuck with serving only one course for the meal. Nonetheless, she set the table out in its entirety. It was set for a multiple-course meal. There were several plates per setting, placed on top of each other, successively smaller in size, one for each course, silverware for multiple courses, candleholders, napkin holders and flowers. When Manfred arrived, he sat at the table. He started with the soup that was first served to him. Gerda had made it hearty and he enjoyed it very much.

"Unfortunately, that is all I have," Gerda said in a somber, sullen tone. There was no bubbliness in that comment. Her effervescence was missing.

VIRTUOSO

"It was wonderful," Manfred said, attempting to be as encouraging as possible. Gerda could tell that he was anticipating more. She felt miserable that he was hungry. He threw his hands up in the air gently. "It's okay." She recognized that expression of his; it was his "that's how it is" look.

"Thank you," Gerda said.

"But why go through the trouble of setting the table for three courses?" He had a look on his face as if he was overwhelmed by the elaborate presentation in front of him.

"What, you think that I would ask you to stand over the stove with me, each of us with a spoon, eating directly from the pot?" Gerda challenged.

"Yeah, that would be fine," Manfred said.

Gerda threw the wooden spoon she was holding onto the floor for emphasis.

"Manfred Ziemer, do you not know me at all? I go through the trouble because that is how a proper table is set," Gerda said with a vigor that underscored her conviction.

"But..."

"What, are you kidding me?" Gerda demanded. "But nothing. I don't know any other way to do it." Her speech took on ever-increasing force with each successive word. "There is only the proper way. No shortcuts."

Manfred responded with an "Ah" that assured Gerda he understood.

● ● ●

Manfred was finally able to save enough money to take Gerda to the opera. Since that first night that he met her, he was eager to take her to hear opera again. It was a magical night; Cupid must have had an overabundance of arrows that evening that he was looking to unload, Manfred reflected. It was New Year's Day in 1951. They decided to attend a production of *Die Zauberflote—The Magic Flute*. The opera had been known for its uplifting revelation and optimistic joy about love and love conquering obstacles.

Manfred picked up Gerda as had been agreed upon. When Manfred saw Gerda, he immediately felt self-conscious about his own attire. She was adorned with a beautiful evening gown. It was the same one she had worn the first night they had met.

"Am I worthy of being able to escort you?" he asked. "Unfortunately, I don't own a tuxedo."

"What, are you kidding me?" came Gerda's response. She then shifted her feet. After a few seconds, she looked up at Manfred. "I am sorry that you have to see me in the same evening gown as before," she stated playfully.

They were both silent for a second as they looked at each other. Both then started to laugh. *Thanks for making me laugh*, Manfred thought to himself.

They had a lovely dinner together before attending the opera. Gerda did her characteristic shower of questions for Manfred. He had come to look forward to it. It was like a pleasant spring rain. She would always remember such nuanced details. How did she remember that student's name? The secretary of the professor, how did she recall the fact that she was very mean? It was a marvel for Manfred. It gave him a sense of being important. As if she was devoting all of this time and attention towards him. *These matters seem so inconsequential*, Manfred thought, *nobody has ever bothered before, but she takes the time and effort to remember them. I suppose it is one of the reasons that I keep coming back for more.*

Manfred tried to reciprocate, but he would mostly just fumble through it. *I am so busy trying to be a gentleman for her, I worry about other things. Maybe we are both getting what we need.*

Neither had seen the performance live before. They had heard many of the arias and the music from the production several times, however. In fact, Manfred had sung some of the arias of Papageno, the baritone part in the opera. However, this night, it would be the role of Tamino that he would feel kinship with, as Tamino was the lover who had to suffer through obstacles in order to be with his beloved Pamina.

VIRTUOSO

As Tamino struggled through the roadblocks, Manfred thought about what he had suffered through in his life before encountering Gerda. While the magic flute helped guide Tamino, Manfred couldn't help but acknowledge that the flute represented music itself for him and his travails. Music had helped him sustain himself and guide him to where he was today.

Manfred thought that Gerda's life could have been re-told as Pamina's story. Gerda's experiences had been similar. From all that Manfred had come to know about Gerda's past, she was also held captive against her own will, by forces and circumstances she had no ability to control. *I suppose too, that like Pamina, Gerda had been awaiting a rescue*, Manfred thought. *Maybe the rescue for her also comes in the form of music. Or maybe it's me.* He smiled to himself.

After the performance, Manfred walked with a bounce in his step that Gerda matched, beat for beat, rhythm for rhythm. The music had invigorated them, giving them a refreshed feeling for life. As they left the opera house, neither was ready to call it a night— they wanted to keep talking and sharing. They began walking.

"After the last aria I felt like I couldn't breathe!" Gerda exclaimed.

"I was enraptured. Everybody was great! What a great baritone they had for Papageno!" Manfred punctuated the end of his sentence by beginning an aria that he recounted the baritone for Papageno had sung particularly well.

Gerda took that as a cue, and the two began dancing together in the streets while Manfred sang. They were not conscious at all of their surroundings. It was as if they owned the streets themselves. As time passed and they became more aware of where they were, they slowed their movements to a halt. Manfred looked Gerda directly in the eyes, a constellation of emotions swelling within him with Gerda's eyes the two stars pivoting the epicenter of that universe of feeling. Manfred leaned in and kissed Gerda. He held her afterwards and whispered in her ear, "I love you."

It was the first time he had uttered those words, not only to Gerda, but to any woman. He felt an immediate weightlessness after the words were spoken.

Gerda looked at Manfred. "And I love you," she affirmed.

CHAPTER V

It's funny being in love, Manfred thought. He couldn't stop thinking about Gerda throughout the day. He would play out conversations in his mind, think what he would say and how she would respond. He would think about how she would react to something in a certain way, laugh here, be frustrated with that, smile upon hearing this. He had a hard time thinking about a future without her. He was also conflicted. He didn't know how he could make a future with her a reality. He stressed about what he could offer her and whether it would be enough.

They continued to rely on their friends to create an aura of music. Heinrich would get together with his colleagues from time to time in the evening and play music together. Gerda and Manfred were always invited to be a part of it. Sometimes, Heinrich let Gerda and Manfred request what was to be performed.

When Manfred arrived one evening, Gerda led him into the living room, where Manfred saw Heinrich already seated with someone else.

"Heinrich, will you please make the introductions," Gerda requested. "I must excuse myself to finish the meal."

"Manfred, come meet our good friend, Dr. Herman Zschacher. Not only is he a renowned surgeon, he is also a stellar pianist," Heinrich relayed.

"It's nice to meet you. Are you living nearby?" Manfred asked, attempting to make some small talk.

"Actually I live in East Berlin. Originally my family is from the Czech Republic, but for decades we have made our home in Dresden, in East Germany."

"As a doctor, Herman is able to come across the border from time to time to visit me. Unfortunately, he is not able to stay long. The Stasi keeps close tabs on him," Heinrich explained.

Manfred had heard about the difficulties that the Stasi secret police were inflicting upon East German residents who asked to visit the West.

"Tell me about your interests, Manfred," Herman encouraged. Herman hovered over Manfred, almost a full head length above him, being over six feet in height. He had a very slender frame, almost a wiry individual. He had a very sharp nose on which rested a pair of beer goggle glasses with thin frames. He had curly, black hair. Manfred noticed how there was a shock of it protruding forward. Manfred found it interesting how he would lean his upper body forward when he talked. Perhaps it came from all of those years sitting in front of a piano. Perhaps it was from bending down to be more eye level with people when he spoke.

"I love singing," Manfred responded.

"Singing is a great art form. I enjoy listening to it very much. Unfortunately, I myself do not have the voice for it."

"Is there something in particular that you like?" Manfred asked.

"I love Schubert's *Lieder*," Herman said.

Manfred nearly leapt out of his chair. "Those are my favorite too."

"Shall we perform together?" Herman suggested with a gust of energy. Manfred noticed how he was moving his upper body back and forth slowly, the shock of hair on his head bouncing up and down in time to his enthusiastic changes in intonation.

Herman walked to the piano. He began playing the music for a song from *Winterreise*. As if on cue, Manfred jumped in and began singing. The two startled Heinrich and Gerda, who were in the kitchen putting the final touches on the meal. They both came out into the living room. Dinner became delayed for several minutes, but nobody amongst them had the heart to interrupt the enjoyment.

After the meal, while they were clearing off the table, Gerda announced to everyone, "Back to your positions, please! There is much more singing to be done tonight!"

VIRTUOSO

Herman and Manfred eagerly made their way to the piano and discussed what they would sing next.

● ● ●

Colonel Kasparov had finally been able to renew his placement in Berlin. He had been there three years already. The Soviet High Command was becoming increasingly more difficult to maneuver around. They had rejected his first two requests, citing unwarranted reasons for the extension. He had to continue to be wily about his desire to remain in the Eastern bloc of Germany and not re-locate to Poland, where he was slated to be and where the original regiment that he commanded had been placed. With his left arm he touched that part of his uniform where his right arm would have been. He wanted to remain a chief Soviet liaison with the East German Stasi. He was very happy—this would provide him with the access he needed.

Sometimes late at night when he was in his own quarters, after drinking several shots of vodka, he would pull out a violin that had been shattered to pieces. It was the only time he ever cried.

The violin had been a gift from his father. It was the last gift he had received from him before his father had died. His father had died immediately after getting that violin for his son. The Kasparovs were a poor farming family. His father had had a dream of his children achieving something other than being a farmer in their lives. He himself had always wanted to be a violinist, but there never was enough money for it. His father couldn't even pursue it as a hobby. He had to sell his violin in order to support the family when Kasparov was young. Kasparov's father swore to him that he would buy Kasparov a violin when he was older. When Kasparov was a teenager, his father made good on that promise; however, the family's financial position had not improved all that much.

Kasparov had never played a musical instrument before—he had only heard music that his father had played for him. He lamented the early loss of his father. He thought about how his father was always more interested in art, poetry, and music and how commercial pursuits were less interesting to him. Kasparov's mother would always fight with his father because of this. She was not as interested in the arts and was constantly upset about her plight in life.

Kasparov struggled to get scenes from that night out of his mind. He kept seeing the image of his mother slapping his father repeatedly and him falling backwards on the staircase into a pool of his own blood after tripping over the violin case that Kasparov had left open.

Kasparov had been determined to learn the instrument left to him by his father. The price of the gift had been his father's life, and he was determined to see what this beauty was about. He wanted to—no, he needed to—understand what it was in order to come to terms with his father's death. And learn he did.

● ● ●

Manfred was ecstatic when he was invited by Gerda again to spend an evening with Heinrich and his friends. This time, Manfred was the first to arrive at the apartment. Manfred noticed that Heinrich had his cello out of the case. Manfred thought that perhaps he would accompany in the performances. Herman arrived shortly after Manfred. Manfred was happy to see him again. Manfred was eager to begin singing with Herman again, but Heinrich asked Herman to accompany him while Heinrich tested some variations on his cello. Manfred stood close to the piano observing them play and taking interest in how Heinrich improvised certain variations. He was getting a little bored, however, as he wasn't a direct part of their activity. Manfred was relieved when there was a knock at the door. "I'll answer it," he quickly offered, happy to have something to do.

He opened the door to see a man standing there. Manfred could tell by the confused look on his face that he thought maybe he had the wrong apartment.

"I'm looking for Heinrich and Gerda," he said tentatively.

"You've come to the right place. I am Gerda's friend, Manfred Ziemer." As he said it, he wondered if he could graduate himself to boyfriend. He decided not to.

"Ah, good. I'm Bastian. Bastian Abramowitz."

He seemed to know his way about the place as he took his coat off and hung it by himself. Manfred just stood idly by and followed as he walked to the living room. Manfred noted that he was already familiar with Herman, given the exchanges.

Heinrich turned to Manfred. "Bastian is a fabulous composer. He focuses on more modern works."

Manfred nodded his head and smiled slightly. Bastian was mid-sized, about the same height as Heinrich. His face was equally round, but he was a bit more portly than Heinrich. He had jet-black hair that was combed back and kept in place using pomade. He was also dapperly dressed like Heinrich. He wore thick-rimmed beer goggle glasses. They were similar to Herman's, Manfred decided, but Bastian's were thicker. His most striking feature was his large nose that took up a fair portion of his face. He was a handsome fellow, but didn't carry as inviting a disposition as Heinrich did.

"What type of music do you compose?" Manfred asked. Realizing that the question was too broad, and not wanting to sound stupid, Manfred followed it with, "Are they orchestral works?" There was something strangely familiar about him, thought Manfred.

"I write mostly modern songs," Bastian explained.

"Are you familiar with the classics?"

"Of course I am!"

Manfred felt suddenly embarrassed for asking. He should have known that Heinrich's friends would be well versed in the realm of music. *But then, why did he have to respond to me that way*, Manfred wondered. *I think he is making me feel more embarrassed than I should be feeling.*

"I'm sorry," Manfred offered. "I didn't mean to imply that you would not be trained classically. I was just curious."

"It is no problem," Bastian insisted, holding his hand up and waving it through the air as though to say *stop* while shaking his head towards Manfred, indicating that his offering an apology was not necessary. *He seems overly expressive*, thought Manfred, *or was Bastian on edge?*

"I trained classically and fell in love with songs. I love all of Schubert's *Lieder* and folk songs from Russia and Eastern Europe," Bastian said in a more relaxed tone. "I use the folk songs as my inspiration to write my modern songs."

"Wow," Manfred exclaimed. He had never encountered anyone with an interest in this kind of music. All the other singers with whom he interacted were purely interested in the classical form of expression.

"Perhaps we can sing something together?" Manfred suggested.

"I am afraid that won't be possible," Bastian declared. "I don't have much of a singing voice."

"Oh I see."

The others had gone into the kitchen, leaving Manfred alone with Bastian. *This isn't the smoothest of conversations*, Manfred thought. Nonetheless, he felt the need to keep it going. Manfred also kept trying to think about how he might know him.

"You seem really familiar to me," Manfred blurted out.

"Maybe you have heard one of my songs," Bastian suggested.

"Perhaps…" Manfred said, all the while saying no to himself. He knew that wasn't it. "How did you develop your interest in folk songs?"

"I was born in Eastern Poland," Bastian explained. "My parents are from Lithuania."

"Where do they live now?"

"They are no longer with me," Bastian said. He fell silent.

Manfred looked at Bastian. He saw sadness in him. Manfred thought back to his own father and when he passed away. There was, however, a freshness to Bastian's mourning. He couldn't speak about it without developing some emotion. It must have been recent, Manfred reasoned.

"They were executed at Dachau," Bastian said in a hushed

voice.

As emotion clearly swelled in him, he offered through a cracking voice, after seeing what Manfred knew must have been an expression of shock on his face, "My last name is Abramowitz, you see. We are a Jewish family."

Manfred was taken aback. He sat there not knowing what to say or do. Words didn't seem enough. He himself had a million questions swimming around in his own mind. None of them seemed appropriate to ask now. He stood up and went to Bastian. He sat next to him and gave him a hug. And then, without saying a word, he got up and walked to the piano. Manfred began playing and sang a song, one of the saddest he had in his repertory. It was a song about losing a loved one. The words of the song said it all.

Everyone at the dinner party came out into the living room, beckoned by the music. Manfred could see it from their faces; each had their own story of loss. They embraced each other and attempted to seek comfort together as a group and through the music.

After Manfred finished, he said to Bastian, "This is what I played when I lost my father." Manfred allowed a few minutes to pass. "I know I can't do anything to bring your parents back," he added, "but I hope this helps you in coping with your loss."

Manfred felt out of his element. Did he just say the right thing or did he put his foot in his mouth? Was it possible to cope with what happened? Manfred felt like a sinking ship. He knew that the circumstances were different. In those few minutes, however, he had a hard time reconciling the murder Bastian's parents experienced with the death due to illness that his own father had experienced. Bastian's parents died before their time, but didn't Manfred's father also—had he not contracted the illness, would he have lived longer? Manfred's head began to hurt as he thought about this. *I have no idea what to say.* He was desperate to say something to make Bastian feel better.

Manfred looked at Gerda. She nodded as if in acknowledgment of how uncomfortable he felt. Manfred was relieved when she threw him a lifeline. She also went to Bastian and gave him a hug.

"Nobody wanted what happened to happen. But we are all here to get through it together. We all have experienced loss. We will build a brighter future together," she declared, looking around the room, seeking agreement from the others.

Through teary eyes, Bastian agreed with all who were declaring their allegiance to Gerda's position.

"Now," she added. "Let's all eat so that we have the strength to survive."

This evoked a laugh from Bastian. Manfred, sensing that it was okay to do the same, also laughed. *How ironic*, he thought to himself. *From the outside looking in, this is a strange grouping of characters, not a gathering that could be found in many other flats in Germany at this time. From the inside looking out, there is no better place to be*, Manfred decided.

After the meal, Manfred could not contain his curiosity. "Your first name does not sound very Jewish," he commented.

"My father was trying his best to integrate into our adopted country, so he gave me a more German name," Bastian explained.

Manfred did not want to stop with his line of questions. He felt emboldened now, and his curiosity was getting the better of him. Bastian seemed to be holding up okay, so he proceeded.

"How is it that you came to know Heinrich and Gerda?" he asked.

However, Bastian was apparently still feeling some of the sorrow from earlier. In being reminded about it again, Manfred sensed that Bastian started to feel those emotions with some increased intensity. Manfred felt like withdrawing the question.

"Maybe I should think about another song to perform," Manfred suggested sheepishly. "Would you have any requests?"

"No, Manfred," Bastian protested. "It is better if I talk about it."

Manfred nodded his head gently and watched Bastian

intently, trying to relay that he was okay with that so long as Bastian was okay with that.

"Our families helped each other out during the war," said Bastian.

"Bastian," Herman yelled out. "Oh, sorry to interrupt, but what is the name of this folk song?" Herman played a few notes as he asked the question.

Bastian stood up. "I think I know the song you are trying to play, but you are off slightly," he said. "Let me show you what I think you want to play."

Everyone became involved in other matters.

Towards the end of the evening, Heinrich turned to Gerda and said, "I meant to mention this earlier, but Kasparov is making noise again." Manfred thought it was odd that he would say this in front of everyone. *I guess he is that comfortable with all of us.*

Gerda was quick to cut him off. "I don't want to hear anything about that. You keep quiet now."

Manfred overheard a bit of it. Later that night he asked Gerda, "What was that thing about Kasparov?"

"I don't want to talk about it," Gerda said, her manner and tone suddenly becoming very cold.

Manfred decided not to pursue it. He then announced his departure as it had gotten quite late and he had some preparation to do for his finals. He turned to say bye to Bastian.

"We will continue our discussion next time we meet." Bastian shook Manfred's hand vigorously. "You have a beautiful singing voice. I wish you the best of luck."

"That's quite a compliment coming from a composer of songs," Manfred stated, showing his deep pleasure to have received the praise.

Gerda walked him out. "Best of luck with your preparations," she told him. "I won't disturb you tomorrow," she continued, "but I will see you before your exam on Monday."

Manfred smiled. He was tempted to ask about Kasparov, but

he decided to let the evening end this way. The emotion of earlier had been a bit draining, and he worried that he might hear something unpleasant. He did not want to ruin the evening any further than it already had been.

He did ask one question. "Gerda, have I met Bastian before?"

Gerda thought for a moment. "He was at the concert with the *Tristan and Isolde* arias. You probably saw him there."

"Oh right," Manfred said, "during the intermission."

"Yes, when you were stalking me."

"Gerda, I wasn't stalking you…I…I was just…"

Gerda kissed Manfred on the cheek. "Go home, Manfred."

● ● ●

Kasparov looked out the window from the Soviet military outpost in Berlin. It was a warm, sunny day during that summer of 1951, but for security purposes, the window could not be opened. The same soldiers that had saluted him several minutes ago as he arrived on site were now saluting another colonel who came to the building. Kasparov was enjoying his new post as liaison between the KGB and the Stasi. He had an office at the KGB building, but he preferred using the army station there. Fewer people would wonder what he was up to. He applied the finishing touches to his letter.

Kasparov had pinned down the location of Sylvester Majowski, Heinrich's and Gerda's father. All the passes that he had available to him got him access to many parts of Berlin. He was able to get an old vehicle that he drove around himself, although a driver was offered to him. He had paid off Sylvester's latest driver, who had not been with the senior Mr. Majowski for long, to keep Kasparov informed of Sylvester's whereabouts. Kasparov monitored Sylvester's every move.

Kasparov sealed the envelope with his latest threatening letter to Sylvester that the Stasi had information that would cause him harm and that he was going to expose it to the authorities. It was a fabrication; there was no such evidence. Thinking of it made him smile sinisterly. But Sylvester knew that the veracity of information was not important to indict people; the slightest hint of improper behavior and you could be called in. If you couldn't maneuver through the system properly, it was hard to get out. Hence, it was best not to be taken in, even under false suspicion. Kasparov prided himself on his clever ruse. He was determined to make Sylvester suffer in order to cause Heinrich pain.

● ● ●

Sylvester opened the envelope at his front door to find a third threatening letter from a Soviet soldier named Kasparov. He sat down on the leather armchair he kept in the dining room to smoke a cigar in the evening. He took stock of the situation. After Sylvester received the first threat, he changed locations. When the threats arrived at the second location, he had a suspicion that one of his staff must be divulging information. Now, Kasparov had found him yet again and was beginning to threaten physical harm to Sylvester.

"I have been loyal to all of you. How dare you betray me like this?" Sylvester yelled at his staff. He asked each one in turn. No one admitted anything. "You are all fired!" he boomed.

All of them left. Sylvester was suddenly without any support or assistance. He spoke with Heinrich. "Father, you don't worry, I will send Gerda right away," Heinrich said.

● ● ●

Manfred loved his time with Gerda, and he loved studying and being surrounded by music. Had it not been for the post-war difficulties, this would have been the happiest moment in Manfred's life. There was one issue that constantly weighed on his mind, though—whether or not he would be able to make a living as a singer once he was done. And whether, as a singer, he would be able to support Gerda. This issue troubled Manfred's mother as well, who did not want either of her sons to have the type of life that she was forced to live.

Several months prior to graduation, Manfred began the search for employment. He checked with all of the major choral groups in Berlin and even in greater Germany. While some musical endeavors were being funded, there just wasn't enough musical activity to absorb all of the new graduates.

He felt shy about doing it, but he went ahead and asked Heinrich if there was anything that could be done with the Berlin Philharmonic. "Unfortunately, there aren't even any auditions which are being accepted," Heinrich told him.

Manfred found himself in a bind. He didn't know what to do or in which direction to go.

Gerda came to Manfred's graduation ceremony. Manfred certainly felt proud of his achievement and what he had accomplished. He was sad that his mother could not make it to see him graduate; she had been busy trying to finalize a dress for a demanding customer. After the ceremony, Manfred went to Gerda's place. He was thrilled with what he found there—there was a party with Heinrich and some of his friends from the Orchestra.

"A very hearty congratulations to you," Heinrich boomed. "I proudly remember the day when I received my degree. It is a great time. You should relish every second of it."

Manfred thanked him for his words.

Towards the end of the evening, Gerda approached Manfred and informed him that she needed to go away to visit her father in East Germany for a while.

"Is everything okay?" asked Manfred. She seemed to display a little anxiety.

"Yes," she said, looking up and directly at him. "Everything is fine, completely fine." Her manner was softer than usual.

She almost tried to assure him too much, Manfred thought. He worried if there was maybe another reason why she was going away. Perhaps her interest in him was waning. Perhaps she too was concerned that he did not have a job.

"Are you sure everything is okay?" he asked again.

VIRTUOSO

She persisted that everything was fine. She smiled for him.
Or maybe, Manfred thought, *her anxiety is because she will
be missing me.* He chuckled to himself. He couldn't make himself
believe it.

● ● ●

Gerda left to be with her father the day after Manfred's
graduation party. "Don't worry, Father," she consoled him. "I will
look after you until we can find a new staff."

Sylvester held his daughter tightly. Gerda looked up at him
with her large blue eyes. He pushed her blond, curly hair out of her
face. He had never thanked his children for anything, so he stayed
quiet. He could tell that Gerda knew he was appreciative. While he
showered them with love, he had always remained stern with his
children. He felt as if physical distance would foster discipline.
This was a rare occasion when he embraced his daughter. He had
purposely gotten her to come by calling Heinrich and not Sylva or
Mia. He wanted his spunky daughter, that she might invigorate him
with her bubbliness.

Their first order of business was to find a new location. This
would have been Sylvester's third house in as many months. They
searched as surreptitiously as they could.

● ● ●

Manfred found himself with more time on his hands. He
was done with school, and Gerda was away. He decided to help his
mother out by getting some of the items she needed for the
household. He had gone through four stores to find the basics: soap,
bread, butter, and sugar. Goods were so hard to come by. Store
shelves remained empty. Manfred saw empty row after empty row
in the stores. The only way to get basic necessities was through a
burgeoning black market that had been started by the Soviets during
their occupation. This was a leftover of the Berlin Blockade when
the Soviets closed off all rail and auto access to Berlin. For nearly
two years, Berlin relied on goods airlifted by the British and
American forces. Although the Soviets had lifted the blockade in

May of 1949 and the airlift had ceased in September of that year, the ordinary flow of goods had not resumed even in 1950 or 1951. When Manfred visited his mother, there were strict rules to follow— only one pass of the hand on the bar of soap in order to wash hands. Holding the bar of soap under running water was a luxury that could not be afforded.

Manfred's aunt in the US would also send care packages because she knew how difficult life was. From time to time, she and her husband called to inquire about their well-being. Prior to the war, two of Manfred's aunts, sisters of his mother, had gone to America. They were the only ones who had not already been married by the time the opportunity to go came up, and they thought they would try for a better life. Both sisters had married Americans and settled down. During Aunt Helga's calls, Manfred's mother would often lament to her about her concern over her two sons. In one phone conversation, Manfred's uncle suggested that Manfred could come to the US where his uncle would sponsor him.

Manfred had to roam the stores again. All he wanted were some potatoes for his mother. After five stores, he was frustrated that he couldn't find them. He remembered his uncle's offer.

Manfred felt that he had some hope for himself in Berlin with the funding by the Americans under the Marshall Plan, so he did his best to stay in Germany. But after completing his studies, he found that it was a real challenge for him to find work. He even looked outside of his passion for singing. The times were still troubled. His younger brother, Horst, managed to find work in a factory, but Manfred struggled.

Manfred took advice from Torsten, Juergen, and another good friend, Jonathon Renstzler. All agreed that they would hate to see him go, but life was bleak and a living had to be earned. Manfred kept debating with himself about what he should do. "I wish I could talk to Gerda," Manfred lamented.

He had heard so much about America. There was still a lot of rhetoric about it being the land of opportunity. His uncle had nothing but nice things to say about the place, and he seemed to have prospered and done well. There were so many American soldiers based in Germany at that time. Manfred spoke to a few of them. All indicated how great the US was.

"Excuse me, sir," Manfred said to a soldier one day as he was walking from near-empty shop to near-empty shop.

The American soldier looked up. "Can I help you?" the soldier asked.

"I just wanted to ask you—how is America?" Manfred blurted.

"What do ya mean 'how is America'?"

"I mean, what is it like to live there?"

"There ain't no other place like it," the soldier declared with a smile. "I'm from Texas. Ya can get everythin' your heart desires there. Ya all don't have much here. And the women—they'll make ya heart beat real fast!"

Manfred was suddenly very shy. He had a difficult time following the soldier in what he was saying. The accent would take some getting used to, Manfred mused. Manfred did take a lot of comfort in the soldier's enthusiasm. Out of necessity he had to rely on the excitement of his voice and not his actual words because he couldn't entirely make out what the soldier was saying. Manfred demurred from asking anything more.

"Thank you," Manfred said, smiling. Manfred walked home deep in thought. He was conflicted. He wondered if he could remain in Germany in the hopes of finding a singing position later. He had already tried to find other jobs to sustain him. Unfortunately, nothing was turning up for him. He wished he could have had the chance to speak with Gerda. It was a Friday night again, and he missed not having Gerda's company. He had to go to the student concert with Torsten and Juergen. During the first part of the concert—Tchaikovsky's String Concerto, his thoughts were scattered. During the intermission, he chatted with Juergen and Torsten.

"If it is meant to be, Manfred, Gerda will either wait for you to return or she will follow you to the US," Juergen stated.

Manfred had a hard time arguing with his reasoning.

"If only I could talk to her," Manfred pleaded.

Both of his roommates convinced him that if he had spoken to Gerda she would advise him of the same thing.

Torsten added:

"For no reason do you fret,
I can say this without regret,
A different response from Gerda
You will never get!"

Manfred always liked the emphasis that Torsten would place on matters when he spoke in song lyrics. It provided much needed alacrity—and perspective for Manfred. He couldn't help but agree with what Torsten and Juergen were trying to get him to see and understand.

After the intermission, when the orchestra began playing Dvorak's Serenade for Strings, Manfred became captivated by the music—it gripped him. Rather than weighing himself down with thoughts, he allowed himself to feel the music and become absorbed by it. He found it so uplifting and full of hope. The music was so characteristic of Dvorak's style—emphasizing the positive and the beauty of life without dwelling on negativity. It was hard to hear this music and be downtrodden, Manfred thought. He even closed his eyes. When the performance was over he opened his eyes, stood up, and led the crowd in thunderous applause. He walked home with a beat to his step. He had reached his decision.

"Uncle, I am coming," Manfred declared into a static-filled phone line. Although Manfred's hands were occupied at the time, he did purse his lips and nod his head.

● ● ●

Kasparov woke up in a cold sweat. He had just had a dream about his mother. His mother was trying to kill him. Kasparov thought back to his father. Those words of his would haunt him. "I am so proud today to bring my son a violin."

His father had been drinking that day. He only drank when he was extremely happy. Those occasions had gotten fewer and fewer. He thought that it was cruel of fate to make him that happy that day.

He remembered asking his mother questions in the weeks and months after it happened. "Why did you have to argue with Papi?"

After she beat him several times, he stopped asking.

He thought back to the time that he broke his mother's second husband's arm. He snickered in his bed. "I taught him to come after me with a knife," he said aloud.

● ● ●

Manfred tried his best to reach Gerda, but was not successful. All she had told Manfred was that she needed to be away for a few weeks to visit with her father. Manfred wanted to go along, but he was not able to. And then a few weeks turned into two months. Manfred couldn't find Gerda at home, and he felt foolish because he did not have her father's address. He made a number of calls to friends whom he thought might have her number. He was not able to reach Herman, whom he thought for sure would have the contact information.

When his calls to Heinrich were not answered, Manfred decided to visit the Berlin Philharmonic. When he got there, he found the rehearsal rooms and the main chamber empty. Eventually he was able to locate somebody from the cleaning staff.

"Excuse me," Manfred said. "I am looking for a member of the orchestra, Mr. Heinrich Majowski."

"You won't find any member of the orchestra here," the man said.

"What happened?" Manfred asked, startled.

"They are in tour in Austria," the man responded.

It was November 1951. The certainty and elation that he had felt the night that he heard Dvorak was now replaced with a nagging sense of loss. He couldn't turn back now. His uncle had already gone through so much trouble in order to arrange the paperwork for Manfred to immigrate. His uncle had also already paid for the voyage and the visa to go to the US. Manfred had to push ahead with his plans.

His heart weighed a thousand pounds. He felt this hollowness, a cavity left in his chest by his heart, which had fallen to his feet, and for the first time, he even felt fear. He wondered why he was afraid and questioned whether he was justified to be feeling that. He could rationalize all he wanted with the words of Torsten, Juergen and Jonathon. Then, he understood why he felt fear. He wasn't worried about this next step he was about to take. But, what if all of his friends were all wrong? What if they were considering the wrong thing? What if they were only grappling with positive outcomes? What if the outcome was in fact negative? *What if Gerda had left him?*

Manfred was all out of sorts as a result of this. He felt bewildered and confused. He needed the benefit of answers, but there would not be any for him to have. *Why did she just leave like that? Why hasn't she contacted me?* The more Manfred thought about the negative outcome, the more he fueled the fire and gave that line of thinking momentum. Eventually he saw the situation in no other way. He had thought about so many ways that he would leave notice for her or try to communicate with her after he was in the US. He saw those plans all dissolve in front of his eyes. He was crestfallen. Perhaps this was his way of protecting himself, he thought, reaching a heightened sense of self-realization. *Or maybe I need to believe this to be true so that I can take this step and not worry that I have walked out on something so meaningful for me.*

"I can't wait any longer," he said aloud, hoping that if he vocalized it, he could make it true. Truer than any of the other statements swimming around in his head or any of the other thoughts in his heart. With a heavy heart and a million unsettled questions on his mind, Manfred Ziemer firmed up his plans to set sail for the United States to begin his new life in Chicago.

● ● ●

Beyond his relationship with Gerda, Manfred was forced to leave many others behind. There was his mother, his brother, and his good friends.

Upon departing, Jonathon gave Manfred a sketch he had made of Manfred singing in front of a large audience. He signed it and wrote the phrase, "Foretelling the future: Carnegie Hall 1960."

Torsten turned to Manfred, and said:
"We are parting with great sorrow,
As we will not share each other's tomorrow,
Keep a smile about you, my friend,
Your sense of humor will carry you to the end."
Juergen left Manfred with a hug and wished him well.

● ● ●

Kasparov had become aware that his informant was no longer under the employ of Sylvester. He stepped up his surveillance efforts and kept near constant watch of Sylvester. Hence, when he moved, Kasparov knew Sylvester's whereabouts.

Kasparov kept Sylvester's newest house under constant continued surveillance. He noticed a young woman arrive at the house. At first he thought she was a new member of the staff. When Kasparov got a closer look with binoculars, he saw that it was, in fact, Gerda.

"So, Mrs. Sabbas surfaces again!" Kasparov remarked aloud to himself.

Sylvester had been subsisting on a pension from the railroad company. After the war, he was relieved of his duties and "urged" into retirement. While the company acknowledged his actions were ultimately good, he had caused the railroad company a lot of damage.

One night while Kasparov was watching Sylvester's house, he saw Gerda and Sylvester at the piano playing together. He saw Sylvester get up and instruct Gerda on a matter. Kasparov could see

Sylvester praising Gerda. He began imagining his own father. He wondered if that scene could have been him and his father, his father teaching him the violin. He remembered fondly those days when his father was alive.

"I would do anything to be able to get you a violin," his father had said. "If I had not had to sell mine to feed the family, you could have used that one."

Kasparov became lost in his thoughts. Why did his mother have to fight with him that night? Why did his father have to drink so much? Why did Kasparov have to leave the violin case at the top of the stairs?

"I drink to live with you. Your life is empty and meaningless. You are an insipid little bitch that has killed all in me that is worth living. How dare you hate music! How dare you hate me!"

Kasparov would never forget those booming words of his father. His mother had venom dripping from her lips. *She hated my father*, he thought, *and she hated me for loving him.*

It was rare for Kasparov to show emotion, but in this instance, he could not avoid it. He began to cry, as if he were holding his shattered violin in his hands. Suddenly, he dropped the binoculars that were in his hands and began driving away.

When he stopped crying, he said out loud with a cold determinism, "I will spare the father. He can't be bad. He is a good father. Fathers are good. They love their children. I will revert back to my earlier target."

He thought back to the image of his mother slapping his father and then seeing him in a pool of his own blood. What he would do to get that image out of his mind.

● ● ●

Ram Sunder Giri was very excited to meet with John Foulds again. He had met with the British composer, now resident in India, a few times already. He had been impressed with John's desire to fuse eastern and western musical styles. Ram particularly appreciated John's *World Requiem,* which premiered at the Royal Albert Hall in London. John had lived for many years in New Delhi where he held the post of Director of European Music for the All-India Radio. John's wife was violinist Maud McCarthy, who was Irish-born, and had traveled to India separately and had spent a lot of time studying Indian music.

This meeting had a very specific purpose. Ram was traveling to Europe and learned that John was in Berlin for a few weeks. Ram made the journey to Berlin. There was one pressing question on Ram's mind – would John be interested in staging a performance of the opera Shakuntala.

"There is a story of Shakuntala that we have in India," Ram began.

John listened with earnest. "I have heard about this."

"Oh how exciting," Ram said. "Schubert developed an opera based on this story... Can you help me locate a recording of it?"

"I will try to track it down," John responded.

● ● ●

Gerda arrived back in Berlin shortly before Christmas, confident that Father would be okay. Father promised that he would spend the holidays in Berlin with Heinrich and Gerda. Gerda was excited about the prospect of Father potentially meeting Manfred. *I'll have to prepare Manfred,* she thought to herself. Father had tried to insist that she did not need to stay with him, but Gerda had a hard time denying her caretaker instinct, which had been with her since her childhood. The threats from Kasparov had to be taken seriously.

When she came back to Berlin, she attempted to look for Manfred. She couldn't find him at his apartment. There was no sign of Torsten or Juergen. She thought they might have moved elsewhere as they all only had a few months to remain on campus after graduating from the Conservatory. She had only ever met Jonathon once and she did not have his last name. Manfred had mentioned his mother several times, but Gerda had never met her. She tried to see if she could find her whereabouts, but Gerda was not successful. Manfred had even mentioned his brother Horst, but it was to no avail. All roads were empty.

"I miss him so much," she cried to Heinrich.

"I know, my dear sister, I know." Heinrich tried his best to console Gerda. "We will do our best to locate him."

● ● ●

Hogitaro Fukiori trembled as he came to Heinrich's apartment. He had his bags packed and with him. He had several bruises on his face and hands. He had only been in Berlin for four of the five years that he had intended to stay. After his military duties, Hogitaro had returned to Tokyo and resumed lessons with his German-educated violin teacher. He had been encouraged to go to Berlin himself to study. But he was too ashamed now to continue with his musical instruction.

"Hogitaro-san, what is the matter?" asked Heinrich.

"I am very ashamed," Hogitaro said. He kept his eyes transfixed on the floor and would not look-up. "I was interrogated by the Soviet police. They thought I was a spy for Japan. They asked me questions that I answered innocently. I just wanted to show them that I was a student. They asked me too many questions about your sister."

"What kind of questions? Where she was living?" Heinrich enquired, suddenly concerned.

"Yes, I answered the questions innocently. I said she came from East Berlin. Did I say the wrong thing?"

"No, I am sure it is inconsequential." Heinrich said this in a reassuring tone.

"That man with one arm kept beating me," Hogitaro added, his eyes swelling with tears.

"Did you say one arm?" Heinrich asked.

"Yes."

"Did you learn his name?"

VIRTUOSO

"No. I am very sorry." Hogitaro bowed down from the waist. A single teardrop fell onto the hardwood floor. "I regret to inform you that this is the second time. Once when I was here only a few months and then again yesterday, after four years. I am very sorry I never said anything to you the first time. It never happened again, and they never beat me, so I didn't think there was a problem," Hogitaro revealed.

Seeing the moisture, Heinrich helped Hogitaro up.

With his head held low, Hogitaro re-traced his steps out of the apartment and left.

● ● ●

Heinrich was pleased that Furtwangler had returned to the Philharmonic and had resumed his role as Principal Conductor. A thorough, grueling interrogation by the Allied de-Nazification Force eventually vindicated Furtwangler and the Orchestra. It was a victory not just for the members of the Berlin Philharmonic, but for music itself.

Heinrich was back to accompanying Furtwangler as they held auditions for a new cellist. One of those auditioning was Juergen, Manfred's former roommate. When the audition was over Juergen walked down from the stage and through the aisle toward the door. At that time, Heinrich, who was sitting in the seat closest to the aisle, was closing his folio and stood up to leave. Several papers had fallen to the floor. Heinrich was engaged in conversation and didn't respond when Juergen called out to him. Juergen bent down to pick the papers up and followed Heinrich to his office. He looked at the photos that Heinrich had on his desk and had a shocked expression on his face. Juergen then smiled lightly. As he handed the papers back to Heinrich he commented, "Excuse me, I believe I know one of the ladies in the photo."

A surprised Heinrich said, "These are my sisters. How do you know them?"

"I believe her name is Gerda. She is a friend of my former roommate, Manfred Ziemer," Juergen responded.

Heinrich who looked like he was about to smile and end the pleasantries, paused for a moment, as if what he had just heard was finally sinking in, and his expression became grave. "Where can I find Mr. Ziemer?"

● ● ●

Heinrich came by Juergen's apartment the very next day. Juergen was able to get in touch with Manfred's mother, who provided the address for Manfred's aunt and uncle.

"He is in Chicago!" exclaimed Heinrich, with a tinge of excitement, that betrayed his mind was considering numerous possibilities. There was a slight grin that even seemed to tease the corners of his mouth.

Without uttering another word, still seemingly lost in his thinking, Heinrich turned to leave.

"Oh, Mr. Majowski?" called out Juergen.

"Yes?" answered a startled Heinrich.

"The audition, Sir. How did I do?" asked Juergen.

"I have a friend in Munich whom you should contact. We can't fit you in here," Heinrich replied in a hurried tone. He scribbled a name on a piece of paper and dashed off.

● ● ●

Heinrich opened his apartment door and was amazed to see Bastian there, unannounced. He was covered with bruises.

"Colonel Kasparov paid me a visit," Bastian said. "He is after Gerda. I am concerned for her safety."

"You know I would give up my life before I allowed any harm to come to my sister," Heinrich declared. "That settles it, I must get her to safety."

● ● ●

Manfred's aunt and uncle were shocked when he divulged that he wanted to bring his girlfriend to Chicago from Germany. He marveled at how he overcame his temerity in approaching them in the first place.

"How can you think of doing that?" his uncle demanded.

VIRTUOSO

"You have to earn enough to have a proper place for her," his aunt declared.

Manfred had a great deal of compunction in approaching them. Their visceral response made him retreat in his ambition even further. He even thought about giving up. Try as he may, however, he was not able to get her out of his mind. Every bit of music that he heard reminded him of her. And then he passed by a poster announcing the performance of *Die Zauberflote* in Chicago. This emboldened him to take action. Manfred saved as much money as possible. He worked hard to get a promotion at his job so that he could earn enough to live on his own. It took him most of 1952 to achieve that target. He was finally able to convince his aunt and uncle that he had the financial means to provide for Gerda.

"I can do it, Uncle," Manfred trumpeted. "I am ready."

Although they were still skeptical, they proceeded to process the papers to sponsor Gerda. Manfred's uncle admitted to Manfred that the deciding factor for him had more to do with the determination on the part of Manfred and not the perceived preparedness from a financial standpoint that made him agree.

● ● ●

Gerda remembered her last letter from Manfred as she walked to the American consulate to collect her visa to migrate to America. She also thought about the last time she had done that walk—the night of the Celibidache concert. Manfred had written to Gerda, "May I always be there to pick up your chair. Let the music of my desire reach you the way Tamino beguiled Pamina with his magic flute. Like Tristan calling out to his Isolde, please come to me."

CHAPTER VI

Manfred arrived in New York to receive Gerda from her transatlantic voyage. It had been nearly two years since he had seen her. He went down to the pier at Fifty-Second Street. There was an excitement in his chest, almost a shortness of breath. He thought that there must be some medical basis for that phenomenon, but he couldn't think much about that. He hadn't received a photo of her since they had been communicating. He wondered if she had changed at all. He imagined what their first conversation would be like or about the first thing he would say to her. Should he say, "Welcome to America"? Perhaps it would be better to say, "Hello, my darling." Shouldn't he say, "I love you," he wondered? All of these questions added to his anxiety, and of course, his shortness of breath. He wondered if he should begin looking for an oxygen tank. The mental image of him standing beside the arrival ship with a mask supplying him oxygen made him laugh. What would Gerda think? *She might think I aged seventy years.* It broke some of his tension. He decided to sing to himself so that he could continue to maintain control over his thoughts and attempt to stem their inconvenient habit of running away with themselves.

He got to the pier on that windy March day of 1953 and caught his first glimpse of Gerda's arrival ship. It was a much bigger vessel than the one he had come in on himself. There were throngs of people, and he wondered how he would be able to spot her amongst the crowd.

Then he saw her moving towards the exit of the boat. He first noticed her eyes. He remembered the sensation he had—he had felt it years before in a concert hall in Berlin. How could he think that those bright eyes would not stick out in a crowd? He should have realized early on that this would be the means by which he would identify her. He held on to that thought—those big blue glimpses of water had just traversed the ocean—water crossing over

78

water.

The sight of her brought back a tidal wave of emotion. The letters between them had been nostalgic and sweet. Two lovers were re-united through the written word after losing touch. Manfred remembered his surprise and delight when he had received Heinrich's first letter. Any news or correspondence from home was welcome and appreciated. And now, her splendor was all there, in the walking flesh. She seemed to have aged beyond the few years that he had been separated from her. He detected strain in those eyes. What should have been a glow was a bit of hollowness. Even from the shore to the deck, Manfred felt like he could have reached into those eyes and would have found boundless space. As if the entire ocean could be found in those eyes, not just droplets of water. When her eyes finally met his—it was like a light switch—she bubbled over with enthusiasm. Manfred was touched; he knew the display was for his benefit. *What a precious gem*, thought Manfred. *This woman has a heart of gold.*

They embraced on the dock beside the great big ship amongst the thousands of people. Years earlier a photo of a sailor kissing a nurse in Times Square by Alfred Eisenstadt appeared on the cover of *Time* magazine. Maybe their inspiration came from that stirring image, maybe from within. As they held each other, it was as if they had gained back those few years of lost time. People, baggage, the world, moved around them. They stood still and savored the moment.

Manfred held her face in his hands and whispered, "I'm glad you are here."

He was relieved that his first comment came to him naturally and he was able to deliver it effortlessly. *So much for planning*, he thought.

Gerda responded with a single tear that flowed down her face and onto Manfred's wrist.

Part II : pre-1949

CHAPTER VII

Manfred and his brother had grown up in a household that worked hard to make it through life. The Ziemers were the enlightened working class. Manfred and his family knew about, appreciated, and understood the fine arts and strived to pepper their lives with it, but their lives were, out of necessity, nearly wholly consumed by needing to earn money in order to survive. Their wages would never amass them wealth. Whatever they earned, they would need to spend in order to maintain living. The next day, week or month, the battle began anew.

Manfred's father, whom he barely had a chance to know, started working in a Siemens factory, a large industrial products company. He was fortunate, however; he eventually found his way into working as a lighting technician in a theatre. Manfred's father was always engaged by show tunes and the music of theatrical productions. He passed away when Manfred was fourteen and his brother, Horst, was ten. In order to support herself and the two boys, Manfred's mother, whom he and his brother called Muti, would sew. She would sew women's and men's clothing and she would at times make women's handbags.

At times, Manfred and Horst would help her, especially with the handbags. "You make these bags too well, my dear little sister," Manfred would tease Horst. "You sew too fast to be a man."

Horst would quietly work away, unaffected by his brother's perturbations, which were actually affectionate as opposed to truly designed to hurt him. Manfred mused that perhaps his brother understood that and quietly accepted them. Not hearing a response would just embolden Manfred to continue. "I will tell your wife that she can work in the factory and you can stay home, cooking and sewing." No response from Horst. Manfred would end the session with a hug for his brother. "Thanks for getting so much done." To this comment, his brother would offer a tiny crack of a smile.

Muti would often claim the severe lung cancer that took Manfred's father's life at a young forty-three was a result of his involvement in the first World War when he was sent to fight in the Balkans. His battle with cancer had been a great challenge. Death was inevitable. Its shadow haunted him like a veil permeating his chest, forcing him to cough incessantly an ephemeral ghost-like substance. The sound would make Manfred cringe. It was the sound of gasping suffering. It troubled Manfred. No matter the extent or vigor of his cough, Manfred's father couldn't shake it. Manfred could see the look of worry on his face for the fate of his wife and two boys. His agony, both mental and physical, was so acute, one night he attempted to end everyone's life by filling the home with gas. Muti stopped the flow of gas before it became fatal. Manfred's father eventually died of natural causes in 1938. Fate had decided to limit his suffering, Manfred had decided; he would not witness another world war.

● ● ●

As a young girl, Gerda had enjoyed all of the privilege and comforts afforded by a family of royal ancestry. The Majowski household that she grew up in was one of the wealthiest in the Rhine-Westphalia region of Germany. Nestled in the town of Herne/Westphalia, near to Dorsten, was the Majowski enclave. Gerda's ancestors had originally come from Poland and now and again Polish could be heard spoken within the Majowski household. Gerda's father Sylvester had amassed a significant fortune managing railroad companies. He benefited tremendously from the increased passenger traffic throughout the region during the 1920s and 1930s and the booming cargo trade that businesses engaged in over land and through ports in the North Sea. Germany in that era was involved in major industrial expansion. Sylvester capitalized on the growth. Berlin was becoming an active cultural center, as were other cities in Germany. The Olympics of 1936 in Berlin were a major push for the government in terms of the building of infrastructure. Manpower and materials needed to move throughout Germany. While Gerda was an adolescent and teenager, Sylvester was there to make it happen.

Gerda's father was not a tall man, barely over five feet tall. Gerda observed, however, that he wasn't so much a man as he was a force. When he walked, people would sense that he was coming. He walked with purpose and intent. He was always a man on a mission. His whole life was about setting out and accomplishing something. Gerda could not recall a time when he was not in pursuit of a goal or objective. He held his head up high when he walked. His handshake was secure, sealed with a tight grip. He looked everyone and anyone straight in the eye. Gerda knew that anyone who interacted with him was always transfixed by his eyes—they declared his steely resolve. His speech was always firm—Gerda never heard any quivering in his voice, any hesitation, any trepidation. He spoke with authority and he commanded attention, and with it, respect. All others in the vicinity tended to be quiet when Sylvester spoke.

When Gerda was a toddler, Sylvester built a large house above a railroad station, just so that he could be nearby work. He always kept a close eye on business. When the house was being constructed, the builder questioned whether it would be too noisy. Sylvester smiled. "I have a solution for the noise problem."

Sylvester was an expert in business, but his true passion lay elsewhere. Gerda and the other Majowski children knew that in his heart he was moved most not by profits but by music. He surrounded himself with musical expression, and he ensconced in each of his six children who filled that house above the station with music. The Majowski household was a testament and homage to the glory and splendor of music—each brick a musical note and the collective whole a stirring symphony, a veritable temple revering music. Gerda always felt that it could stand proud next to the grand opera houses, La Scala in Milan, Covent Garden in London, and the grand concert halls of Europe, as a sacred, hallow space for the expression, production, and development of music. And unlike those public arenas, music was not confined to set times of performances or practices; no, music lived and breathed in the Majowski residence throughout the day. Anyone calling on the Majowski household was guaranteed to hear and enjoy music in some form or another. Even passengers on trains pulling into the station would marvel.

"Is there an orchestra performing at the train station?" conductors would ask.

"No," the stationmaster would reply, "it is from Herr Majowski's residence. His orchestra is comprised of his six children."

Within those divine walls, music was deified. It was elevated to an exalted level within that structure. For Gerda and her siblings, in that Majowski house, life was music, and music was life.

Sylvester himself had shown a strong affinity towards music at a very young age. Gerda knew that everyone had regarded him as a musical prodigy; he became well versed in all instruments from childhood. He developed a strong passion for conducting. Gerda knew that had his family not experienced the hardship it had while he was growing up, he would have pursued music as his full-time profession.

Gerda struggled to vie for her father's attention in that setting. It was a challenge as her siblings exhibited a great deal of musical talent to rival hers. Gerda had to resort to other means to attract, and retain, her father's attention.

As a young girl of seven, Gerda approached her father after he came home. She was the only one who dared approach him. The other children scurried away in fear. "Father, why do you love music so much?" Gerda asked.

Sylvester stalled a few seconds before putting the paper down to face his child. Gerda sensed that he needed the time to recover from his shock that one of his children had the audacity to start a conversation with him. It had always worked in the other direction. After another few seconds, he put the paper back up and continued to read. Undeterred, Gerda came back to him the next day. The other children were aghast. None of them dared approach their father that way. After one week, he pulled Gerda onto his lap. Gerda could tell by the look in his eyes that he didn't know what to do with her.

"It gives my life meaning and a purpose to live," Sylvester told her. In a rare show of affection, she hugged her father and kissed his cheek. The other Majowski children were in awe as they witnessed their father reciprocate this affection. Gerda remained the only one to break through Sylvester's austerity. Within days of answering Gerda's questions, he confessed to her that he had made a promise to himself, as a young boy with his family suffering financially, that his children would be afforded the opportunity to make their lives in music.

Sylvester was the oldest of sixteen children. Although Gerda's grandfather had been knighted by the Polish prince and the family boasted a coat-of-arms, tough times had fallen on the family, and all of the property that they owned had been lost due to the Prussian wars in that region. Gerda's grandfather had to work in a coal mine to support the family. He struggled, but knew that beyond titles and nobility, education would be the salvation of the family. He sent all of his children to the best schools possible. Sylvester knew he had to have a job where he could earn as much as possible. He told Gerda that at the time he felt that his best opportunity to do so would be in Germany so he traveled there to attend one of the most prestigious military academies. He didn't know German at the time, but he exhibited great skill in linguistics. He also wouldn't allow his lack of German to be an impediment.

After graduating, he joined the national railroad company. He worked his way up the ranks, surpassing many of his peers. He had more and more people reporting to him over time. Eventually he was named president of a region.

"Look at this gold watch I was just granted," he said to his children, starting with Gerda. When he had been promoted to president, he was given a gold watch as a gift. He kept that watch with him at all times. Gerda couldn't recall an image of her father without that watch; it had become so ubiquitous. For Sylvester, it was a badge of honor, a medal that he had been awarded. It was the physical representation of the success he had worked hard to attain. Gerda sensed that every time he looked at the watch it was a reminder to him of all that he had struggled to accomplish in order to reach the post that he held. All of his children knew how important it was to him. Over time it was a curiosity for the children. Sylvester could have bought hundreds of gold watches with the wealth he had accumulated. But they knew that this one had a special significance. Sylvester would often quip to Gerda, "Your grandfather received a knighthood. I received a gold watch."

Sylvester used the money he earned as a railroad executive not only to provide his family with a very comfortable living but also to pursue his true love—music. In the town of Dorsten, he commissioned and paid for an orchestra that he himself conducted. Every Sunday there would be a performance by Sylvester's orchestra in the town center. Not only the townspeople would enjoy it, but people came from the surrounding areas to enjoy the concerts. Sylvester took great care to select the best musicians he could afford. Over time, he was able to attract musicians of ever-greater caliber. His concerts were always free, however. It was his gift for people to enjoy.

All of the Majowski children were trained in music. Each learned to play the piano. In addition, Wilfred, the eldest, was trained in rhythm as a drummer and in conducting. Sylva, the next oldest, became an opera singer. Ernest became a composer as well as a conductor. In addition to her musical instruction, Mia was also trained as a nurse. Gerda, the fifth born, focused exclusively on the piano. And of course, young Heinrich learned the cello. Sylvester believed strongly that each child should be encouraged to pursue what their natural abilities showed they had an inclination towards. He supported them each and encouraged them to pursue what they were fond of and the arena in which they would have the highest probability of attaining success.

Sylvester was also their first music teacher. He would collect all of the children in the living room. He would play music for them and encourage them to appreciate what they were hearing. "Allow yourself to be swept away by the music—don't resist," Sylvester encouraged the children. "The beauty of music is that it can control your emotions—if you know how to listen. Let the conductor take control over your senses and your heart; he will navigate you. At first, it will be natural to resist. But just imagine each stroke of the bow on the string instruments is wiping away your resistance, each gust of air in the wind instruments is blowing away your reluctance, and each wave of the baton is banishing your inhibition. If you feel joy, smile. If you feel sadness, cry. Don't be afraid to let your emotions go. That is the gift of music. It will move you if you allow it."

He could see a wave of understanding soak his children. Intuitively he knew that Gerda would be the first to grasp this, and she rewarded him handily by allowing a smile to creep on her face while her eyes were tightly closed as she listened to the piece of music Sylvester was playing. Soon all of the Majowski children were attuned to what he was attempting to instill in them. He could tell by watching the reactions on the rest of their faces. When he saw them naturally change their expressions to suit the music, Gerda leading the charge, he knew that they had an understanding and appreciation for the gift of music.

While Wilfred and Sylva were twelve and ten years older than Gerda, the other children were much closer in age. Ernest was two years older than Mia, who was two years older than Gerda, who was four years older than Heinrich. Gerda was born in 1920.

Every night, after dinner, the children would take turns at the piano or in singing a song or playing their instrument, playing for the family. This was a proper recital for the children where they were supposed to display their talents. Each would practice during the several days prior to their designated day and during the day prior to the meal so that they could deliver the best performance possible. The children were all aware of their father's strict standards, and none of them wanted to disappoint him. If they made mistakes, Sylvester would instruct them on how to improve.

"You have five days to practice and rehearse this piece," he instructed them. Sylvester would make them perform the piece again. They would keep going like this until they had mastered the work. Then he would require them to move on to another piece that was even more challenging.

"This is how you will improve," Sylvester would say. Gerda was always proud of the fact that she had the lowest repeat performances of any of the children.

Heinrich would be encouraged to play the cello and Sylva would sing. On two separate occasions, Sylvester would speak for weeks to the townspeople about how there would be a guest conductor at his orchestra on Sunday. To the audience's surprise, it was first Wilfred and then Ernest in the conducting role.

"You have to get this right during your first performance," he told his two sons, "You are performing to a large audience, not just the family."

● ● ●

Ram surveyed the premises like he did every morning. It was a bright summer day. The production lines were set to run. The materials had arrived a few days earlier. The shift would begin any moment. The customer had been pushing him for several days now to receive the product.

Ram owned a factory that made brass idols. The idols were of Hindu gods and goddesses. The pantheon of possibilities in this polytheistic religion was good from a business sense as well: there was a wide range of products that could be sold. Ram had considered other materials. There were idols made of marble, granite, or onyx and some that were made from the precious metals of silver or gold. Ram preferred brass. He could make the full range of sizes that way; a six foot marble idol would be prohibitively expensive to try to sculpt. Also, brass would be cheap enough to sell to the masses.

The smaller format, more popular idols were made in the production line. The larger format idols, over eighteen inches tall, were made using traditional hand methods employed by master artisans highly skilled in working with metal. Ram had assembled some of the finest craftsmen in the trade.

Ram came from a large family. He alone had six children. But, he also had five younger brothers. Each had been married and had their own children. There were fifty-two people in all, and he was the head of the whole group. This made him, ultimately, responsible for their collective well-being.

Growing up, he had a desire to move beyond the traditional agrarian base that the family had been involved with for generations in the northeastern part of India. "There is opportunity in metal working," he had declared to the family one day. "We shall move to find the right situation for us."

None of the family members said anything negative. Two of his brothers said in unison, and that too only when Ram looked around the room and locked his eyes with theirs, "If you think it is best, *Bhaiya*"—a term meaning respected elder brother.

All of the women in the household stayed quiet. His own wife kept her head bowed down when Ram would speak at such gatherings. The wives of his younger brothers all kept their faces veiled with their *saris*, the Indian traditional dress, six yards in length, folded and manipulated around the female form in an artistic display that could be at one instance demure and another instance provocative. In Ram's presence, it was always the former. Ram had never seen his brothers' wives faces except for the first day that he had met them. That was the day he had decided that they would be the right wife for each brother.

Karachi and its surrounding areas were the industrial base of the country. It was nestled in an area called Punjab in the northwest. With some family members in tow, Ram set out for Karachi, leaving behind his home and the plantation.

"You must continue to plant and harvest the fields," he instructed two of his younger brothers. "If there is no success in metals, we will have to come back to farming."

Ram had considered opening a metal manufacturing facility on the plantation. "I'll never be able to procure raw materials at a reasonable enough price to make it worthwhile to stay in this part of the country," he lamented out loud. His family listened to his reasoning. The men nodded their heads in agreement. The wives remained silent.

Ram reflected on his brothers' behavior to his good friend, Akbar Khan. "It's not that they can't think for themselves. Sometimes they think too much for themselves. Remember how many times I had to bail my brother out of prison for protesting against the British?" Ram had relayed the story to Akbar many times. He was the one who arrived first to bribe the 'brown' constable at the prison.

"And then the protests that my other brother, the officer in the British Army, made. What a ruckus that was!" Ram chuckled as he reminisced. "His most endearing comment was 'Come on, brother, if the British quit India, I will be out of a job, please have some mercy.'" Ram laughed as he recounted the story.

"He didn't even laugh as he said it. Invoking brotherly love! That little rascal," Ram added. "They are all good boys. They lost their father at a young age. To whom were they going to turn? It was me."

"You lost your father as well," Akbar reminded Ram.

"Yes, but I wasn't so young. These boys, anything related to family matters, they always defer to me. They never question."

"It is good that they respect you, isn't it?"

"They are smart boys. Sometimes having their thoughts to help shape mine would be a good thing," Ram commented, his voice trailing off. "Turn the record over, the last movement of Beethoven's Seventh is on the other side," he instructed Akbar. "You know, the Eighth Symphony is so short that its four movements plus the fourth movement of the Seventh Symphony all fit on one side."

Ram often sought the sanctuary of music to put his mind at ease. At home, when he had to make tough decisions, he would isolate himself in his study with his phonograph. When he wanted to air something off his chest, he would visit Akbar and listen to the music there. Sometimes he would bring his own records as Akbar's collection was limited.

"It reminds me that there is beauty in the world," he would quip to Akbar and his other friends and associates who found his love of music intriguing. While he certainly was appreciative of the Indian musical tradition—in all of its folksy splendor—western music had its unique, beguiling appeal. For him, it was structured spiritual reverence.

Just as Hinduism had taught him a pantheon of gods and the central edict of respect for all religions—all were paths to the same higher spiritual being—so he reasoned the same would be for the realm of music. He digested and consumed all forms of world music. Ram never discriminated.

● ● ●

Gerda's mother, Christina Majowski, maintained a strict order in the house. The children called her formally as Mother. While Sylvester would see to the children's artistic development, Christina would see to it that the children learned the fine art of living. Sylvester was fond of living well; it was a high priority for him. Gerda knew that in his mind it justified the long hours spent managing the railroad. She could also detect that it was a vindication for the hardships that he had faced as a young man and with which he saw his parents struggle. It was also a return to a standard of living that Gerda's forefathers had enjoyed at the time they were anointed royalty. In Christina, Sylvester had found the perfect companion to instill those virtues in the children.

Gerda's childhood house was impeccably organized. There was a set purpose for each room in the house, and Gerda and the other children had to adhere to that purpose. Each child had their own bedroom, and there was a set room designated for playing. Toys were only allowed in that play room. There was a separate instrument room where they could make whatever noise they wanted. But when they entered the rehearsal room or the recital room, they had to preserve the house rules of staying quiet and sitting still unless they were spoken to or they were performing.

One day Gerda brought a toy into her parents' bedroom. The whole next week she was required to organize all of the toys in the toy room. Christina was adamant that she learn her lesson. Christina also insisted that all of the children had to abide by a strict schedule of chores, studies, and practicing of their musical instruments. There was no wavering from this. There was no sleeping late allowed, even on days of relaxation. The children each had their stated times when they had to be in bed and their set times when they had to wake up.

While there was an extensive house staff, the children were not allowed to remain idle. Gerda and the other girls learned how to manage a household and prepare proper meals, clean the house, and sew clothing. In addition to mending their clothes, they also learned how to make new clothing. For holidays they were required to make themselves elaborate dresses to fit the occasion.

Gerda's brothers learned about managing resources, allocating funds and establishing priorities—things that would enable them to be the head of a household when they grew up. However, there was always time dedicated to music, and it took the highest priority.

When Sylvester arrived in the evening, each child had their responsibility—one had to bring father's slippers, another the evening newspaper, another his evening jacket, etc. All of the attention and focus would be on him.

The day would start with the family having breakfast together. The table always had to be set the night before by the girls in the household. Each girl would be assigned a night. In the morning Christina would run a ruler along the edge of the table, each of the plate edges and the edges of the silverware had to be flush with the end of the table. If any went over or were too far in from the edge, Christina would first scold and second educate the girls.

From Gerda's memory, Sylva always got her table settings right—that suited Gerda fine. She was pleased enough to be their father's favorite. Gerda was comfortable that another sibling could be their mother's favorite, except when it came to Mia. Gerda and Mia always competed to see who would get the most praise, and Mia would always be resentful whenever Gerda received a lot of praise. Gerda had to admit, that was part of the fun. The tables also had to be set with the finest linens—linens which were changed frequently, as were the newly cut flowers on the table, in order to provide a fresh look everyday.

Floral arrangements were where Gerda would excel. She would always strive to find the most exotic flowers from the town that she could get her hands on, while Mia would always just pluck from the garden. Gerda wouldn't even leave the house; she would have one of the town boys bring it to the door. All marveled at how she pulled it off. "I'll never tell where I got them from," she boasted, while shooting a glance—a modified victory lap—towards Mia.

When all would assemble at the table at mealtime, Christina would keep by her side a large wooden spoon. If the children displayed any behavioral problems, Christina would threaten with the wooden spoon. "I don't like what we are eating," Gerda would complain. Christina would hold the wooden spoon in her hands, tapping one end of it on the palm of her hand, and look straight at Gerda. Without saying a word, Gerda would turn back to her food and eat. Christina would then look under the table and say, "One leg is missing." She grabbed a hold of the wooden spoon again. Gerda quickly put her leg down. If the children did not finish the food on their plates, the wooden spoon would be in hand yet again.

For breakfast, the family always started with a fresh fruit dish. Then came the "sweet course"—either apple pancakes or crepes. Sometimes the sweet dish was replaced with an egg dish. Then they were served the bread course. A wide range of breads were made at home—white, wheat, rye, pumpernickel, muffins, etc. There were also always a broad assortment of jams and jellies to choose from. Some were quite common—strawberry, grape, orange—while others were more exotic—plum, gooseberry or boysenberry. Some came from France, some from the UK. Gerda assisted her mother in looking for the most exotic marmalades they could find. Additionally, Gerda and Christina preserved a number of different fruits on their own—apricot, peach, and even pear.

Lunch was always the main meal of the day. Christina would lead Gerda and the other girls to always make them elaborate affairs with multiple courses. There would be a soup, a salad, a main dish and a dessert. The same would be repeated for supper, although it was much lighter. The meals would always be the highest caliber meats or exotic feasts inspired by refined cuisine from Europe—German, Polish, Italian or French cooking. In the evening a home-baked cake was usually served. The children's mother and father would enjoy coffee. Later in the evening Sylvester would sit in the corner of the dining room and enjoy a cognac and a cigar.

Holidays were a grand celebration in the Majowski household, particularly at Christmas. Sylvester would go with the boys to select a tree from the forest. They would have it cut down by a member of the household staff and brought to the house. All family members would participate in decorating the tree. Gifts were either purchased or made by hand. Sylvester would prepare his orchestra for a special Christmas day gala. An elaborate meal was always planned, typically five to seven courses versus the usual three or four. Particular attention was paid to the Christmas treats. Cookies and other treats were especially baked for the occasion. Gerda was always a little resentful of Christmas as she always felt shortchanged for her birthday, which happened to fall on December twenty-sixth. All of her siblings would wrap up the Christmas gifts that they received which they liked the least and would present them to her as her birthday gifts. One year, when Gerda was seven, Heinrich gave her a toy wooden soldier that he had received. "What, are you kidding me?" Gerda demanded of him and chased him around the house with it. It was the first time she had uttered the phrase.

Every New Year's Eve the family would listen to Beethoven's Ninth Symphony after midnight. It was how the family rang in the New Year.

● ● ●

Although the children had to adhere to schedules, maintain certain behavior standards and be disciplined about their musical pursuits, their years were largely full of the carefree days of an idealistic, halcyon youth. There was ample time for them to be children and display their individual traits.

Propped by the disproportionately large amount of affection she received from her father, Gerda became a bit of a daredevil and a tomboy while growing up. In contrast to Mia, who was frequently sick, Gerda was rarely sick. She had a lot of strength as a child. This led to Gerda being more adventurous outdoors. Somehow, Sylvester and Christina must have had a sense of their youngest daughter's future proclivities, for the name Gerda meant "woman of the garden."

She was notorious for playing practical jokes about town. She would even be adventurous with Sylvester's weekly sponsored concert in the marketplace of the town. One day, Gerda poured lemon juice and several lemons down the opening of the tuba player's instrument, ending his ability to play. The incident angered

VIRTUOSO

Sylvester a great deal. His performance for that week was sub-par as a result of it. Had it been one of the boys, or one of the other girls, he would have disciplined them harshly. When he approached Gerda, she heard the pounding of his footsteps in the hall. As he came closer, he seemed to slow down. His determined walk had become less emphatic. She thought she could feel his eyes piercing through her, but as he approached he seemed almost confused. The confidence with which he began the action seemed to wane. Gerda felt a sense for what was transpiring. Maybe he was appreciative of her audacity to stage such a stunt, she thought. Gerda's siblings would never have dared to do such a thing.

"Gerda, don't you ever do that again," Sylvester said to her, his tone surprisingly even. Gerda then noticed the look of disappointment on his face and in his eyes. She had let him down. She immediately felt shallow. *That was stupid,* thought Gerda. She instantly felt remorse for doing what she did.

This wouldn't keep her from engaging in other mischief, however. *Next time, I won't cause any harm to Father,* she reasoned as she merrily went about her way. In the evenings, she would repeatedly turn off the gas-lit street lamps. This would make the local townspeople livid. Because of Gerda, they at times had to roam around in the dark. In order to do this, Gerda had to remove her shoes so that she could climb up the lamppost. One evening one of the other town boys who had a crush on Gerda, distinct from the boy delivering the flowers, stole her shoes. Before she had a chance to chase after him, Heinrich whistled Beethoven's Ninth Symphony from the window of the house, which he did every night to alert Gerda that she should come home. Their mother was looking for her. Gerda came running home and had to explain why she did not have her shoes. She came up with an excuse that she had lost them. To Gerda's dismay, when Christina went to church the following morning, Gerda's shoes were there outside the church door.

The other children were also not without mischief. One evening Heinrich sat at the dinner table wearing a cap. Gerda could sense that Christina was not pleased. "Heinrich, are you aware that you are not dressed in appropriate attire to be sitting at the dinner table?" she questioned him in a stern voice.

Heinrich nodded his head yes, but did not remove the hat.

"Heinrich, do you know what you are supposed to do?" Christina continued.

Again Heinrich nodded his head yes, but did not remove the hat.

Their mother lost her patience at that point.

"Heinrich you remove your hat immediately!" she scolded him.

Heinrich removed his hat. Gerda was the first to notice and started laughing. Before Christina observed Heinrich, she disciplined Gerda. "That is not appropriate behavior for the dinner table, young lady!" she boomed. And then their mother looked upon Heinrich. He had shaved off his eyebrows. "What in God's name?" asked Christina, exasperated.

"I wanted to shave like Father," said Heinrich in a meek voice. "I didn't have any other hair on my face to shave."

Christina tried her best to hold her laughter in. Sylvester was the first to break. Then all the children laughed. Gerda felt a little resentful for having been scolded. She knew she was not allowed to make mention of the incident, but Christina threw a glance at her while she started to laugh, one of the many instances of their silent communication, a look that without saying anything condoned Gerda's earlier reaction.

Sylvester kept his ties with his family, including his close brothers, whom Gerda and the children knew as Uncle Franz, Uncle Wilhelm and Uncle Heinrich. Uncle Heinrich was quite close to Sylvester and was the namesake for Gerda's brother, Heinrich. Uncle Heinrich had played the cello in his youth, but had to give it up when the family hit upon hard times. Sylvester would also visit his mother in Poland once a year. Gerda would always accompany him. She was the only one. She would meet her grandmother, who only spoke Polish, and would try to communicate with her although Gerda spoke only German.

On one trip, Gerda decided to tease her father. "Father, how come I am the only one that you bring with you?" Gerda knew from the silence that ensued that she had either stumped her father or he wasn't comfortable in answering.

"Because you are available," came the terse response.

Gerda smiled to herself. She was secretly pleased that she did not have to wait one week for a response. She also understood by the response that her father never wanted to articulate definitively that she was his favorite.

● ● ●

As a young boy, Manfred showed an acumen for mechanical aptitude. He had an intuitive understanding of how machines worked and functioned together. He could have effortlessly become an engineer. As a result, Manfred also spent some time in a factory, trying to earn some extra money. In one incident, Manfred was working with a steel cutting machine and he accidentally cut the tip of his finger off. This had a lasting impact on Manfred as he found it a challenge to manage playing the piano when he studied at the Conservatory. The nerve endings in his finger never healed properly.

Even at a young age, Manfred's passion for music was evident. Being an ace engineer was second nature for him, but his passion was in singing.

While Manfred was a fit young man, Manfred's younger brother Horst was sickly. He was tiny when he was born and struggled to put on weight as an infant and toddler. His frail body would contract numerous illnesses, making it a rarity for him to be feeling well.

During one episode of illness, a doctor had declared to Muti upon his examination that Horst would not make it and that the family should prepare to lose him. Manfred saw the expression on his mother's face. This was a call to action for a very determined

Muti. Horst was always very picky with his food choices. Amongst the small number of foods that he would take, he did enjoy eating bananas. She began feeding Horst large quantities of bananas. Even when Horst would resist, Muti kept feeding him. The lad would kick and scream but Muti would force the bananas down his throat. She returned to the doctor that had foretold of Horst's death. The doctor insisted that it was not the same child as he had examined before.

Times were often tough in the Ziemer household. Often, all that Muti had to feed her boys were turnip sandwiches. Muti had a strength of will that infused her with a determination that survival was the only option. Muti relied on her passion and love for music to help her get through raising two boys with no husband to support her. The purchase of instruments was out of the question because money was tight, and the thrill of experiencing live musical productions would elude the Ziemers for some time. So Muti relied on her voice to create music, to enjoy the listening of music and to impart the wonder of music to her two boys. When she could spare any time, she would sing as a part of a choir. She earned some money doing this, but it wasn't enough to be pursued as a full-time profession. She felt as if she had not had the proper training for it. She was not shy about articulating her dream to Manfred: that one of her sons become a professional singer.

Muti was one of thirteen children. She had ten sisters and two brothers. Most of her siblings had settled throughout Germany, and two sisters had migrated to the US. Muti was closer to some siblings than others. Their upbringing had been similar to how they managed their own lives. They came from a working household that took the time to appreciate singing and music.

Manfred followed in his father's footsteps in two ways—he worked for Siemens for a while, plying his mechanical proclivities, and he became a soldier. In his heart, though, he wished to fulfill his mother's dream. He was driven not so much by the desire to please his mother, but because the joy that he felt in singing stirred something in Manfred that he arrived at on his own.

● ● ●

Ram had trouble keeping tabs on all of his brothers. They each had diverse interests and jobs that they were all pursuing or had shown interest in pursuing. There were so many possibilities available for them to explore. "I have the least luxury in that regard," Ram said, ruefully.

Ram had too many responsibilities. As much as he wanted to be free, he always had to think about providing for such a large family. He knew he couldn't take any risks in terms of his career pursuits. He needed something secure to rely upon.

"I wonder how things would have been for me if I had a choice in what I could do?" Ram wondered aloud to Akbar.

Ram actually had a sense of what he would have done. In his travels, Ram would come across many people from the West who were passionate about music. Ram always enjoyed speaking with them to learn what he could about the latest recordings.

On one visit to New Delhi, Ram had his very first meeting with John Foulds. "I would love to write pieces that fuse Indian and Western music," John told Ram.

Ram was intrigued by this. "It would be interesting to hear how it sounds," Ram said. He tried to be a bit more enthusiastic. He couldn't help it, though. Ram was a purist.

"In many ways," Ram said, "I feel that a fused music would have its own place, that wouldn't necessarily fit in with the separate identities of Western and Eastern music."

John looked like he was lost.

"That is to say, I don't know that lovers of Western or Eastern music individually would necessarily like the fusion of the two."

John had to agree with the premise. "I have had that revelation as well," he admitted. "I will attempt to appeal to both sides. That is my mission."

CHAPTER VIII

Gerda always felt that her father had to pay a price for his success. Sylvester had been doing business so well in the Dorsten area that the railroad company wanted to send him to all of their troubled spots. Because of his knowledge of German, Polish, and Russian, they posted him back to Poland in 1937, in a town called Llazy. It was in the northwestern corner of the country, close to the border of Germany. Gerda was seventeen at the time. Once again, Gerda watched in wonder as he established his musical palace by the rail station.

Llazy was a very different town than Dorsten. It was much more rural. Gerda sensed that part of her father enjoyed the bucolic surroundings. But she also knew that part of him missed the greater cultural center that Dorsten was. It was a bit more cosmopolitan and gaining access to larger cities was easy. In Llazy, Gerda observed her father struggle. By then, Wilfred, Sylva and Mia had been married, and only three children were at home regularly. Ernest would likely get married soon, so most of the time it was Gerda and Heinrich with Sylvester and Christina at home. Had his children been younger, Gerda knew that her father would have made a decision not to go to Llazy for fear of limiting the children's access to culture and the arts. Since he had already exposed them extensively, Gerda surmised, he felt comfortable in making the move.

Sylvester had little very time at this point to devote to other matters beyond work, such as setting up his local orchestra. Gerda also had a suspicion that father wasn't sure that a local orchestra would have quite the following that it did when the family was in Dorsten.

"I am getting on in years," Sylvester replied to Gerda, when she pushed him on why he would not be starting an orchestra. "Perhaps my sons can take over the conducting of orchestras. It is my turn to enjoy as a member of the audience." Gerda had a hard time arguing with his reasoning.

When Sylvester arrived at Llazy, Gerda saw her father work hard to get the operations of the railroad into shape. It absorbed most of his time. Gerda barely saw him. The previous president of that region had allowed the company to fall into severe disarray. Sylvester had problems with workers being agitated, trains breaking down, and trains not running on time. There were a lot of issues he had to address. One of his biggest difficulties was with his coal supplier. Gerda marveled at his resourcefulness. She observed as her father went to the one place he remembered – the coal mine where Gerda's grandfather had worked.

The current owner was Sylvester's age. The man's father had operated it when Gerda's grandfather worked there. Both had passed away by then. The current owner did, however, recognize the name Majowski. "It is impressive how far you have come, Herr Majowski."

Sylvester eventually developed a good relationship with the family, and their business thrived as a result of adding Sylvester's rail territories to their business. The family had a son named Uli. He was their only son and he had not yet gotten married. At various gatherings at the Majowski home in Llazy, the family that owned the coal mine caught sight of Gerda. They asked Gerda's hand in marriage for Uli.

Gerda saw how hard her father was working at the time and the number of obstacles he was forced to overcome. She had seen Uli only once or twice before at social gatherings. She had never spoken to him. She didn't know if she would have much in common with him. *He does have some qualities*, thought Gerda; he was very handsome and he came from a good family. "Father, what should I do?"

"Gerda, my dear, this is your decision," he said to her. "Wilfred, Sylva, and Mia have been married already. They all made their own decisions about whom to marry."

"Would it make you happy if I were to marry him?" Gerda pursued her line of enquiry.

"Yes, Gerda, it would," Sylvester revealed. "They are a very good family, and we have some historical ties with them. Additionally, from a business standpoint it would be very helpful. I can introduce their coal into other regions. I will receive a hefty commission from it myself, and you will become more wealthy in the process, as Uli is the only son."

What Sylvester was saying made a lot of sense to Gerda. She appreciated his honesty tremendously; she didn't expect anything else. She thought about how it would have been so much easier if he had just said that he was indifferent. "Father, I accept their proposal," she proclaimed to Sylvester.

They were married on the coal mine grounds in 1939. It was an extravagant affair. She was poised to live the life of a princess, and the wedding was staged to properly announce that new status for her. It was a fairy tale story—she was now the owner of the coal mine where her grandfather worked to re-build the family's lost wealth. Gerda's wedding procession was lined with all of the coal miners holding up their lanterns. The life of a princess that Gerda was about to step into was a natural extension of the privileged life that was her upbringing. Her new house was palatial, and she had a staff at her disposal to manage the household and to provide her with all the comforts befitting her position.

At the wedding itself, Gerda for the first time saw her father become emotional in front of a crowd of people. With a glistening droplet of moisture in his eyes, he turned to Gerda. "This is the happiest moment in my life. If my father was alive now, he would be so pleased. As a family, we have accomplished so much. Your forefathers are proud of you, my dear."

Gerda felt a sense of pride. She was thrilled that she could do this for her father. He had provided so much for her and the other children. It was something Gerda could do to show her appreciation.

VIRTUOSO

But all was not well in this seeming paradise. She should have seen the clues early on. Every time he was supposed to visit her during their courtship, Uli would come late, and it was seldom that he actually offered up an excuse as to why he was tardy. When he was with her, he would be aloof and distant.

"What did you do today?" she would enquire with her characteristic earnestness.

"Oh...not much," came his desultory response.

"Was there anything interesting at your work?"

"Well...yes and no," he would mumble without any effort at elaboration.

"Isn't this wonderful music that Father is playing?" Gerda would persist.

"What? Oh the music. Yes, there is music playing," Uli answered halfheartedly.

On the night of their wedding, Uli disappeared after the first dance. Gerda went to her bedroom by herself. She waited several hours. He finally showed up; he had been drinking excessively.

"Where have you been?" Gerda demanded.

"Oh...uh...something came up. Yes, something came up urgently," he responded with some difficulty in enunciating the words.

"What could be more important than your wedding?" She cornered him in her pursuit of the answer.

Uli mumbled a response.

Gerda was too stunned, hurt, and disheveled in terms of her emotions to keep pursuing the questions to which she was so desperate to have the answers. She felt resentment growing towards him. After several minutes of consideration, she realized that her resentment was more directed at herself rather than at him.

"What have I gotten myself into?" she posed the question to no one in particular, sighed and went to bed. The silence was answer enough. She tried to recall a soothing cello suite by Bach that Heinrich had played for her prior to her wedding—it was his way of saying goodbye, not being able to articulate his sadness by any more effective means.

And so a very lonely life ensued for Gerda. She missed being home, being with her siblings, and most importantly, being surrounded by music. There was no honeymoon planned for the two of them. Several days after the wedding she lamented to her father in a letter, "There is not even a piano here." Sylvester fixed that problem and immediately had a piano sent as a gift for his daughter and son-in-law.

At New Year's Eve, Gerda was once again very sad. She spoke to her family and revealed that there was no recording of Beethoven's Ninth in her new home. That night, Sylvester set out with the family's recording. He arrived at her house six hours later at seven AM.

"Father, I can't believe that you came all this way," Gerda exclaimed after seeing Sylvester. Tears began rolling down her face. She was overcome with emotion, and her body started to shake as a result of it, making her embrace of her father a very animated encounter. Gerda was touched by how her father did his best to console her.

"No little girl of mine will be without Beethoven's Ninth on New Year's!" Sylvester proclaimed.

They both listened to the entire symphony that morning after having been up all night. Gerda recalled how when they lived in Dorsten, her father would commission his orchestra to do a live performance of Beethoven's Ninth shortly after midnight. Nonetheless, this was one of the most meaningful New Year's that Gerda would experience. Uli was not with them. He had gone to sleep several hours earlier, and although Gerda insisted he wake up when her father arrived, he did not bother to come downstairs.

Gerda's empty life continued. "Father parceled us a beautiful cello concerto. Heinrich is learning it," Gerda pronounced to Uli. She presented the cover of the phonograph record to him as she spoke. He ignored it.

VIRTUOSO

That evening at dinner, Gerda made a suggestion to her in-laws. "Perhaps we can listen to the music that Father sent after dinner." She was met with silence. She was the only one who seemed to feel awkward about the silence. The others quietly continued their meals. Just to be sure, she raised her voice and repeated her idea. There was no reaction whatsoever from the three of them. Uli looked up when the butler entered the dining room to serve the next course. He didn't even bother to look in Gerda's direction. After dinner, all went their separate ways. She sat in the drawing room, her only companion the tears in her eyes, and listened to the music.

Gerda rarely saw her husband. During those times when he would make himself available for family gatherings many topics were discussed, but there was not a focus on anything artistic, let alone music. Gerda always felt that something was missing. The discussions would inevitably involve business or science. This wouldn't have bothered Gerda so much in and of itself, but she had grown accustomed to greater depth, and that was sorely lacking in her current situation.

Gerda also had to contend with the fact that Uli was frequently inebriated. He drank excessive amounts of alcohol. She could only remember a few times when he was sober. He would regularly consume vodka—that was his drink of choice. Often, he would carry a flask full of it, starting in the morning. He did not have a violent temperament. Gerda took some solace in that. But what good was a marriage to a man who slumbered through most of their time together? This began to take its toll on her.

"There is a problem with our customer in Warsaw. Get on the train tomorrow and solve it," Uli's father instructed him one evening. Gerda watched her husband attentively. She knew that her father had arranged for Uli to meet with government officials the following day. Uli had indicated with enthusiasm that he was looking forward to it. Gerda was certain he would protest, but no such luck. Gerda listened in horror as her husband's response reverberated through her.

"Yes, father," Uli acquiesced.

"But the meeting my father arranged," Gerda reminded him.

Instead of Uli responding, his father interceded. "That meeting is not that important. Uli must attend to the customers."

"But my father..." she protested.

Uli's father gave her a stern look, "Enough."

Gerda looked to Uli, but he kept his face down.

The frequency of such events initially shocked Gerda; for months she was troubled by them, but eventually she just accepted that her husband was a coward and she was powerless to change him. He never defended her when it came to his parents. He always allowed his own father to bully him. It was hard for Gerda to bear witness to this. Her father-in-law did not have the strength of character or the moral compass that her own father possessed. He often led Uli down a fruitless path so that his own agenda would be achieved. He rarely considered or advocated the path that would be the most beneficial for Uli. Over time, Gerda came to realize that Uli was likely coerced into marrying her so that his parents would benefit. It was hard for Gerda to cope with this realization. She was not accustomed to this display of weakness; this behavior was very foreign for her. He was nowhere near the man that her father was.

CHAPTER IX

Shortly after Gerda was married, political events began to dictate all of their lives. Their own ambitions, desires, hard work, initiative, perseverance or passions were meaningless. Soon, they lost all control over their lives. For a while, life continued in the magic of musical artistry of the Majowski household. The trains came and went beneath the house full of passengers or cargo. There had been a fair amount of isolation from the events that Sylvester heard about through the news brought to him via the traveling railroad conductors or that he read in the newspaper.

Germany entered Poland on September first of that year, 1939. Poland became split into three. The Soviets on the East, the Germans on the West and the middle territory to be contested. Sylvester had noticed that there were not many Jews in prominent positions in Poland, unlike Germany or France, where they had achieved a great deal; in fact, many of his colleagues had been Jews. The government seemed to be providing subsidized housing ghettos to the Jews in Poland. This was characterized as a positive that was being done to look after the country's downtrodden. But laws began to change. There were rumors that all Jews had to register and wear identifying marks. Sylvester had never witnessed any of this. He also heard a rumor that there was a new law stipulating the death penalty for any gentile that helped a Jew.

And then life changed immeasurably at the Majowski household. One day, a cargo train came through the rail station. Gerda was visiting her parents at the time. She, her mother, Heinrich and Ernst, the last remaining of the Majowski children living at home, saw not crates but eyes looking through to them when they looked inside the train cars.

Gerda sought out her father. She didn't come across him until dinner. In unison, Gerda and her brothers asked their father and their mother for an explanation. Christina didn't have an

107

explanation, and Sylvester's face was grim.

Later that night, Christina asked Sylvester when they were alone.

"I really don't know what is happening," he said, "Ever since Germany occupied Poland, I can't get any answers to my enquiries. I just keep hearing the same pronouncements from people. It's always said the same way without any further explanation. It's like a singer who only knows one song and repeats it continuously. Nobody is explaining anything."

From that day forward, music was not played loudly at the Majowski household. Trains pulling into the station heard silence.

The trains with the people kept coming. They were packed in like cattle. Some remained huddled in the corner when the train stopped at the station, others stood and looked out at the surroundings. Gerda, Heinrich, and Ernst asked more questions.

"Those are government trains. They are refugees," Sylvester responded one day after several more trains were seen. He shrugged his shoulders towards Christina to indicate that he didn't know what else he could say.

While the experience was traumatic for all them, Gerda knew her mother was especially moved by the plight of the people they were seeing. Christina began instructing the workers in the household to hand food to the people on the train, whenever one stopped at the station. Gerda never saw her mother cry so much as the day she stumbled upon a baby's corpse by the side of the railroad tracks. Christina was violently ill for days, vomiting what she had eaten prior to the incident and refraining from consuming any food immediately after. Gerda sat with her and nursed her back to health. Christina and Gerda developed a plan of action. In addition to the food that they were distributing, Gerda and her mother took bed sheets from their linen closet and cut them into makeshift diapers for the babies. Christina also ordered bottles of milk to be handed to the young mothers.

"I have looked into some of their eyes," Christina lamented

one day, after they had been supplying the trains for weeks. She was not able to focus her glance on any of her family members. "They seem hungry and cold."

Later to Sylvester she admitted, "They also seemed really scared."

"Of course they are scared," Sylvester retorted, his tone elevated, "You would be too!" He was screaming now, his voice reaching a heightened state of anxiety and exasperation. "What the hell is going on!" he demanded to the open air. He took a few seconds to breathe deeply. "I wish I had some idea," he said with resignation. "I just don't know if these people are in any danger. I feel miserable that they are coming through my territory and I have no idea where they are going."

One day Gerda prepared a package for Heinrich to take out to the train. Heinrich observed a young man roughly the same age as him.

The young man asked him, "Do you know where we are going?" He spoke with perfect diction. He seemed educated, and it looked like he had taken great pains in the past to be well-groomed. Now, he had black marks on his face, and his hair looked unkempt. But it had been cut stylishly and his hands looked soft—there were no noticeable calluses. Heinrich easily could have seen him at his own school. He would have fit right in. He didn't seem like a refugee.

Heinrich was so surprised he nearly jumped back. "You don't know where you are going?"

"No."

"Well, aren't you refugees?" Heinrich cringed as he asked the question. He wore an expression on his face that made it seem like, after the fact, he wanted to make the question rhetorical.

"I suppose we are," the young man said. The young man handed Heinrich his handkerchief. It had the initials DD inscribed on them. "Thank you for your kindness," said the young man.

Heinrich waved to the young man as the train pulled away.

Gerda came out to see what was taking him so long. She watched as the train became a speck on the horizon and visibility was completely lost and saw her brother continuously waving his arm. She approached him.

"Did you talk to one of them?" Gerda enquired.

Heinrich relayed the conversation. "I can't get him out of my mind," he confessed to Gerda while they stood there on the tracks.

Heinrich went into his room. He brought his cello there. He took his cello out and played a very somber tune. Gerda knew that she should be advising her brother not to play in the wrong room; it was against their father's wishes. But she sensed something that day and let him proceed. "Who cares about the instrument room," he shouted when the butler came to his bedroom. He then played a fierce, violent tune. At the last note, he threw down his cello and bow.

Other changes were occurring. Sylvester kept receiving demands to free up his rail line capacity for use by the German government. He had to deny some of his industrial customers access to the lines in order to comply with the government mandate. This was of course, far less lucrative for Sylvester and the Majowski family. He began making less money than he had before.

At the same time, supplies were becoming more difficult to come by. Cloth, toiletries, even food was becoming more scarce.

As war waged on and the situation became more difficult at home, Christina insisted that they strictly adhere to their daily routine. Gerda visited more frequently. Tutors and musical instructors continued to come to the house, Heinrich and Ernest, who were young men continued to practice their musical instruments. Life did not change or miss a beat in any way. Even when there was only soup to serve for dinner, a full table setting was laid out. The structure and rhythm of life was not compromised.

Except for the evening musical performances. And the open practices and rehearsals throughout the day.

VIRTUOSO

"I can't stomach our enjoying of music so blatantly at a time of seeming human suffering," Sylvester declared to his children. "I don't know where those people are going or why they are there, but they are there against their will." He paused a few seconds as he looked down and deeply inhaled. Gerda couldn't remember a time when he had been more distraught. He looked to her and while holding his gaze, seemingly drowning in the blue ocean of her eyes, he was speaking to all of them, but delivering the comment to Gerda. "Sometimes it is okay to have music be very personal." He proceeded to close the door and play a somber piece on his phonograph.

News about what was happening to the country was becoming increasingly more difficult to come by. Great Britain, France, and the Soviet Union had declared war on Germany. But there was no further news. Nobody knew what was going on. There were reports of troop movements and there were the trains, but nobody had any clue what was happening. Sylvester did his best to learn what he could through his railroad and military connections.

Gerda did her best to learn what she could through her cousin, Helmut Majowski, who was an officer in the military. He was the son of Uncle Franz, Sylvester's closest brother. Uncle Franz was living in Berlin. Among other pursuits, he owned a bar in Berlin called the Majowski Bar. It had become famous as a venue for secret meetings against the Nazi government. Gerda wrote Helmut many letters asking him for information. Each letter's purpose was clear—when would it all end so that they could go back to their lives as they had been?

● ● ●

Gerda tolerated the behavior of her husband for years. She never dared mention anything to her family for fear that they would be overly worried for her. When she found it hard to cope though, she did seek solace and refuge at her parent's house. As time went by, she found herself escaping there more frequently. Eventually, Gerda knew that her parents suspected that something was not right.

111

Gerda's marriage anniversary would come and go and there would be no activity on the part of Uli to commemorate the day. Gerda attempted to honor the event in the early years, but she too grew tired and weary. Eventually, she also gave up on holding those special occasions dear. Gerda found it frustrating, and would vacillate between giving up and struggling to make things right. At the end of her internal debates, she would reason that she should struggle to try to stay with him.

● ● ●

Being called off to war put a hold on Manfred's musical ambitions. Horst was also sent to war. Horst didn't qualify as an infantryman, so he went as an administrative clerk. He was sent to a command post close to Denmark.

It was a difficult time for Manfred while he was away. Several times he almost lost his life. Throughout the years, *I have become adept at cheating death*, he would reflect to himself. Manfred had joined a unit that was akin to the Army Corp of Engineers—for which he was a natural fit given his innate engineering abilities. His unit was responsible for building bridges. In one incident, he was marching with a tank and his commanding officer ordered him to move to the tank in front. As soon as he did that, there was a huge explosion as the tank he had been marching with went over a landmine. All of the soldiers on and marching alongside the tank were killed. Manfred would have also lost his life had he not moved.

He had been thrown to the ground because of the impact of the explosion. As he stood up and tried to untangle the black soot from his hair of miniscule curls, he looked around himself. His eyes locked with the commanding officer. Both stood there, eyes ready to pop from their sockets. Manfred had to remind himself to breathe. When he finally did it came out in swift, frequent bursts as if he were gasping. Music suddenly came to him, in his mind. The others around him looked at him quizzically. It was only when the commanding officer came to him and shouted at him, "Stop your silly singing!" that he realized he had begun to sing aloud. Manfred kept going however, internally. He kept singing to himself as he was instructed to assist with the moving of corpses. He only stopped when he and the remaining members of the unit walked away. After feeling lightheaded, as if he was going to faint, Manfred went back to singing. It allowed him to avoid falling over.

In another incident, Manfred and his unit were moving large I-beams. Every motion was set to the shouts of a commanding officer. On command, all members carrying the I-beam bent down to put the I-beam down and on command came up. Just as Manfred stood up according to the command, a bullet went into his wrist. The group was under attack by sharpshooters from the Soviets. Manfred was too stunned to feel any pain. All he could think about was that had his commanding officer not yelled the command, his head would have been where his wrist was as he was bent down, coming up at the time. His head likely was the target, he later realized. He would have been gone. The music first, and then the lyrics of the song, came to him again.

Manfred left the site on a stretcher and was transported first to a mobile medical tent and eventually to a hospital. As he suffered, emotionally and physically, Manfred turned repeatedly to a tune in his mind—a song that he loved to sing when he was at home in Berlin. As the pain intensified, Manfred kept going through the song, until he realized he had been singing it aloud. Everyone in his hospital ward dubbed him the "Singing Wounded". After a few months in the hospital to allow the shattered bones to heal, Manfred was sent home.

● ● ●

Gerda cried incessantly when Sylvester phoned her with the news. She knew it was a possibility, but she had wanted to avoid coping with the reality. All three of her brothers had been drafted into the army. Gerda informed Uli and was met with apathy. Without informing her husband, she instructed one of the drivers to take her to her parents' home.

Wilfred and Ernest were sent into infantry divisions. Wilfred was posted in the north, near to Denmark, and Ernest was sent to the southeast, close to Austria.

Heinrich had become an officer and was sent to the Soviet front. As an officer, Heinrich was permitted to carry with him a certain number of personal items. Gerda knew he would be taking his cello. She knew that he never left his cello behind. Gerda held the cello with her as Heinrich packed his other things. She clutched the handle tightly and while they all stood at the door, she was embracing the cello case. She imagined she was holding her kid brother. It kept her from crying, she thought. Once she did embrace Heinrich, she made his shoulder wet with tears.

● ● ●

At night, Heinrich would sometimes play his cello to remind himself of home. This worked best when he was at the base or enclosed barracks. He played for an hour or two at a time when he could. He thought fondly of Gerda holding his cello case before he left, the life he had with his family before he took his commission as an officer, and the boy who had given him a handkerchief from the train.

Heinrich was not always posted to a barracks. Even when he had to be out in the field, Heinrich would seek out some seclusion, taking two of his best soldiers with him for protection. He would swear these two soldiers to secrecy. They knew not to tell any others in the unit what their commanding officer was up to. Heinrich didn't want any superior officers finding out and specifically forbidding him from doing it. This way, he wasn't disobeying any commands. He just couldn't imagine being without his cello. He wrote letters home to Gerda indicating what he was up to. She encouraged him, in every response, to be extremely careful.

Heinrich's unit was given duty to carry out surveillance in the field for several weeks. As the commanding officer, Heinrich was given his own tent. He had his soldiers report back to him continuously on any activity in the surrounding area and the movement of enemy troops. Two weeks went by; to be safe, Heinrich resisted the urge to play his cello. He thought back to all of Gerda's entreaties in the letters she had sent. However, it was becoming increasingly hard for him to continue denying himself. One night, he emerged from his tent. It was a crisp, cold night in the winter of 1942. The temperature was below freezing. Heinrich could see his breath take shape about his mouth and nose. The stars in the sky were clear, crisp, as if icicles suspended in air.

Heinrich reviewed the intelligence reports from his unit and from headquarters. It was the same as it had been for the past two weeks. There was nothing happening. Heinrich decided that there was no imminent danger. Hence, he felt comfortable in taking out his cello and playing in the woods for a while. As they sought a site for Heinrich to play, Heinrich had his two usual men stand guard with him. As he looked about, he was surrounded by an army of tree trunks stripped naked, standing in seeming disarray, obeying nature's order and not man's neat rows of a marching army. Heinrich thought it a plus; it increased visibility he felt. In his heart, he knew he was taking a bit of a risk, but Heinrich felt out of sorts not being able to play. He stayed out for less than an hour and came back to his camp and his tent.

The next night, Heinrich engaged in the same routine. He reviewed the reports and determined that he would go out again. The night was as still and serene as the night before, but the temperature was slightly warmer. The snow that he and the soldiers trekked through had now become solid on the surface. *Perhaps some rain sneaked in that we did not notice*, reasoned Heinrich. As they approached the site where he had played the night before, very faintly, in the distance, Heinrich heard a violin playing. Heinrich and his men approached closer towards the sound.

Heinrich looked about the sky, seeing if there were any birds in the air. And then he scratched his forehead. He checked if he was having a fever. "Do you hear this sound as well?" he finally asked his soldiers. They indicated that they did. There was a look of relief in Heinrich's eyes.

Heinrich dropped his jaw and opened his eyes wide at what he then saw. There was a Soviet officer playing the violin in the distance, flanked by two soldiers. Heinrich and his men approached closer, slowly and very cautiously. Heinrich and his men stood ready to shoot. Heinrich stopped them.

"This is a trap," said one of Heinrich's soldiers, the one carrying the chair that Heinrich would sit on to play.

"They know you are a musician, sir, they are going to take you out," the other proclaimed.

"This is more significant than a white flag," Heinrich said, in a tone that strived to reassure both his soldiers and himself with equal effort. Seconds passed. Heinrich studied the situation. He observed the man's technique, his facial expressions, although he was looking down, and Heinrich thought about the music he was playing. Every few seconds he would repeat the same refrain. It was misplaced because it didn't belong in the piece he was playing. As Heinrich listened again for the next refrain he sang under his breath, "*Alle Menschen Werden Bruder*—All Men Will Be Brothers." Heinrich gasped. *This was from Beethoven's Ninth Symphony.*

"Our enemy is speaking the language of music. There is no hostile intent," Heinrich declared with an affirmation and confidence that surprised the soldiers.

Heinrich opened his cello case. He began to play. The Soviet officer acknowledged Heinrich's joining him, and they played a duet together. They kept such a distance that they were barely in the audible range of the other, but there was something more magical about the music they were creating together that night than if the world's greatest musicians had been in a celebrated concert hall with the finest audience in attendance.

They then moved on to another piece. One would start and the other would follow—all from memory. This went on for several hours. Heinrich was the first to stand up. He knew he needed to get back to camp. Heinrich turned partially away from where they had been sitting and began walking away. He watched from the corner of his eye as the Soviet soldier did the same.

The next night, Heinrich was eager to set out again. It was a strange day; no reports came through from headquarters. Heinrich questioned his officers and his troops, but no reports had come through. The weather had changed. It was warm again, as it had been the night before. However, in the early evening there had been a lot of fog, which had dissipated some, leaving a light mist. Heinrich worried about the chance of rain.

Heinrich decided to set out once again. He had a nagging thought of whether he was allowing his love for music to blind him to potential risk. He reasoned through it again, and after convincing himself, he marched out into the night with confidence. As Heinrich and the soldiers were making their way to the location from the night before, the campsite they had left behind went abuzz with energy. Headquarters had just sent a series of messages saying that there were Soviet troop movements near their location. The soldier managing the communications tent enquired about the whereabouts of Heinrich. Assuming they had gone on a patrol, he took his gun and set out after them with the message in hand. He caught sight of Heinrich and the two soldiers with him ahead in the distance. He began running towards them. As he approached something in the distance caught his eye. He reacted quickly.

Just as the soldier with the telegram was approaching, Heinrich was facing the Soviet officer and soldiers, and the Soviet officer was moving his hand. What Heinrich saw was him pointing to himself as he shouted out, "Kasparov."

The soldier approaching from Heinrich's camp with the message assumed that the Soviet officer was reaching for his weapon, and he immediately fired several shots from his gun. The Soviet officer was struck in his right arm.

Heinrich heard the twanging of strings. It sounded like the violin had been hit as well.

The Soviets responded with their own shots, and Heinrich's soldiers also volleyed several additional shots. In the chaos, Heinrich was able to escape, brought to cover behind several successive trees by one of the soldiers charged with protecting him. Unfortunately, Heinrich had dropped his cello and bow in the snow. As he fled the scene, he saw one of the Soviet soldiers take his cello. He was sad to be estranged from his instrument—his only source of joy. He was also concerned because his name was inscribed inside the cello and now it was in the hands of the Soviets.

CHAPTER X

Hogitaro entered Singapore with his Japanese Imperial Army regiment. The intense heat and the sweat constantly dripping from his forehead were getting to him. *Southeast Asia is so different than Japan*, he thought. *Even in the humid summer, Tokyo is not this bad.* He thought back to the last few days and not being able to bathe. He entered the pleasure tent, where the army kept comfort women so that the men could go and relieve themselves. He was desperate for a bath.

His second urge was wishing that he had a violin with him. He missed playing it terribly. As he thought about the weather in Tokyo, he thought about sitting with his musical instructor, practicing his violin. His instructor had been trained in Berlin and was a close adherent to the German method of teaching. His instructor had taken the trouble to learn German. Hogitaro was attempting the same. At times, his instructor would teach him in German.

Hogitaro wondered if he should have learned English instead.

● ● ●

Colonel Kasparov was taken back to his camp. Two soldiers carried him, one by the shoulders, the other by the legs, and the third carried the shattered violin and the cello that Kasparov had ordered him to take. When they got back to camp Kasparov was taken to the medical tent. Despite his injury he remained aggressive with the soldiers carrying him and the medical staff in the tent. The doctors and nurses were busy in the tent performing an amputation for another soldier whose leg had become infected and needed to be removed.

"Get over here and give me attention," roared Kasparov as he entered the tent.

One of the soldiers who had suffered Kasparov's invective back to camp joined in. "You'd better do as he says, he is a

Colonel."

"I outrank him!" Kasparov shouted.

Several nurses came over, followed afterward by a doctor. One of the nurses tried to remove the Colonel's coat so that she could look at his right arm. Her pulling on the sleeve created a sensation for Kasparov as if his arm were being pulled off. He yelped in pain, "I need to keep that!" In a flash he thought of his mother and her second husband. He then reached for his revolver with his left hand. He struggled to hold the gun—he was not left-handed—and clumsily shot the nurse.

The other nurses gasped and stepped away.

"Do you want to be next?" he challenged one of them. She immediately went to work trying to cut away the coat so that the wound could be examined. When the doctor approached, he had with him an injection. Kasparov knew it was intended to sedate him, perhaps put him out. Kasparov raised the gun to the doctor's head. "Don't even think about it." His voice had a booming cadence to it, delivered with a strength that Kasparov had to dig deep within him to deliver. He dropped his hand to his side, but the intense stare of his eyes never waned in intensity. The doctor was stunned, and his initial reaction was to step back. Kasparov scanned the room to look for another doctor. Seeing none and his desperation rising, Kasparov used whatever energy he had in him to lift the gun once more. He coldly aimed the gun at the doctor in the tent again. "You save this arm or I will do you in as well." There was a power in his voice that shook the doctor and the other nurses. Kasparov could see them tremble. Kasparov was beginning to feel faint, the lights in the room turning more bright with each passing second until all he saw was white. He kept shouting, "You save this arm! You save this arm!" hoping it would allow him to remain conscious. Within minutes he was out.

When he finally came to, he was by himself, cordoned off from the other chatter in the room by white sheets hung from metal scaffolding. It took him a few minutes to recall why he was there.

VIRTUOSO

He looked with dread to the right side of his body. He saw the empty space where his arm used to be. With force he moved his left hand over and confirmed what his eyes had feared. As he grabbed the stump, he yelped in pain. Tears began to stream down his face. The shout prompted a nurse to appear. His crying stopped, and his screaming began. "What did you do to me?" By then the news of him shooting a nurse had spread to every one in the camp. The nurse scurried away. Kasparov looked for his gun. It was nowhere to be found.

Kasparov could rationalize that in the field there weren't enough means to preserve the arm or impede the spread of infection. But his grief was too much to bear, and his anger consumed him. Although weak, Kasparov pulled himself out of bed. Hunched over, and moving sloppily as if he were a deranged beast looking for his kill, he stormed through the tent, shouting, "Where is he! Where is he!" The doctor sensed the danger to his life; he had already escaped to headquarters to demand a new assignment.

Kasparov felt a pinch in his right calf. He fell forward, colliding with a cart of medical supplies. Before he landed on the floor, he heard the sound of breaking glass, and the smell of alcohol filled his lungs. Within seconds the light in the room went dark.

● ● ●

Manfred was sent on another tour of duty. It would become another two opportunities for him to escape death. He was sent to the north on this occasion and was in Lithuania. One day his camp came under heavy attack by an advancing Soviet army unit. They launched several grenades at Manfred's unit. One of them exploded close to Manfred. Unfortunately, he suffered a very difficult injury. A piece of shrapnel was lodged into his thigh. When the surgeon removed the shrapnel, Manfred lost a small piece of his thigh as well, including a piece of the bone. He was sent to Poland where he could be attended to. When he first arrived, the doctor informed him that Manfred's leg had to be amputated. The removal of a portion of his thigh and fragment of his bone in the field had caused an infection, the spread of which could not be constrained. Manfred fainted.

When he came to, he was thrilled to learn that his leg was still there. It had not been removed. He stayed at that location for one month and was placed in a cast so that his leg would heal.

While he was in Poland, one of his mother's sisters came to visit him.

"Hello, Aunt," Manfred said.

"My dear boy, what has happened to you!" she shrieked.

This is probably my least favorite aunt, thought Manfred. *Of all people, why did she have to come? I thought the point was to make me feel better, not more miserable.*

"Well, I suffered an injury," Manfred told her matter-of-factly.

She knocked on the cast. "Is there still a leg in there?"

Manfred rolled his eyes. "You see my foot sticking out at the bottom of the cast, right?" Manfred asked. He tried his best not to sound like he was putting her down. She was his mother's sister, after all. He didn't want to be disrespectful.

His aunt began weeping. *Here it comes,* Manfred thought.

"You mother is worried sick for you and you can talk like that!" She sobbed even louder.

And then my mother wonders why I don't like her, Manfred thought to himself. He tolerated the rest of her visit, but was not shy about exhibiting his glee with the nursing staff after his aunt had left. When the nurses showed shock at his reaction, he suddenly felt remorse for his behavior and thought that he should be penitent. As soon as the nurses left the room, however, the smile appeared back on his face and he sighed in relief.

Manfred was eager to get back to Germany and tried going on the first ship out from Poland. Unfortunately, he couldn't make it on that one and had to wait another week to get on the next ship. When he boarded his eventual ship, he noticed that there was no emblem on it—the traditional red cross was missing. He asked one of the ship-hands; they informed him that a week ago, the first ship that had left had a red cross on it and because of that, the Soviets had bombed the ship and sank it along with all of the people it was carrying. Manfred was spellbound. He was without words. All he had was the words to that favorite *Lied* of his, *Lebenslied*—"Song of Life", by Schubert, going through her mind.

When he was transported back to Germany, Manfred had to rest in a hospital for one year, only getting around by using crutches once his cast had come off. Here again, Manfred had adopted the name "Singing Wounded."

As he was singing one day, one of his bunkmates, whose leg had been amputated and whose hip was in a cast, commented, "I heard about a guy like you in Poland. Always singing. As the pain increased, the singing would intensify."

Manfred responded, "I was in Poland."

The man grew excited. "Then it must have been you!"

Manfred now had a singing partner. His name was Gunther. Manfred's singing partner and he were eventually well enough to be housed in an apartment on the campus of the hospital, outside the ward, but still in a place where they could receive medical attention nearby.

In helping Manfred to heal, a weight had to be added to the leg so that it would be roughly the same length as his other leg. Without that, his injured leg would have been two inches shorter.

● ● ●

Gerda answered the door when the messenger arrived with news for her father. She was spending more and more time at her parent's home.

He hesitated when he saw her. "Please, it is for Herr Majowski."

"I am his daughter. You tell me," Gerda demanded, panic entering her voice. Gerda knew that her father kept tabs on news about her brothers while they were in the war. He would talk to the military personnel that came through the stations that he was

123

managing in his region.

"I am sorry, Heinrich has been injured. While engaging with the enemy, he took a bullet to the leg," the messenger said.

"Where is he?" Gerda pleaded. She attempted to maintain her composure, but she found it difficult to. Tears began streaming on her cheek.

"I am afraid we don't have that information," the messenger said.

Gerda walked away from the door, without closing it. She got to the foot of the stairs and wailed. She needed to use the banister and railing to support her. Her mother was the first to hear her and came running down the stairs.

"What are we going to do?" Christina pleaded after she became apprised of the situation.

"Is there anyway we can find out any news?" Gerda beseeched her father. She sat at the edge of the sofa, bent forward, her arms wrapped around herself. She rocked back and forth gently. She found it strangely comforting. She had the image of Heinrich at the front door, the last time she saw him, in her mind.

"I will find him," Sylvester declared, and he walked out the door without another word to Gerda or the family.

Gerda did not think that what her father was saying was reasonable, but she was desperate for any news. She also knew better than to try to stop him. Gerda assumed that he would use his connections in the railroad company, which was involved regularly with the military, to learn about Heinrich's whereabouts and attempt to get him closer to the family that way. When he disappeared for days, Gerda and the family became frantic.

Gerda pieced together that her father must have been extremely dissatisfied with the lack of a firm response about Heinrich's whereabouts. Sylvester proceeded to take one of his steam engines and went from town to town on the war front to search for Heinrich. Eventually, he was able to find him. Sylvester was able to maneuver through the towns of Poland and Russia as he spoke both languages.

● ● ●

"Hello, my dear son," came the voice that Heinrich heard. Heinrich thought that he was dozing off in his sleep again. He opened his eyes wide to see his father in front of him.

"Father! I can't believe it! How did you get here?" Heinrich asked.

"I took the train, my boy. The best way to travel," came Sylvester's cheeky response. He had a broad smile.

"How did you know where to find me?"

"I have my own questions," Sylvester boomed. He became stern in his expression. "Why didn't you inform us that you had been injured?"

"I'm sorry, Father, I didn't want to worry you," Heinrich explained.

"Well you had us plenty worried. We had no idea what had happened to you!"

"The wound is not severe, Father," Heinrich explained. "The bullet went through my thigh and the entry was so shallow that it did not even touch the bone. Nonetheless, I have been ordered to recuperate in this military hospital." Thinking to change the subject Heinrich asked, "Father, how did you get to me? Did you have a military escort?"

"No," Sylvester replied. He pulled out a gun from his pocket and showed it to Heinrich.

"You intended to protect yourself?"

"Yes."

Heinrich opened the gun. There were no bullets in it. "Father, either you used all of these bullets or you never loaded it," Heinrich stated, knowing full well which of the two had actually transpired.

"I had no intention of using it, I just wanted to scare people off," Sylvester stated, matter-of-factly. He left Heinrich for a few minutes and sent a telegram home that he had located Heinrich.

Sylvester indicated that he would bring him closer to the family. When he came back to Heinrich, Heinrich enquired about news from home.

"How are Ernest and Wilfred?"

"They are okay from what I hear," Sylvester stated.

"How about our cousin Helmut?" Heinrich asked, "I try to communicate with him through the officer channels, but I have not heard from him in a while."

"I have seen my brother Franz in Berlin. He is frequently at his Majowski Bar. He says that everything is okay with his son Helmut." Sylvester then added, "Imagine having our name affiliated with a bar of all things. I can understand, the Majowski Orchestra or the Majowski Opera Company, but Majowski Bar just doesn't feel right."

Heinrich shrugged off this line of commentary from his father. He was eager to keep asking questions. "How about Mia and Sylva? And Mia's daughter Crystal?"

"All are okay," Sylvester declared.

"And, and, how is Gerda?" Heinrich hesitated with a timidity that was uncharacteristic of a military officer, let alone Heinrich.

"She is very angry with you." Sylvester's slight chuckle betrayed that he was thinking with affection about her reaction to Heinrich's situation.

"I know," Heinrich said. He then confessed, "I mostly didn't tell the family because I didn't want her to worry."

"I know," Sylvester stated grimly. After a few minutes, he turned towards the nurse attending to Heinrich. "Please bring my son's cello," he instructed her. "You shall play something festive to commemorate the joy we both feel in our being re-united," Sylvester said, facing Heinrich.

The nurse did not move. Sylvester tried another language. The nurse looked up at him with a bewildered expression.

Heinrich finally spoke up. "Father, my cello has been seized by the enemy."

VIRTUOSO

"What?" Sylvester asked in a state of alarm and concern.

Heinrich explained to his father what had happened.

"I am proud of you son," Sylvester said. Heinrich sighed in relief.

"I thought you would be angry with me for losing the cello," Heinrich stated.

"No. You recognized that this man was coming to you with peaceful intentions to share together in the performing of music. You did the right thing," Sylvester affirmed.

"It is a tragedy what happened to the other officer."

"Indeed it is. He likely will never be able to play the violin again," Sylvester observed.

● ● ●

Hogitaro wasn't sure if he had heard him correctly. One of the Japanese officers patrolling the district by the Singapore waterfront was saying that he found an abandoned British officer's house intact with all of its furniture. *Did he really say he knew where to get a 'white people's string instrument'? How would he know what it looked like?* thought Hogitaro.

He approached the officer. "Where is this location?"

The officer looked at Hogitaro up and down. Luckily for Hogitaro, they were of equal rank. "It's right next to the Keiko command center," the other officer declared.

"What kind of instrument did you see?" Hogitaro pressed him.

"It is not like a *koto*. I do not think it is played flat. It is more like a *shamisen*. But I don't know this instrument. It is for the white people."

"Is it a violin?" Hogitaro asked. He said the word slowly.

"I don't know what that is." The other officer walked away.

Hogitaro thought for several minutes. He made a plan to visit this deserted house.

● ● ●

Kasparov looked out the window of the hospital he had been

127

placed in. It was a challenge for him to get accustomed to life without one arm. The most challenging part for him was not being able to play the violin. He had struggled as a teenager to master the instrument. There was a determination in him to learn it—the same determination that contributed to his advancement in the military.

He had always been a relatively quiet man. He had now fallen into a cold, retaliatory silence. The attendants and nurses hated assisting him. He would never speak, except to verbally abuse whomever it was who did something slightly off—bringing a meal too late, not positioning his slippers in the right spot, taking too much time to change a wound dressing. He felt naked without a firearm. He knew that they were intentionally keeping one from him. He had attacked the orderly who didn't have a fresh towel brought to him. He attempted to strangle him, but there was only so much force he could exert with one arm, his weaker arm, so the attempt was clumsy and the orderly easily got away.

Kasparov didn't see much action for the rest of the war. Once he was released from the hospital, his assignments were close to the military headquarters. Everyone assumed that he would head home once the war was over. They were surprised to learn that he had applied to stay on and seek a position in the Post-War occupation.

Kasparov eyed the cello that was in his quarters. He imagined playing it, but he only held it in front of him with his left hand. He had no appendage to draw the bow. He threw the cello down. As he did, the angle was right for him to be able to look inside of it for the first time. He saw the words "H. Majowski".

● ● ●

Life was becoming more difficult for Ram. His brother was involved in ever-greater uprisings against the British government. He had become a real Gandhi devotee. He had taken rank in Gandhi's movement. He participated in the salt march. He had been arrested several times. It was hard on his wife and children when he would do this. Ram wished he could convince his brother otherwise. Sometimes his brother's convictions were so strong.

Ram thought about the situation himself. He didn't know which he preferred: rule by the British or without. Yes, they had stolen many national treasures and a lot of resources, but they had also done a lot of good. They had built the railroads. They established a university system based on the British model. They brought English as a primary language, which Ram and all of his brothers had learned. And they brought with them music. There was no way Ram would have been able to get his recordings in India if they had not been shipped to be sold to the British living there.

Of course, they treated Indians very badly. It hurt him to see his countrymen abused or treated as second-class citizens. It was hard for him to be idealistic, however. He had a large family to worry about.

He was also conflicted. His other brother was getting promoted through the ranks of the British military. And now, Ram just came to know, he had just received news that his brother would be shipped out on the war front. He was being assigned to a base in the Pacific theater. The British had just surrendered the port and city of Singapore to the Japanese. It was the first time a Western power had surrendered to an Asian country. It was a strategic location though, an important trade route for access to Asia. The British must want it back, Ram reasoned.

● ● ●

Hogitaro had the address: 13 Robinson Road. He arrived at the house. The other officer was right; indeed it was abandoned. He walked through it. He had developed the cover of needing to place land mines throughout the house, given its proximity to the command center, in case there were any spies lurking about.

He placed a few land mines, so that he could say that he had accomplished it.

Then he went to the drawing room. There he saw it. The violin that his fellow officer had indicated. He was ecstatic. He played and played and played. He thought of taking it back to the barracks with him, but he knew it would probably be found and be confiscated.

When he got back to the barracks he told his superior officers that there was communication equipment inside that house and that in addition to the land mines that he had planted, he needed to make regular patrols of the area to be sure that the equipment was not being used to spy on the Japanese. He was thrilled when his superiors agreed.

CHAPTER XI

After locating Heinrich, Sylvester brought him back to a hospital in Poland. They utilized the same steam engine that Sylvester had used to locate Heinrich. They were stopped a few times, but Sylvester indicated that he was transporting a wounded officer and they allowed him to pass.

When they arrived at the hospital in Poland, doctors indicated that Heinrich would need a blood transfusion. Sylvester was the first to volunteer; however, his blood type did not match closely enough.

"We need to get one of the siblings," the doctor instructed.

Sylvester sent a telegram to Gerda. The maid took the telegram to Gerda's in-law's place in person.

"I am sorry to disturb you, madam, I have word from your father," the maid announced to Gerda. Gerda leapt up from the dinner table where there were seated many guests of her husband's family.

"Come right away," was written on a telegram.

Gerda did not even turn around. She abandoned the party, the table, the house of her in-laws. Her in-laws were celebrating a wedding anniversary and were throwing a lavish party for the event. As Uli was their only son, Gerda and her husband had to be there. She did not take the time to seek out Uli or offer an explanation to her in-laws. She ran outside of the house and called for the driver. She told him to not stop until they got to the hospital where Heinrich was, as relayed to Gerda in the telegram, a distance of four hours.

As she had done in the past, Gerda thought of some of the concerts that her father had made his orchestra perform when she was younger. She replayed her favorite pieces in her mind. It was the only thing she could do to keep her from thinking devastating thoughts or from crying. She worried that something had happened to Heinrich.

When she arrived, she saw Sylvester in the hall. "What is it, Father? What is wrong with Heinrich?"

When she heard about the need for a transfusion, Gerda grew very angry. "Why did you wait for me? This was urgent. Wilfred is stationed nearby, and Sylva lives closer!"

Sylvester sat Gerda down. "Gerda, Wilfred and Sylva have a different mother than you, Ernest, Mia, and Heinrich," he finally revealed to Gerda. "Their blood may not be an exact match, and we are running out of time."

Gerda was amazed. "All those years…" she began to say to him.

Sylvester looked into the distance. Gerda understood. She walked into the room they had been standing outside of, removed her coat, rolled up her dress sleeve and offered her arm to the nurse for the removal of blood. She lay in bed after the first batch was taken.

Gerda heard the rest of the story from Sylvester. "My first wife died after giving birth to Sylva. Her name was Anna Woolf. She was from a prominent family in the town where I was studying when I came from Poland to study in Germany." After a brief pause, he added, "She is the one who taught me German."

Gerda remembered going to "Grandma Woolf's" house as a child growing up. She had an extensive castle with an enormous plot of land surrounding the residence. Throughout the home were lit candles. When Gerda was really young, it would scare her. Now those visits made much more sense to her.

"I was still very young at the time of my first wife's death. I also knew that Wilfred and Sylva would need a mother to raise them properly," Sylvester concluded.

Gerda suddenly felt a newfound appreciation for her mother, who never made it seem like Wilfred and Sylva were not her own children.

● ● ●

News of an assassination attempt against Hitler reached the

Majowski household in early 1943. Gerda was again the one to answer the door when the messenger requested the audience of Herr Majowski. Gerda soon learned that there was a sect within the German High Command that was becoming horrified with the actions of Hitler. They wanted to put an end to Germany's war activities. Gerda became gravely concerned when she learned that her cousin Helmut was involved.

"I am afraid that he might be caught and killed or that he may attempt suicide," Father declared to Gerda.

After more digging, Gerda came to learn that an elaborate assassination plot had been conceived. Initially, word had reached Berlin that the bomb had been placed under Hitler's table. There was initial rejoicing at the news. Unfortunately, their plot failed. Hitler appeared on the radio and made a speech. His escaping the assassination attempt only served to embolden him further. The plan had backfired. The news was that a few officers had been caught, but it was unclear to Gerda and Sylvester whether Helmut was one of them. Gerda knew that all involved had made a pact that if it were not successful and they were caught, the plotters would be forced to take their lives. Gerda was wrought with anxiety, worrying that her cousin had been forced to follow through with that.

She was also unnerved to learn another detail—the plot had been conceived at the Majowski Bar in Berlin among senior officers in the military.

Gerda cried as she gathered all of this news with her father's help. She was troubled that she was not able to learn about what had happened to Helmut. She remained on edge as days passed and no further information was obtained. Gerda was also becoming concerned for her three brothers. She worried that Heinrich might be sent back.

Gerda watched as her father did what he could to console Uncle Franz. Gerda could tell that the anxiety of not knowing whether his son was alive or not fueled greater anger in her uncle. Sylvester called Franz frequently, but Gerda could tell that he felt disconnected from his brother.

"I am not satisfied with the answers I am getting," Father announced to the family after four days.

Gerda understood what that meant. She knew she couldn't stop him. "I am going with you."

"What?" Sylvester and Christina exclaimed in unison.

"That's right," Gerda said. She didn't wait to engage in a conversation with her parents. She went to her room and started packing her belongings.

Sylvester tried to convince her otherwise. "I'll be back soon," he pleaded.

"Okay," Gerda said, "then I'll be back soon with you."

The remaining family members begged both of them to be careful.

They traveled to Berlin on one of Sylvester's trains. Gerda knew that her father wanted to be with Uncle Franz to see if anything more could be learned about Helmut. Sylvester conceded feeling miserable for Uncle Franz.

"I can empathize with Franz. I experienced the same level of concern when I went out in search of Heinrich, not knowing if I had lost my son or not," Sylvester explained to Gerda, in a rare display of what he was feeling. "Heinrich had been shot by the enemy," Sylvester continued to reflect to Gerda prior to their departure. "Helmut may have been forced to kill himself! Why was he trying this assassination attempt? I need some answers."

Sylvester and Gerda found Uncle Franz at the Majowski Bar. Gerda's uncle explained to them what was happening.

Sylvester cut him off shortly after Franz started to speak. "Why was Helmut attempting to assassinate Hitler?" he implored.

"Haven't you been noticing your Jewish friends disappearing?"

Sylvester was silent for a moment. "Yes, Franz, it is true. There are several of my Jewish friends that I have not heard from in several months."

VIRTUOSO

Gerda reflected on this is well. *It's true*, she thought. She hadn't given it much thought before.

"But in the current war environment," Sylvester argued, "nobody is doing much socializing."

Gerda had to agree with her father's reasoning.

"They are being killed!" Franz boomed. His voice resonated with an anger that shook both Sylvester and Gerda.

"WE ARE KILLING THEM!" Franz shouted even louder, sweeping his arm in front of him and pounding the wood bar with his fist. There were a dozen glass *Steins* in front of him. All were swept aside, and several broke on the wall adjacent to the bar.

Franz's eyes were ablaze. They were bloodshot and distressed. He didn't bat his eyelashes at the sound of breaking glass. Shards of glass flew back and pierced the skin of his arm. Blood flowed down the side, but he didn't react to it.

Gerda had been struck in the crossfire. Sylvester noticed and was making a motion to get a towel but Gerda signaled to him not to. She took out a shard of glass from her arm and threw it on the floor. She pressed down on the cut with her thumb. "We thought that the official reports from the government were true, that Jews were being sent from urban slums to country campuses," said Gerda to try and avert any attention to her wound.

"Our friends are being killed and we can't do anything to stop them," Franz stressed in a more hushed tone, shaking his head. He struggled to get some of the words out, his voice wavering as his body attempted to let all emotions flow through. Speaking and crying competed with each other. One would occasionally take the lead, but at times the other would prevail—Franz would move his mouth but no words would come out as the tears could not be held back any longer. The dam had given way.

"My little boy was so brave to try to stop them, but he was not able to make it end," Franz said after several seconds had gone by, in a voice that admitted defeat.

"What if he has forsaken his life for nothing?"

● ● ●

Gerda was in the front of the house when Helmut passed through its doors after three days. Gerda was brought to tears. She embraced him, without saying a word and quickly moved out of the way to let her uncle and aunt see their son.

"Oh, my son!" Franz was intermittently crying and talking. "You are alive! You are alive!" Franz kept shouting.

Sylvester looked as elated as Franz. Gerda wondered if this was the expression he had on his face the day he found Heinrich.

Helmut and his mother began a lengthy exchange— vacillating between an endearing embrace and verbal chastising.

Gerda was thrilled to see him. She helped him take his coat off. She brought a bowl with warm water and a towel and wiped his face clean.

"You don't have to do that," Helmut said, his voice clearly strained.

"You stay quiet," Gerda demanded.

Helmut managed a smile. "Remember when we were kids, I would always refer to you as 'big blue eyes'?"

"Don't strain yourself," Gerda insisted, in a softer tone now, his reminder of her nickname drawing a smile on her face as well. When food was ready, Gerda brought the bowl of soup out and began to spoon-feed Helmut.

Sylvester looked agitated and was now pacing. Gerda could tell that he was itching to ask his questions.

"Give him time, Father," Gerda finally stated.

"Oh, yes, yes," Sylvester said, going back to his thoughts.

Franz was so pleased to see his son. He sat next to Helmut, holding his hand.

Gerda observed how run-down and haggard Helmut looked. It was clear he was under duress. He was a tall man—six feet and two inches of height. He had blue eyes and blond hair that he combed straight back. A prototypical Aryan. Ready to end Hitler. This last thought made Gerda smile faintly. She hoped in her heart that justice would ultimately prevail.

Helmut held up his hand to Gerda to say that he had eaten enough for the time being.

"This is just a break. Only until the next course is prepared," Gerda informed him. Helmut kissed her on the forehead. Helmut had no sisters; he was an only child. Gerda loved how he would dote on her.

"It is good to see you, Uncle," Helmut finally said to Sylvester. Gerda detected with satisfaction that his voice had a bit more life to it. Nonetheless, she could still sense the strain.

After the other pleasantries were over, Sylvester asked Helmut to sit down with him.

"Helmut," Sylvester asked, "what is going on?"

"It is true, Uncle, Jews are being killed by the hundreds of thousands," Helmut said. Gerda was transfixed by what she was hearing. Helmut's voice exhibited a mix of anger and excitement, marked by his shortness of breath.

"They even took my Marisa and her family," Helmut said. Gerda felt pain in her heart at hearing this. She watched as Helmut's jaw got tight, and his eyes began fixating, with laser-like intensity, on a point in the middle of empty space.

Sylvester touched Helmut's shoulder. Gerda and her family had met the girl and her family at the engagement party that Franz had hosted years prior. Gerda was startled at the news. She thought that Marisa was a good fit for Helmut.

"I see, my son," Sylvester said to Helmut. "You have done the right thing."

Gerda recognized her father's tone as consoling, supportive.

"I am very sorry to hear that it did not work," said Sylvester.

"Not this time," said Helmut. His eyes were still bloodshot from the emotions of his coming back. Gerda noted that he looked into empty space again with the same concentrated effort as earlier. Gerda knew that Helmut was not a naïve officer. He had attained sufficient rank and controlled enough men where he could speak with authority on the matter. He had enough access to the highest ranking officials.

"How did you manage to escape getting caught this time?" Sylvester asked.

Gerda knew what her father was doing. He was signaling to Helmut that he understood what Helmut was trying to relay.

"I can't say anything more except that several very senior military officers are aware of what we are doing even though they won't take any direct involvement in it," Helmut explained. "They help us by turning a blind eye. When Hitler demands names, they attempt to spare as many of us as possible," Helmut noted. "I can't say anything more about it, Uncle."

"No," Sylvester said, "Of course not." He offered a smile towards Helmut as he spoke. Gerda thought it was an odd expression. It didn't seem to come from within him. It was sincere, but perfunctory, thought Gerda. Her father had been exposed to the military. Based on his own experience and that of his sons, Gerda knew that he had learned the rules.

"Enough talking," Gerda said. "Now you must eat something."

They all sat at the table that Gerda and Helmut's mother had set.

Sylvester repeatedly looked down at the floor as he spoke with Helmut. When Sylvester spoke, he would look at Helmut; when Helmut spoke, Sylvester looked down.

I know what my father is going through, thought Gerda to herself. *I know that he is glad to see that there was someone, especially in his family, who was so determined to put an end to these atrocities. But, he was glad that it was not one of his sons that was risking his life.* Gerda knew that he sensed the conflict. *He always loses his confidence when he feels like he has not thought through something or if he finds his thoughts contradictory. I bet he feels selfish for feeling that way and it bothers him.* Gerda wished that she could tell her father, *I know that you want this nonsense to end, that you want this war to end, but that you don't want to lose your family in the process. I want to tell him that it is okay to feel that way. I want to reassure him that there should be a time after all this. There* will *be a time after this. We have to think about how we will live and survive when that time comes.*

Gerda asked Uncle Franz for his phonograph. Gerda played Beethoven's Sixth Symphony. She knew that the first movement would soothe her father. It had always worked in the past.

Sylvester's face remained ridden with an unconsoled expression on it. *I must try harder*, thought Gerda.

I can tell he is conflicted. Maybe he is thinking something else. Perhaps he is feeling that he wants Helmut and his colleagues to stage another attempt, as Helmut had just revealed he would. How else could it all be stopped? Gerda had received news about Allied troop movements, but from where they were sitting, there was no information on whether the Allied troops were experiencing any success or not. *I bet Father feels like he should be discouraging Helmut instead and telling him to preserve his life.* Gerda sensed that this could be it. Had it been Wilfred, Ernest or Heinrich, he would have told them not to do it. *I hope he doesn't live to regret this moment*, thought Gerda.

Luckily Sylvester's brother Franz took up the role of trying to convince his son otherwise. Her father looked noticeably relieved. *I guess he can't ever shake that paternal instinct*, thought Gerda. But, then, Gerda could tell that Uncle Franz was not being as harsh or domineering with his son as she thought Uncle Franz should have been.

"You really should consider all of the possible alternatives to end this nonsense," Franz said in a very even tone.

Looks like there is a part of Uncle Franz that wants this to end as well, Gerda thought to herself.

Helmut's mother was hysterical in her saying that Helmut should give up on the war.

● ● ●

On the way back to Poland, Sylvester asked the conductor to stop the train. They had not reached the Polish border yet.

"What on earth for?" the conductor asked.

Gerda was about to ask him the same question, but before she had a chance, Sylvester responded to his question fiercely.

"You work for me, you do as you are told!" Sylvester scolded. Sylvester went out onto the track. He instructed Gerda to wait for him. He had himself and his gun. This time, Gerda noted, he had loaded the gun with bullets. He was intent on using it. He shot the connecting mechanism that the train had already passed. He damaged the switch that would allow trains to come towards his part of Poland.

"Let's see how long that slows them down," he said to Gerda once he got back to the engine.

Gerda was gushing with admiration. Even at this age, her father was a soldier, no, a crusader.

Once they crossed the Polish border, Sylvester instructed the conductor to stop again. Sylvester had re-loaded his gun and went outside again to do the same.

When he got back home, the following day, he took a crew of twenty men and traveled a distance of five kilometers west of where his rail station was.

"We need to replace this part of the track," Sylvester declared.

"But sir, this will put the line out of commission for several days," the foreman said, "And also," he added after scanning the premises, "there doesn't seem to be anything wrong with this section of the track."

"Are you questioning me?" Sylvester asked, waving his finger in their faces. They were all taken aback by his behavior. "You do as you are told," Sylvester commanded.

The men got to work. When they had ripped out the old track, Sylvester instructed them to stop. "We are needed urgently back at the station," he declared to his men.

"But no trains will be able to pass through," said the foreman. "There is a gap of more than fifty meters."

"It can't be helped," Sylvester declared, "Hurry up and go!"

When they got back to the station, the foreman asked Sylvester what needed to be done.

"You will await my instructions," Sylvester told them.

But those instructions never came. That night, the phone at the rail station was ringing constantly. In the morning it was the same thing. The stationmaster came to the residence when Sylvester had not gone into work.

"I am not to be disturbed," Sylvester said.

"Herr Majowski, there is a line of rail cars waiting to pass through the station," the stationmaster insisted.

"I AM NOT TO BE DISTURBED," Sylvester insisted. He was listening to music on the phonograph.

After one week without a single train passing through the station, a train arrived.

"How did you get through?" Sylvester asked.

"The government has fixed the problem with the tracks," the conductor said.

"What are you carrying?" Sylvester asked with trepidation.

"We have steel from one of your frequent customers."

"Ah."

"We need to re-load on coal," the conductor said. "Can you supply us some as you always have?" asked the conductor.

Sylvester told him to wait a few minutes. He disappeared for a while. He came back to the conductor and said it should be there soon.

Soon turned into one hour, which became four hours, then twelve hours. Soon a whole day had passed.

The conductor came to the residence.

"Herr Majowski is not to be disturbed," the butler said, "but he did ask me to prepare accommodations for you in the guest house. We also have room for your crew here. Follow me, Sir."

That night, Sylvester hired a crew of men to unload all of the steel on the train and place it on the platform.

"It must have been bandits," Sylvester said to the conductor the following morning.

"Herr Majowski, you are impeding our delivery, and you are blocking any other trains from entering," the conductor declared.

"You and your men are welcome to stay here as long as you like," Sylvester said blithely. He walked away from the conductor at a hurried pace, being sure not to turn around, so that he wouldn't have to be involved in any other conversation with him.

The next day there were numerous phone calls to the rail station. "Herr Majowski is not in," was the response.

The following day, there were numerous calls to the residence. "Herr Majowski is not available," was the response then.

Within three days, military personnel arrived. They brought their own coal. They did not engage Sylvester in a discussion. They simply re-loaded the cargo, filled the train with coal and left.

The next day, another train arrived. Sylvester had one of his workers dislodge the locomotive from the rest of the train. He had his worker destroy the connection. And so it continued: Sylvester would do whatever he could to prevent the flow of trains. He had such great support and such a strong following within the railroad company, that few made open threats to him.

Gerda was immensely proud of their father.

"I don't know how much of an impact this is having," her father would say in dismay. "I won't let them pass through my station, but I know they are choosing alternative routes around me. I don't understand my countrymen," he would bemoan. "They are prepared to turn a blind eye towards me? How dare they turn a blind eye on the executions! I wish I could do more." He had a forlorn scowl on his face, and his eyes were bloodshot. "How much risk am I going to expose my family to?"

● ● ●

Several months passed like this. Gerda had gone back to her

home with her husband. After a brief period, Gerda showed up again with her driver. Sylvester came outside. He could tell that she had been crying.

"Uli is having a baby with his secretary," she declared. Her voice and tone showed her anger, not her sadness.

"Oh, my poor daughter," Sylvester said embracing her. When he got inside, that's when he found his anger.

"Stupid, good for nothing, piece of shit!" Sylvester was screaming. Christina attempted to calm him down. He had his coat on, and his hat and cane were in his hands. Gerda knew what he was up to.

"You will not, Father," she told him.

"YES, I WILL," Sylvester commanded. "I WILL TEACH HIM A LESSON."

"NO, YOU WILL NOT." Gerda took the hat and cane from her father's hands.

He stood there dumbfounded for a while. His jaw moved twice, but no sound came out.

Gerda knew why he wasn't moving. He was flabbergasted. Nobody spoke to him that way. *Had I been his son or one of his employees, he would have let me have it.* Gerda could tell he was about to launch into a verbal tirade, and then he stopped short.

Sylvester took off his coat.

CHAPTER XII

Early in the evening of New Year's Eve 1944, Sylvester had been accosted. While he was in the office part of the railroad station building, his office was stormed by six Soviet soldiers.

Sylvester sat quietly at his desk as they entered. Two railroad personnel followed in after them, looking flustered and confused. Two of the Soviet soldiers immediately stood in front of them.

"I am sorry, Herr Majowski," one of the workers said in a quiet, sheepish voice.

"Why are you here?" Sylvester calmly.

"We are here to seize your property," one soldier said. He spoke in Polish.

"On what grounds?" Sylvester asked. His tone was still calm, but he stood up as he asked the question.

"We don't need any," came another soldier's response. Sylvester knew from his uniform that he was the commanding officer. Sylvester watched as the officer observed the mahogany humidor that Sylvester had on his side table. He nervously looked back at Sylvester, as if returning to the situation.

Sylvester turned to him. He studied the man's face. His comment seemed forced, delivered with a certain hurriedness. Sylvester wondered if that was a sign of him being uncomfortable and desirous to complete his task quickly. Sylvester remained intentionally quiet.

"We must go to your house immediately and take possession of it," the commanding officer said. His voice stammered slightly as he spoke. Sylvester maintained his gaze, adopting a sympathetic expression on his face.

"Don't come to my house right now," Sylvester said in a low voice that exhibited quiet strength.

"That's ridiculous," the commanding officer said. "We go

144

now." He stressed the last three words and continued to speak at a hurried pace, as if he was stumbling over his speech. He came across as sloppy and not fierce.

Sylvester walked to his side table. He saw the officer stiffen. He took the humidor and presented it to the officer.

"You may take anything else of value here that suits your fancy," Sylvester declared. He unclasped his watch and handed that to him as well. "Take my watch as well. It is made of gold."

The officer greedily swiped the watch from Sylvester's hands and studied it. A smirk began forming on his face. Sylvester continued, "Come back some time in the future for the house and its possessions."

Sylvester worried about whether the man could be trusted or not. Sylvester had traditionally had a good feel for people.

The soldiers were not aware that Sylvester spoke Russian. While the officer was nodding his head slowly and methodically, as if his thinking was deliberately making the motion slow, Sylvester overheard a lower-ranking soldier argue, "Colonel Kasparov will not be happy."

The officer stopped nodding. He examined the watch again. Sylvester seized on the opportunity. In Russian, he asked the officer, "Do you have a family?"

The officer and the soldiers were all stunned. The officer nodded his head. His motion was more emphatic in this instance.

Sylvester continued in Russian, "So you know how important family is. Please give me some time with them. After several weeks you can come back."

The officer kept his head still. Without saying another word, he made a swift move towards the door. The others followed. "You will all keep quiet about this," Sylvester overheard him instruct his men as they left the building.

● ● ●

Gerda would never forget that evening. She knew that the situation in the part of Poland that housed the Majowski mansion was becoming increasingly more difficult. Although her in-laws had requested her presence at their home that night, Gerda was determined to stay at her parent's home to celebrate the New Year. Her father had arrived a little late that evening.

"Father, where is your watch?" Gerda asked Sylvester as soon as he entered the home.

Sylvester wore a grim expression on his face. After several seconds, which Gerda sensed as an eternity, he responded. "I am afraid that we will need to leave the house."

Sylvester relayed the incident to Gerda and the family. He mentioned to Gerda when they were alone together, "I detected one of the soldiers smirking while they were leaving. Perhaps that indicates that we do not have much time."

Gerda knew that her father could not turn to his work colleagues, other executives with the railroad company, for assistance. They were the ones that told the Soviets to come after him, Gerda was certain of it. Because of his antics over the last several months support for Sylvester had dwindled beyond apathy to resentment. Gerda knew that this was a price that he had to pay.

"This is a strange sense of justice," Sylvester commented to Gerda. She understand exactly what he meant, but he went on to explain himself. "The group that hands me over to the Soviets has become disgusted by my deeds. Those deeds would be lauded by the non-Soviet Allies if the proper authorities ever came to know about them; however, it wouldn't be enough to spare us, because ultimately the Soviets see us as Germans and they are on our heels."

As was their tradition, the Majowskis listened to Beethoven's Ninth Symphony that night.

Gerda saw that Heinrich, Mia, and Sylva, who had assembled for the holiday—Heinrich on leave from the military to recuperate—had a look of fear on their faces. Gerda realized that she likely had a similar expression. Sylvester said to them, "We will not let our enemies destroy every part of us. We will hold on to what is the most dear. When you listen to this performance, know that we must feed the hope in our hearts that we will survive this and everything, eventually, will be okay."

After the performance, the family packed their things and prepared to leave. As they assembled in the entrance foyer about to depart, Sylvester spoke to the family. "I have decided not to go."

"It is more accurate that you are declaring your intention not to go, which you knew all along," Gerda accused.

"Gerda you will stay quiet," her mother said.

"I will not," Gerda protested. "If Father stays, I will stay," she insisted. Gerda adopted a combative tone. For only the second time in her life she had an aggressive stance with her father, careening on the precipice of impertinence.

Sylvester closed his eyes. He nodded his head slowly in reluctant acquiescence to Gerda's demand.

"You stay behind and look after your father," Christina said, in support of Sylvester's decision.

"I shall stay as well," Heinrich piped up. He was leaning on a cane that he needed to assist him in walking.

"No," Sylvester said. "You are still recovering and you are needed to escort the rest of the family to safety."

Sylvester then took Heinrich aside. "I am giving you this locomotive," he said to Heinrich. "Take the train to southern Germany, close to the Austrian border. You will pass through Czechoslovakia, but try to avoid Prague. Your Uncle Wilhelm will meet you in the town of Rosenheim with his family. He will help you get to Salzburg. I will meet you in Salzburg and all of us—you, me and Wilhelm, will work on going to Zurich."

Heinrich had not had a chance to get a replacement cello. Gerda saw the expression on his face; she could tell he looked a bit lost without having his cello nearby him. He wouldn't be leaving the house without one, under normal circumstances. Gerda lamented that there was no other way for her brother.

"Don't worry, Heinrich, you are escaping. You don't need your cello." Gerda tried to console him as best she could.

"I always need my cello," Heinrich said ardently.

Sylvester stayed mostly with Gerda at the house during the weeks after the family's departure and with a much-reduced staff of one butler and one cook. Gerda was so proud of her father. He was defending his territory. He wouldn't leave without a fight.

However, there came a time when Sylvester had to leave for a meeting. He had heard that the locomotive carrying the family had come back to Poland. Gerda knew he wanted to make sure that the family had arrived safely in Rosenheim and that they had connected with his brother Wilhelm. It meant leaving Gerda alone in the house during a very volatile time. Many residents of the town were fleeing, fearing for the safety of their lives. Gerda knew that Sylvester had always had a keen sense of each of his child's temperaments. He also knew what each child was capable of. Gerda felt a sense of pride that her father knew she had the strength of will to persevere there. When Gerda said goodbye to Sylvester, his parting words were, "Whatever you do, do not leave the house."

Sylvester was away for days. He had said that he would call her, but Gerda never heard from him. The Soviet soldiers were infiltrating the town. Gerda could hear the rumble of their tanks. There weren't many people left in the town—it was virtually empty. Gerda had to make a decision. She'd heard horror stories of people being captured or killed, even rumors of rapes. She knew she had to flee. When she saw the soldiers marching into the town, she knew she had no more time. Either she left or she placed herself in harm's way. She packed whatever family valuables she could and made an escape.

She went to the rail station in a neighboring town. There she saw one of her father's allies. She asked him to take her to her father. He knew where Sylvester was.

"We need to wait awhile, the track won't be clear for another three hours or so," he informed Gerda.

"You will take me there now," Gerda demanded.

They set out on a single locomotive immediately.

Sylvester's friend had been wise to recommend waiting. Coming at them at fast speed from the opposite direction was a speeding train. As much as her father's friend blew the whistle, the opposing train did not hear it in time. By the time the other conductor did hear it, there wasn't enough track left to stop completely. Gerda looked with horror at this train coming at them.

"Brace yourself," her father's friend said.

The two trains collided. Luckily, the speed of the opposing train had slowed sufficiently. Gerda was thrown into the air and landed with a thud against the furnace, the side of her head striking it. She stood up after a few minutes, dazed, but feeling lucky to still be alive.

"How long before we can continue?" Gerda asked her father's friend.

"This will take a few days to repair. First of all, we have to get out of their way so that...."

While he was talking, Gerda was already moving about. She grabbed two cases and surveyed the outside surroundings. Gerda, without saying a word, jumped from the train and started walking. Eventually she reached a road heading towards a town.

She had to rely on the help of gypsies who allowed her to travel with them to take her the rest of the way. They wouldn't let her take both cases; Gerda could see that there was no room in their over-stuffed truck. She had to trim down to one. She tried to keep with her the most valuable of what she was able to take. She felt a little exposed as she consolidated her belongings into one suitcase. She assured herself though, *As long as I keep the case in my sight, I should be okay*. The gypsies seemed considerate about helping her with the remaining bag that she had. She was so exhausted, she fell asleep in the back of the truck. She woke with a start, but felt relieved when she remembered that she had used the case as a pillow.

Gerda heard on the truck's radio that Dresden had been destroyed by the Allies. That was the neighboring town to Berlin.

She worked her way to the town where Sylvester was. She found her father at the train station. When she approached him, he did not say a word. All he did was slap her across her face. Gerda saw instant remorse in his eyes. He, of course, did not know the full story. Gerda also knew that he never would have wanted his daughter's life to be at risk or her well-being threatened. Gerda knew what was going through his mind. He must have been horrified at the thought of Soviet soldiers trampling through his musical palace. The dream that he had made a reality—that he had built from the ground up for his family—fell away. Gerda knew that he did not blame her. It was the cursed war.

Gerda reciprocated her father's deep understanding of her and the other children with a deep understanding for him and his temperament. Gerda knew his sense of loss was immense. She waited patiently to be able to explain to him what happened.

Sylvester looked at his daughter. He finally opened his mouth to speak. "What an ordeal you must have been through," he said to her. "You even forgot to put on one of your earrings."

Gerda touched her ears. *Oh*, she thought. *I must have slept on the other side of my face, and the gypsies could only get one.*

When they got to a safe place, Gerda opened her luggage. She wanted to show her father what she had been able to salvage. When Gerda opened her bags, the two looked not upon their family's heirlooms, but upon rocks the gypsies had inserted in their place as they looted the Majowski treasures.

Her father did not seem as troubled as Gerda would have thought. Gerda herself was distraught.

"The train with the rest of the family stopped before entering Prague," Sylvester said, "Heinrich was concerned because of an increasing number of checkpoints. They got off the train and never came back to it. I need to find them."

"We need to find them," Gerda corrected.

● ● ●

Manfred had been eager to get back to Berlin to visit his

mother. At that time in Germany, there was no way for him to be able to cross the border into the Russian-controlled area and make his way into Berlin as he was currently in the American sector. He knew he would have to rely on black market methods. He also needed a way to generate some cash.

He and his singing partner, Gunther, came up with an ingenious idea. They began producing handbags using materials that they had available to them. The idea had its genesis in Manfred witnessing his mother make handbags at home. Hence, Manfred knew how to make them. Gunther knew how to get a hold of the materials. Manfred would then take these handbags to the American base and barter with the soldiers and the soldiers' families to sell them for cigarettes. In turn, they would sell the cigarettes on the black market for cash.

They naturally needed some assistance from the inside in order to be able to pull this off. Manfred and Gunther had become friendly with one of the nurses, Heidi. She had grown very fond of their singing. Her family came from Stuttgart, where her father had been a singer. He had been killed in the war. Heidi would listen to Manfred and Gunther intently. They would often ask her to request songs she liked to hear, and they referred to her adoringly as 'Our Number One Fan'.

Heidi was very young. She was barely fourteen when she began training as a nurse. Because of the huge demand, at eighteen she started working for the government. She had only been working as a nurse for a few months before she met Manfred and Gunther. She was tall for a female—five feet eight inches. She had brown hair that she kept long and brown eyes. She had a very slender frame. She had a classic beauty to her face. Someone whom everyone would notice as pleasantly pretty. Even without make-up she was sweet to look at. She always wore an expression of warmth about her, and her mannerisms were extremely courteous. She was not very emotional, in the sense of being overly dramatic, but she was sensitive.

Heidi was the first recipient of a handbag. She provided cover for them when they wanted to visit the military base to sell the handbags. She would also help them procure some of the materials to make the handbags.

The cash that Manfred and Gunther earned enabled Manfred to pay off a railroad engineer to hide him in the coal railcar with his suitcase so that he could enter Berlin through the Russian-controlled zone. Manfred noticed something glisten in the coal storage area. He touched the metal surrounding it. It felt hot to the touch. He quickly put his hand in and pulled it out. It was an earring. He thought of selling it to get more cash.

When he reached his mother, she wept as she opened the suitcase he was carrying. It was full of vegetables and potatoes—key necessities for survival that had been nearly impossible for Muti to find. She made a few great meals for her sons—Horst had made his way back home—and they sang together during Manfred's stay. Manfred decided to give his mother the earring he found, as a way to commemorate his visit.

"Let's have it melted and have two smaller earrings made or make a ring," Manfred said. "One earring isn't going to do you much good."

Manfred paid off another railroad engineer so he could sit in a coal car to get back to the hospital.

• • •

Gerda and Sylvester were desperate to re-connect with the family. They went into Czechoslovakia to look for them. They had no idea where to look. Sylvester took a locomotive and stopped at every rail station between the Czech border and all stops north and west of Prague. The railroad managers knew of Sylvester's name. They were willing to help him out on the sly. Thankfully, he was able to confirm the last train station that they had been through. He began making enquiries in the restaurants and cafes of that town—places where he thought it might be safe to make enquiries.

Gerda and Sylvester also scanned the letter boxes of

residences, hoping to find a Polish household. When they found one, Sylvester would knock on the door and ask them for help in Polish, explaining that he was from Poland. One such Polish household said his brother had a butcher shop in town. He enquired with him and said that there had been a young man with a cane who would come in every few days. Sylvester instructed the butcher to tell him that his father was here for him.

"Father, Heinrich may not trust this man," Gerda worried.

"I know," Sylvester said and then he turned to the butcher. "Tell him that he held a viola as a cello when he was four."

The butcher did the same the next time Heinrich walked in. Heinrich scribbled on a piece of newspaper. Sylvester and Gerda arrived at that location a few hours later. It was a Jewish family's home. In the basement was Mother, Mia, Mia's daughter Crystal, Ernst's son Klaus, and Heinrich.

As Gerda and Sylvester entered, she observed her father studying the name on the door. It said "Abramowitz". At the time they arrived, only the young son of the household was there. After several hours they heard someone else enter. Christina calmed Gerda and Sylvester down. Both remained on edge from their journey.

"It's okay," Christina said, "Herr Abramowitz usually comes home at this hour."

"Ahh," Sylvester said, "I must meet him!"

"Wait here," Christina said. "He will come to us when it is safe for him to come down."

After twenty minutes there were footsteps coming down the stairs. Sylvester moved forward to meet the man who had provided shelter to his family. Gerda was moved as she watched her father with tears in his eyes.

"How can I ever thank you?" Sylvester asked, trembling.

Herr Itzhak Abramowitz embraced Sylvester. He was a short, stocky man. He had a round belly and a receding hairline. His face looked like it had extra layers of flesh on them, their purpose unclear. They created a layering effect about his cheeks and mouth. When he talked they would jiggle.

"My brother," Itzhak started, "you spared my life so that I could be here today to provide shelter for your family."

Sylvester was bewildered. He had never met the man. "You must forgive me, brother, I do not recognize you," Sylvester said, feeling embarrassed.

"There is no way you would," Itzhak said. "When the Soviets freed us, we were stuck outside of the station at Llazy, unable to get by for days," Itzhak explained.

Gerda saw a look of shock, amazement, and awe consume her father's face. He stood there speechless. *He must be dumbfounded*, Gerda thought. And then the first hint of a smile appeared. It was coupled with a look of disbelief. Sylvester moved his face in and out of a smile several times, at first seeming to believe, then not believing, what he was hearing.

"I had no idea I had been able to actually save anybody," Sylvester said, his voice breaking as he spoke.

"So many things have gone badly for us lately," Sylvester exclaimed. His voice and arms began to shake. He began to loose the stability of his legs. He looked as if he was going to fall over. Gerda and Heinrich dashed over to his rescue.

Gerda thought to herself, *This single event has done so much to restore all of our faith in life.*

After Sylvester was seated, Itzhak continued, "While we were parked there, the German officers kept condemning you. We heard 'Damn Majowski' so many times."

"I recognized the name. My elder brother had lived near Dorsten. He would attend your concerts, and he took me one time when I went to visit him," Itzhak continued. "I could never forget the man who gave concerts for free," he added. "Your love for music is moving and your altruism is inspiring. When your wife and children arrived, it is a good thing I looked at the case that your wife was carrying and began to ask questions." He suddenly sounded shy. "You know, it is just that we can't hide everyone. I hope you understand."

Sylvester nodded his head vigorously. "I will be eternally grateful to you for what you have done."

There were a few minutes of silence as the two embraced again.

"Is your elder brother here?" Sylvester asked.

"No, he did not survive. He was one of the first to go. He was executed at Dachau," Itzhak revealed.

Sylvester fell silent. "I am sorry I could not do anything to save him," he said.

"No need to feel that way," Itzhak said. Gerda sensed he said it with the resignation of a man who has been forced to come to terms with a situation he wished with everything in him that he never had to face.

"There were only a few like you, Herr Majowski," he added. "God protected some of us thanks to angels such as you, Oscar Schindler, Raoul Wallenberg and others."

All members of the family were overwhelmed with what had just happened. They couldn't find the words.

"I wish I had my cello," Heinrich softly mumbled, but loud enough to elicit a smile from Gerda, who was within earshot.

"This is my younger brother's house," Itzhak said after a pause. "You met his son already, the young boy who was here when you arrived. My nephew, Bastian, is also living here. He was the son of my elder brother." Itzhak offered, "He is a great lover of music, just like you and your family."

When the Majowski family was alone together again, they embraced for a very long time. All stayed quiet—there were plenty of tears, but no words were spoken.

Gerda was the first to speak. "Music has saved our lives, Father."

All reflected on the comment and said nothing more.

From that day forward, Itzhak would visit with Sylvester

every day. They would talk extensively about life, the war, music. He smuggled a phonograph downstairs and rigged some electricity to it. Thanks to Bastian's help, he was also able to get a piano there. Bastian would join them in singing. Itzhak had hope in his heart. "Maybe when the Soviets cease their manhunt, you can settle down here."

"Nothing would make me happier," Sylvester said, "but the reality is that we need to get back to Germany—the American, British or French-controlled sectors."

"My brother and I can probably help get you to the Soviet zone of Germany," Itzhak offered.

"I think you would be putting all of your lives at risk if you tried to help us beyond that," Sylvester said, completing Itzhak's thought.

● ● ●

Heinrich approached Gerda one day when he came back from the butcher.

"The butcher claims that your husband Uli is looking for you," Heinrich informed her. "I don't know whether to believe him or not," he added.

Gerda said nothing to Heinrich. In her heart she was feeling betrayal that it had taken him so long to surface—wasn't he concerned? She then thought to herself that perhaps it had just taken him this long in order to locate her. Finding people was not easy. Gerda decided to do nothing with the information.

One day a Soviet soldier arrived at the Abramowitz house. He didn't say a word to Itzhak; he just left a box. The name Gerda Sabbas had been written on the front.

Gerda opened the package. It was a pendant that Uli's mother had given her. She now knew that Uli was truly searching for her.

"Now I have to decide if I want to go back," she said to Heinrich.

"Father is eager to get back to Germany. He thinks he has

found a way to get to East Germany first and then into West Germany. He doesn't want to go to Switzerland anymore," Heinrich indicated to her. "I think you should come with us."

The same Soviet officer came to the house the next day. Gerda gave him a letter.

After one week, he came back. He had a letter for Gerda.

"Uli is asking me to wait here," Gerda read to her family, "He thinks he can get to me in two weeks."

"We were planning on leaving in four days," Sylvester said, now lost in his thoughts.

Gerda knew why her father was stating that. He wanted her to go with the family. Gerda thought about it for a long time. She was strangely touched by what she saw as her husband's attempt to get her back. *Did she wait for him? Or did she go?* She decided to wait for him. She could see the dismay and concern in her father's face.

"I beseech you, Itzhak," Sylvester pleaded. "Please look out for my daughter."

"Do not worry, brother," Itzhak said. "She is in safe hands."

Heinrich turned to Bastian, "I am counting on you," he said.

Bastian hugged Heinrich. "It's because you can."

Gerda said goodbye to her family. She had tears in her eyes. She had faith though. She was confident that soon they would all be together again.

● ● ●

Kasparov entered the barracks late at night. It had taken him months to determine the precise location of the doctor who had amputated his arm. He had stalked the field headquarters almost daily until he found the person with the information. Threatening the clerk for the information was easy. One simple motion of the gun to his head, and Kasparov had all he wanted to know.

The war was turning in favor of the Allies, and there weren't many of the enemy afoot as Kasparov made his way through the countryside to the remote region where the doctor had asked to be posted. As a colonel, Kasparov had ample clearance to enter the barracks, and didn't raise suspicion that he arrived at two in the morning, alone. Kasparov worked his way through the building until he arrived at the sleeping quarters. Luckily each room was labeled with its inhabitant. Kasparov heard footsteps down the hall and concealed himself in the entryway of his target door. As the footsteps got further away, Kasparov opened the door and entered. He left the door slightly ajar to allow a little light in. Kasparov edged his way to the bed. He pulled out his gun and prepared to aim it at the doctor's head. He began drowning in his thoughts. He recalled all evil: his mother, his stepfather, the nurse. He moved forward less cautiously now. As he leaned in, his leg brushed against the end table with enough force to cause it to move and for a glass resting on top of it to come crashing to the floor. The body lying asleep instantly shot up. With the light from the hall Kasparov caught a glimpse of his face. Kasparov was immediately taken back to when he had been shot and brought into the medical tent. A tidal wave of anger gushed forth within him, crashing with impact onto the metal shore of his weapon's trigger. Kasparov pulled twice for good measure. The look of horror on the doctor's face was satisfying. Instantly, the doctor was dead.

Still reeling from emotion, images of hate—his mother, stepfather, the nurse, the recently deceased doctor—yielded to a vision of his father. He imagined him playing the violin. Kasparov's hand was still shaking violently. *Why don't I feel better?* he asked himself.

Kasparov didn't detect the footsteps coming towards the room he occupied from the hall, so deep was his immersion in his thoughts. A man in a white overcoat, presumably another doctor, swung open the door and turned on all the room lights. Kasparov was stunned. He instinctively moved towards the door, aiming his gun at the doctor. The doctor reacted quickly, stepping backwards into the hall and tactically slamming the door on Kasparov's hand. Kasparov tried to move his hand and drop the gun in the process, but he was not quick enough. The door slammed shut, wedging Kasparov's middle finger between the gun, the door and the door post. It was the middle finger of his only hand. He was in too much pain to pursue the doctor. Kasparov had to escape; he knew that the doctor would announce his presence. Kasparov was barely able to lift the gun up and place it into his pocket. He exited the living quarters building and ran across the courtyard, holding his sole hand against his chest. There was no hope of getting a glove on, he covered it with the sleeve of his overcoat, and marched through the security gate, not returning the salute given to him by the soldier standing guard. As he clambered into the jeep and began driving with the palm of his left hand, he waited to hear the sound of an alarm coming from behind him. It never came.

Kasparov escaped to another camp and invented a story about his injury. He was treated by the medical team there. The incident permanently injured Kasparov. Several bones in the tip of his middle finger were broken. Although the finger was intact, he lost most of the sensation in his finger as there was extensive nerve damage. It also impacted his mobility. He couldn't move his middle finger on its own; for the middle finger to move, he had to move his ring finger.

It was morning by then, and Kasparov made his way to the military base where his official post was. He became lost in thought once he arrived back and had entered his room. He was disgusted with what had happened to him in his life. On one hand, he thought that maybe he should feel lucky that he was not a double amputee— that he still had a hand that mostly functioned. But then he just felt more angry. *Why don't I feel satisfaction? The doctor who took my arm is dead. I have my revenge.* He reflected on the loss of use of his finger as a cost for retribution. But then what price was being extracted from him for the loss of his arm? He pulled out the shattered violin and ran his hand over it.

He thought again of his mother and her second husband. "I came after the wrong person," he said aloud. He had picked up and was now holding a cello with a name inscribed on the inside.

● ● ●

Gerda waited the two weeks for Uli. There was no sign of him. Another week passed. Yet another one. The butcher pulled Bastian aside and indicated that many Germans were heading for cover. The Soviets were stepping up their search efforts.

Bastian came to Gerda. "Gerda, it is not too late. I can get you to your family."

"No," she said to Bastian with some hesitation. "N-Not yet."

"I will give you a few more days," he told her.

It was too late. The next day, Soviet soldiers stormed the house. They beat Itzhak and Bastian severely but spared the young boys.

They found Gerda in the basement and dragged her upstairs. They pulled her onto the street. She was thrown into a truck with other women and was taken to a prison.

For the first time in her life, Gerda worked hard to look as ugly as possible. She let her blond hair go wild, running her hands through it, covering her face—killing all attempts to keep it orderly. She knew she had to cover her blue eyes. She didn't want to draw any attention to herself. She tried her best to act as if she was insane. She beat herself against the prison wall for added effect whenever soldiers would be within earshot. Her temples were the most frequent victim. Banging both sides of her head repeatedly caused her head to hurt a great deal. She was careful to not draw any blood—she didn't want an infection. She added some theatrics to make it seem as if she were striking with greater impact than she was. Periodically, women were being taken from her cell. They were returned after a while. When they got back, their hair was disheveled, their clothes were torn, and there were streaks of black on their faces.

The door opened again. Gerda was banging her head repeatedly against the wall. To her horror, the Soviet soldier pointed at her and three others. He pushed them out of the cell.

Gerda took to screaming and flailing, all the while being sure to keep her eyes covered. They were taken to the front door and shoved through it.

The soldier went back inside. Gerda also soon had streaks of black on her face. She shivered as she cried. She collapsed from exhaustion. Hers were tears of relief.

• • •

When Manfred and Gunther were discharged, they both made their way to Berlin. On the day of their departure, Manfred made one final visit to the American base to sell off the last of the handbags that they had made. Gunther was going to meet him at the train station. When Manfred arrived there, he was surprised at what he saw.

"Heidi! So nice of you to come," said Manfred. "Are you seeing us off?"

"No," she said, "I am coming with you."

It was only then that Manfred noticed the bag she was carrying. Manfred was flummoxed. He turned to Gunther. "Can I speak with you?" he asked, pulling Gunther aside. "This is additional risk," Manfred pleaded. "Already you have to move around on your crutches. This will slow us down even more!"

Gunther responded, "I know, Manfred."

"We will need extra cash," Manfred added.

Gunther patted his pocket. "I have it here."

Manfred looked into empty space for a while. He was frustrated with his friend, and he was not keen on putting at risk his chances of making it to Berlin. He saw the determined look in his friend's eyes.

"Well," Manfred said, pursing his lips and shrugging his shoulders, "that's how it is."

They walked back towards Heidi.

"Why are you going to Berlin?" Manfred asked, turning to Heidi.

Heidi reached for and held Gunther's hand. They looked

clumsy, she with her tall, slender figure, and Gunther slumped over on his crutches. Gunther had a big smile on his face.

"Ahh," Manfred said, *"THAT'S* how it is." Instead of pursing his lips, Manfred smiled and shrugged his shoulders.

CHAPTER XIII

Hogitaro regularly received news of Japan beginning to lose its battles. It caused a shift in mood at the camp where he had been stationed. Triumphant songs were sung less often. Most nights, people retired early, not enjoying sake at the officer's quarters. Even visiting the comfort women tents had decreased in its intensity. Hogitaro recalled the night he heard about the dual bombings in Hiroshima and Nagasaki. He felt badly for the people there, but relieved that he had no family in those regions. He then heard about Emperor Hirohito publicly announcing Japan's surrender.

Hogitaro took advantage of the more lackadaisical atmosphere these events provided. He escaped to the Robinson Road house when he could to play the violin there. Now that his country had surrendered, his thoughts turned towards going home and what he might do with the rest of his life.

By September of 1945, arrangements had been made for Japan to relinquish control of Singapore back to the British. It was a lawless time in Singapore. Hogitaro witnessed a lot of looting and the locals running about without a care for law and order. He and his Japanese associates felt no obligation to continue their patrol and the maintenance of order for a territory that they had been forced to forsake. The British had not arrived yet to assume control of the island.

Hogitaro thought of the house on Robinson Road. He knew he had placed the mines there for his own benefit; he knew that the honorable thing to do would be to take them out. It would be irresponsible not to. Hogitaro entered the house as he had always done. He thought of playing the violin first, holding it in his hands. He then felt that he should finish his work, then he could play freely. He began disarming each mine, taking his violin to each mine location as he worked.

Hogitaro heard the sound of a jeep approaching. He

assumed it might be looters. He had one last mine to disarm. He quickly went to it, set down the violin and began working. As he worked, he heard approaching footsteps. He stood up, instinctively reaching for and holding the violin. Hogitaro could tell by the uniform that it was a British officer, but he was of Indian origin. He was squat and stocky with thick black hair and a moustache.

Hogitaro watched him. He was shouting at Hogitaro in a language that Hogitaro did not understand. Hogitaro kept watching him. The British officer must have assumed vandalism, thought Hogitaro, because he immediately took out his gun and pointed it at Hogitaro. Hogitaro began shouting back. It was of no use. It was clear he didn't speak Japanese nor the token German that Hogitaro knew. Several more words were exchanged; words that meant nothing to the other person. *I wish I had learned English*, thought Hogitaro.

Hogitaro saw the officer make the motion of pointing his gun down to the ground. *Perhaps he means the violin*, thought Hogitaro. He put the violin down.

Hogitaro then tried to explain that there was one mine left that he had to disarm. With his arms raised, he kept pointing to the black object behind the bookcase where Hogitaro had placed it. He tried to make an explosion motion with his hands. It was of no use. The British officer wouldn't listen. He began pushing Hogitaro out of the house with force. Hogitaro protested, but it was to no avail. He eventually left, and he waited in the grove of banana trees behind the house. He thought he would go back in once the British officer left. He was hoping that the mine would not be triggered before that. As he leaned against the tree, to his horror, he heard a large explosion.

● ● ●

Gerda managed to find her way back to the butcher and from there to Itzhak. He hugged her deeply when he saw her.

"Oh my child," he wailed, "I have failed you!"

"No, Herr Abramowitz," Gerda said, "I am okay. They

never touched me."

Itzhak and Bastian were overjoyed.

Bastian turned to Gerda. "I am not asking this time."

• • •

As Gerda made her way back to her family, she was reviewing letters from her father. Several were short. One was multi-page. Gerda began reading it. It was regarding her beloved cousin Helmut.

The internal resistance movement that Helmut was a part of had been gaining more and more strength. It was clear that Germany would lose the war. All in the military seemed to understand that, except for a select group at the highest levels of power, including Hitler. There was new leadership in the ranks as well, her father explained in the letter. Colonel Stauffenberg had led yet another assassination attempt in July 1945. At that point, her father explained, so many lives had been lost, they didn't know if they could preserve any more of their Jewish friends, but the war had to end.

Her father went into detail describing the event. A similar staging transpired as in the earlier assassination attempt. Stauffenberg placed the bomb under Hitler's desk and was airborne minutes after it detonated. He called Berlin prior to his taking off and announced the launch of Operation Valkyrie, which was a full-blown takeover of the government and all other leading military outposts throughout the country. Her father wrote that Helmut had a role in this mission, and it could not be turned back. Chaos soon broke out as people learned that the bomb had gone off but that Hitler had survived. Gerda looked up as she read. She had a large, sinking feeling in her heart.

By nightfall, after a full day of Operation Valkyrie, Hitler went on the radio. At that point, all knew that he was still alive and the assassination attempt had failed. Helmut could not be spared this time. He had arrested a senior military officer in order to assume command of the outpost where he was located. This senior military officer was not sympathetic to the cause. "He sacrificed our Helmut," Sylvester wrote.

Gerda shared the letter with Bastian. He closed it with a grim look on his face.

"Have you heard anything about this?" Gerda asked.

Bastian looked away. "There have been rumors and reports of what happened. Nobody speaks officially."

Gerda put her hand on his arm. "Tell me," she instructed him.

"Those loyal to Hitler were instructed to arrest and keep the plotters on site and wait for the arrival of the military police," Bastian relayed. "Before the military police arrived, it was not uncommon for the officers to be beaten and tortured extensively. There was likely not much mercy exhibited towards him."

Gerda maintained her composure as Bastian studied her face for a few minutes.

"Helmut would then have been led to the German High Command headquarters where two hundred officers were assembled in the courtyard."

Gerda wondered how many of them Helmut might have recognized. She thought of all of their faces and bodies, bruised, tattered, broken. Gerda wondered how many of them had frequented the Majowski Bar in Berlin.

Bastian continued, "Each one of the officers in turn was handed a gun. 'You know what to do', they were instructed. 'If you don't, we will do it for you.'"

Gerda cried at the image of Helmut taking the gun in his hand.

● ● ●

Ram got the news that his brother had been killed in Singapore. It came in a telegram. It had the words "Ministry of War" emblazoned across the top. "We regret to inform you," the telegram started. Ram worried at first that his brother had been injured. He read on. His hands trembled. He took off his reading glasses and placed them in his pocket. He saw his face in the mirror. His eyes were now bloodshot, and his jaw was shaking. He went to his cabinet. He pulled out an album. He tucked it under his arm and walked straight to his friend Akbar's house.

Ram's servant had been coming up the stairs with his afternoon tea. "Sir, your tea." Ram walked straight past him, not even acknowledging his comment.

As "O Fortuna" played on that squeaky phonograph, Akbar folded the telegram and embraced his friend.

After he heard the song a few more times, Ram stood up. "Now I must inform his wife and children."

● ● ●

Gerda and Bastian entered the town in East Germany where the rest of the Majowski family was.

"You can not tell Father that I was imprisoned." Gerda's tone was firm.

Bastian looked straight ahead. "I don't like it, but I'll agree to it."

Sylvester and the family were in a small, two-bedroom apartment on the second floor of a building. They had to be in hiding again. Sylvester tried to locate Wilfred, Ernst, and Sylva. He wanted the family to re-group there. When Sylvester was not trying to locate his children, he began working a scheme to get the family back to the western part of Germany.

Gerda announced to the family, "Uli never came. I got tired of waiting."

Sylvester looked at his daughter. Gerda watched as he stared directly at the bruising on her temples. There were several black and blue marks that she was not able to mask. According to Bastian, they looked more blue than black. She wondered if the color of her eyes enhanced the blue.

Sylvester held his daughter's face with his two hands and pushed back her blond hair. "What are these blue marks?"

"Nothing, Father," replied Gerda, meekly.

Sylvester put his hands down. He looked in the distance, and Gerda could tell by the way his shoulders made a slight jolt that he was fighting back tears.

"It is the blue blood that shows you are royalty, my princess," Sylvester declared. Gerda embraced her father.

● ● ●

The loss of the Majowski home was painful on Gerda and all members of the family. Gerda had a sense of security from it, from the veil of music the Majowskis enshrouded themselves with and had all thrived on and reveled in. But that was now gone. Gerda found her father always very despondent as a result.

"I had built up so much," he would grieve. "Is it all lost?"

The only one he would really lament in front of was Gerda. "Perhaps these are lofty ambitions at this point," he confessed to her. "Trying to recover what I had would be nice, but now I must be concerned about survival."

Gerda nodded her head knowingly. "I am very concerned for Mother," she said. "I think that the loss of order has been too much for her. She doesn't cope with chaos well."

Gerda sensed that the toll taken on her mother of losing the house was probably the most severe. After being on the run, from house to house, first Poland, then Czechoslovakia and then East Germany, Gerda saw that there was a lot of wear and tear on both her mother's person and spirit.

All of them still had a hope and desire to get to West Germany, but Sylvester had to concede to Gerda, "It may take some time." Gerda saw all of the effort he was putting into establishing their move; he would spend a lot of time going into West Germany frequently to see what he could set up for the family.

Gerda saw that what helped raise her mother's spirits, and certainly Gerda's and her father's as well, was that the family re-grouped and re-connected in East Germany. All six children came together there. Wilfred and Ernst had been taken to prisoner of war camps. They escaped to make it back to East Germany. Sylva had been sent to work in a munitions factory. She also made her way back. Heinrich and Mia and the children of Mia and Ernst, Crystal and Klaus, had always been with Sylvester and Christina.

Klaus's mother had left Ernst when Klaus was young, abandoning her son. Gerda would never understand why, but Ernst declared he wanted nothing to do with the boy. Many thought that Gerda could look after him. Mia intervened. "Gerda's situation with Uli is too unclear," Mia protested. Gerda had to concede.

Gerda watched as her mother's spirit was raised temporarily, but soon came plummeting down. For Gerda, it felt like a precipitous and continued decline for her mother. "The strain must be too much for her to bear," Gerda would lament to her father.

Gerda would plead with her mother, "At least we haven't lost any members of the family."

Mother tried several times to take her life. Her will to live had gone, Gerda realized. Gerda had intervened on many occasions and had taken her to a hospital where she was able to recover. While there, she was cared for by a Dr. Herman Zschacher. Herman gave special attention to Gerda's mother. He was a concert pianist and had great fondness for anyone who appreciated music as much as he did. He tried to get Christina to talk about better times. He had been very impressed when he heard about the concerts that Sylvester would sponsor in Dorsten and the devotion of the entire family to music.

To help lift Christina's spirits, Herman brought a piano to the hospital and performed several pieces to lift her up. Gerda was quite moved by this display. It meant so much to her.

Herman's favorite piece to play was the Piano Concerto in A minor by Grieg. Sometimes Gerda would join Herman at the piano, and the two together would play Schubert's Fantasie in F minor. This lifted Christina's spirits and pumped some much-needed life back into her. Gerda, and the whole Majowski family, were grateful to Herman for his kindness and consideration. Eventually, Christina left the hospital.

● ● ●

When the British had decided to divide the Indian sub-continent into two—India and Pakistan, Ram had to uproot his family from the city of Karachi, which was now part of Pakistan, and re-locate back to his ancestral lands in the northeastern part of India, near the foothills of the Himalayas.

He was still coping with the loss of his brother.

"I can't get over the fact that Singapore was back in the hands of the British," Ram lamented to Akbar, knowing that his time with his friend would be limited. "The objective had been achieved. He died without there being a proper cause." The Japanese were only there for three years before the British reclaimed their colony; nonetheless, regaining of the territory had cost his brother's life.

"I suppose it is appropriate for us to re-trace our steps to where our forefathers were," Ram said, thinking back to his current situation. His close confidantes were aware that this was his means of coming to terms with what had happened to him. It was his mechanism to assuage his sense of loss. Those close to him also understood what he meant; Ram's last name, Giri, was Sanskrit for mountain.

Ram was a Hindu in a Muslim-dominated region at the time of the partition. He feared for his life and the lives of his family. He was the oldest of the family. His Hindu friends were all leaving, and several had been killed. He was torn as to what he should do. He decided to err on the side of safety.

"Large groups of people can hate other large groups of people," he lamented to his Muslim friends. "They become the faceless enemy. It's easy to blame them for everything that is wrong with your life. But one-on-one interaction rarely breeds hate. Give your enemy a face, a name, learn about his family, understand that he is a son, a brother or father and you'll never be able to pull the trigger." He embraced his Muslim friends when he had to say goodbye.

VIRTUOSO

He had to abandon all of his assets back then in 1947. When he came back to his old home—which was now his new home—he reverted back to his agrarian roots once again and set-up the sugar cane plantation that had been there for generations. His passion was in working with brass, however, and he survived in agriculture as long as he had to in order to set up, once again, a brass factory.

● ● ●

Gerda heard from Bastian. Uli was searching for her again. Bastian apologized profusely for not being able to come to her earlier.

Gerda responded to Bastian, "He has two weeks. If he is not here, I am going with my family."

Uli showed up. Gerda had thought so much about that encounter and what she would say to him. When he arrived, she had no idea what to say. She couldn't find the words.

He had flowers with him. He looked gaunt and run down. He was thinner than Gerda had remembered. His eyes looked sunken. His clothes looked sloppy on him now, loose and hanging over his shrinking frame.

"Gerda, Gerda," he kept repeating.

Gerda's first thought was that he looked repulsive. She also found his offering of the flowers a pathetic display. She thought that he was genuine about his despair, but she wanted to be sure that she was reading him properly. She didn't want to be hurt again, or left to cope in a vulnerable situation. Gerda began to feel more sorry for him at that point than sorry for herself.

"Please come back to me. I have been so wrong," he beseeched her.

Gerda still hadn't said anything. She took a deep breath. She reminded herself that she had committed to giving it a try.

"Come in," she said finally.

After being served some food, Uli wasted no time. "Please follow me back to East Berlin."

Gerda looked at her father. His expression was even. "I will follow you," Gerda finally said. She looked at her father again. He maintained the look on his face.

Sylvester had been successful in securing a new location for the family in West Germany. The remaining members of the family made their way to a farmhouse where they lived next to a cow stable. It was a dilapidated setting, Heinrich reported in a letter to Gerda. A far cry from the palaces of music that they had become accustomed to, Gerda thought.

Christina named each one of the cows in the stable and would call out to them periodically.

● ● ●

Heinrich was disciplined about keeping in touch with Bastian. One day he came to the Majowski farmhouse to pay a visit.

"Something is on your mind," Heinrich said. They were sitting at the dinner table, enjoying a meal.

"My uncle Itzhak is encouraging me to get married. I feel like I don't have a choice in the matter." He was silent for a while, looking down at his stew. "They have found someone already. Her name is Sara."

Heinrich sensed he mentioned her name for his own benefit, as if somehow it would help him to come to terms with it. Heinrich stayed quiet, watching his friend.

"My uncle insists that 'life must go on'," Bastian mimicked.

"He is right, you know," Heinrich offered. He watched as Bastian stopped chewing momentarily and then went back to his food. "But you are not pleased."

"I don't mind getting married," Bastian said, "I just want somebody who is a bit more involved in music. Unfortunately, I have had no luck finding that on my own."

"That would be better for you," Heinrich admitted.

"I worry about honoring my parents. I think they will be at peace knowing that I married somebody that they were fond of."

Heinrich put his hand on his friend's shoulder.

Once Bastian did get married, he made a decision to go back

VIRTUOSO

to Germany. He moved back to Berlin. West Berlin.

● ● ●

Kasparov tried to keep a low profile. He awaited any inquiry or persecution as a result of the doctor spotting him after he'd killed the doctor who had amputated his arm. It never came. Kasparov had to live in fear about possibly getting caught. Perhaps that was punishment enough, he thought to himself. He couldn't resolve the matter in his mind. He didn't know why the doctor who had seen him was showing clemency towards him. He had likely seen Kasparov's face—he had turned the lights on. It would have been easy to do a search of treatments for hand injuries conducted in the military camps. For several years, Kasparov coped with this internal debate. He couldn't reconcile his bloodthirst for retribution with the kindness that the doctor was showing him. It also disturbed him that he did not feel satisfaction from his execution. He decided that killing wasn't the answer. He couldn't cope with the strain of possibly getting caught. No, he decided. He would destroy lives the same way his life had been destroyed.

In 1947 he eventually got married. It was at his mother's behest. She had selected his bride-to-be, Anna. His mother had been nagging him incessantly that she needed someone to take care of her.

I'd like to take care of her, thought Kasparov to himself, full of macabre images.

No, he realized, *I couldn't take my mother's life.*

Despite his mother's insisting that he come to meet Anna, Kasparov met her on their wedding day. Kasparov found Anna as plain looking as his mother. She had brown hair that she kept tied back. Kasparov noticed that her left eye was slightly larger than her right and her nose was bulbous to match his. He became agitated looking at her too long.

They slept apart on their wedding night. It was only when Kasparov came back home drunk one night that the marriage was consummated. It had been five months.

He continued to pursue his military career, back at home, after being married. He came to despise his wife as much as he despised his mother. The two seemed to have a united front in nagging Kasparov. Sometimes, at night, he would fantasize about killing both of them. And then he would hear the voice *No, I couldn't do that to them.*

Kasparov's drunken antics yielded a daughter. Kasparov felt nothing for the little girl. He didn't bother to hold her when she was born. He signed up for as much away duty as possible. He aimed to be based in Berlin.

● ● ●

Hogitaro was ecstatic to have arrived in Berlin to study music at the Conservatory. He was now at the school where his instructor in Tokyo had studied. His German would be of use to him. There were a handful of other musically-inclined Japanese soldiers who were there with him. What a privilege he thought. Most of his countrymen had been shamed and did not want to leave Japan. Hogitaro knew that it was important for him to study in the west or he would never become the world-renowned violinist that it was his dream to become.

His first concert while there had been that of a modern song composer named Bastian Abramowitz. He was able to meet him at a reception that was held afterwards. Bastian's biography talked about the loss of lives he had experienced. Hogitaro felt kinship with that. He had lost many members of his family as well. They began to talk and formed a friendship.

Through him, Hogitaro met a cellist named Heinrich. Heinrich honored him by playing a duet with him.

"Anything to honor the glory of music," said Heinrich.

● ● ●

Gerda decided to sneak across the border into West Germany for her father's birthday in 1948. While Gerda was crossing the border, she was captured by the Soviets. She had heard rumors that Germans were being randomly captured when they were found to be crossing the border, but she had taken her chances. She had to spend a week in prison where she peeled potatoes. She constantly had anxiety regarding any of their attempts to rape her. She once again tried to look as undesirable as possible and resorted to her act of being insane. She would hold her head down while peeling, pulling her blond hair over her blue eyes. Fortunately, she was released without harm.

When she got out she was determined to continue on her journey. The possibility of turning back was available to her, but she pressed ahead.

She was stuck to traveling by foot. Gerda found a road and tried to look for a vehicle that might be able to take her to her parents. She eventually hitched a ride with a milk truck from Holland. She recognized the flag on the truck and felt that it was safe. She made it to her parent's farm.

Upon arrival Mia told her that their mother was in the hospital. Gerda made it to the hospital by evening. It was a bit of a distance from the house where the family was staying. When Gerda got there, her mother looked frail. Her situation seemed desperate. Gerda felt lost. This wasn't like the other times when her mother had been hospitalized for attempting suicide. Gerda knew how to deal with that; she knew what to say, how to be supportive, and she knew ultimately that her mother would be leaving the hospital. This time, it seemed different. Gerda felt helpless because she could not convince herself that this time she would be able to get her mother out. Nonetheless, she adopted that as her game plan and end goal. The doctors indicated that Christina had fallen sick because of natural causes. Her lungs didn't react well to the air, the fertilizer, the fumes. Gerda couldn't reconcile in her mind how the air at a railroad station with the constant coal burning would be more palatable. *It got down to one's will to live*, she realized.

That night, Christina held up with pride a watch that she had on her bedside table and said, "Here is a gold watch for Father for his birthday." Gerda was so happy. Christina was so proud. Gerda sat with her mother as her mother fell asleep. At two o'clock in the morning Christina woke up with a start. She reached for Gerda's hand. She uttered the words, "My dear daughter." Gerda thought that she was starting a sentence. After several seconds of silence, Gerda realized that it was actually the end, the finale to her life.

● ● ●

Kasparov reviewed the list of names that surveillance was being done on in Berlin. There were some Japanese names, some Russian names and several German names. Kasparov began reviewing the Japanese names. He saw the locations that the dozen or so under surveillance had been going to. He saw something that caught his eye "Residence of H. Majowski" had been written in one of the entries.

Bring this man in," said Kasparov, pointing to Hogitaro's name.

● ● ●

Hogitaro could barely breathe. The cloth bag over his head had finally been pulled off. He was immediately taken back to the images of fighting the British during the war. He had been beaten a few times. The energy had been taken out of him.

"What are you doing here?" demanded a voice.

Hogitaro, who had taken great pains to learn German, responded. "I am a student. At the Conservatory."

"What were you doing at the Majowski residence?"

"Visiting. He is just a friend."

"Whom did you meet and who else was there?"

"I met his sister," came the response.

The man with one arm hit him repeatedly.

"Tell me about her. Where does she live?"

● ● ●

Kasparov put Gerda on surveillance, tracking her every move. He studied her husband Uli, understanding the work he did, the places he went, what could influence him.

He noted with interest the number of phone calls and the

176

frequency of visits that Gerda made to her brother, Heinrich. They must be close, he concluded.

How can I make this as painful for Heinrich's sister as possible?

Part III: post-1953

CHAPTER XIV

On the train journey from New York to Chicago, Gerda relayed all the details of what had transpired in her life, filling in the details of what Manfred had read from her and Heinrich's letters.

"Let me answer the question you posed to me two years ago—'Who is Kasparov?'" Gerda started.

Gerda revealed to Manfred how she had been married once before. She watched his reaction. He was listening intently. "I had been betrothed to one of the wealthiest families in Poland. He was the son of a family that controlled a number of coal mines. I met him through Father. His name was Uli Sabbas. He had a penchant for studying and reading works on science and metals. He became fascinated with metallurgy and although he didn't need the income, he worked for the large steel conglomerate Krupps as a new product development expert." Gerda realized that she was talking very fast. She knew that she just wanted to get it all out as fast as possible. As if it were burdensome luggage and her arms and legs were beginning to shake and buckle under the weight. She took a deep breath.

"The marriage didn't last, Manfred. It is a story for another time, but please understand that it didn't work." She looked at Manfred pleadingly with her blue eyes wide open.

"I believe you," Manfred said.

I knew he would be trusting, thought Gerda. "My husband was simply not devoted to me."

Gerda went on to provide some detail, "Uli was fourteen years older than me. He failed to take me seriously or be thoughtful about what my needs or desires might be. It was clear he had received pressure from his family to take a proper wife and he viewed it as fulfilling his duty. After the wedding, he would spend countless hours at work and in reading and would be away for long periods of time." She paused momentarily to take a deep breath. She didn't know why she should feel nervous. "I never felt like it was a marriage. I had merely attended a grand function and then changed addresses."

Manfred chuckled at this last comment. Gerda took another deep breath. The train made a station stop. Gerda became lost in her thoughts. She remembered those scenes—the images were haunting her now. She was a young, bubbly bride full of hope for the future. The castle of a home. The stunning grandeur of the wedding. Her elaborate wedding dress was the envy of all women in attendance. And yet she was about to be bound to a statue of a man experiencing famine of emotion. Wasn't she right in what she did? she wondered. *Did I give up too soon?* She worried that Manfred might think she gave up on the marriage too quickly.

The sudden movement of the train as it left the station brought her back to the present day. "I really tried my best to save the marriage," she stated. Her voice was now more calm and collected. She thought she better explain her actions. She continued with her story.

"I decided to make an effort to be more involved in my husband's work life. If I were to show interest in all that he was studying and researching, maybe he would look at me in a different light. I went to good schools, I was fluent in English and I would often spar with my brothers on intellectual matters. I wanted to show him that I was intelligent too."

"One day, back in 1943, I went to the Krupps steel factory with a packed basket lunch to surprise him. Nobody was outside his office so I entered the door. I found my husband in the arms of his secretary. The second shock of that day came when the secretary turned to face me. I saw her large belly. I dropped the basket I was holding. The wine bottle in my grip also fell to the ground and shattered into several pieces. Red wine flowed everywhere." Gerda paused to let the drama of the event sink in.

"I ran out to the car. I told the driver not to stop driving until I reached my father's house, which took six hours." Gerda recalled that during the entire car ride she thought about a Bach cello suite. It was from the most recent performance she had heard of Heinrich's, and now the music played again in her mind. At the time it was the only thing she could think of to keep her calm. She thought of sharing this with Manfred, but suddenly felt shy and decided not to.

"It was the end of love in my mind," she said to Manfred.

Gerda remembered thinking, like the wine leaving the bottle that day, her affection for Uli had left her body.

"There is something else I should tell you." She looked up at Manfred. She thought he might wince or show concern. Instead, the expression on his face showed his concern for her. He was listening intently and keenly. He showed no visible signs of anxiety.

"I had been experiencing perpetual conflict with my husband because of another matter. After years of attempting to, I was not able to conceive a child. With the wealth we had available, we exhausted all medical possibilities known at the time. It was to no avail," Gerda recounted. She paused briefly, ran her hand through her blond hair, bit her lip and admitted, "I will never be able to have children."

Manfred maintained an even expression as he heard the news. Gerda paused, waiting for Manfred to react. Manfred seemed to take note of the gap; after several seconds he looked up and suddenly uttered "Oh." Gerda remained still. He followed that with "Uh..." and looked as if he was searching for something. He looked like he was about to say something, as he adjusted the glasses on his face and ran his hand through the miniscule curls of his hair. And then he stopped fidgeting his body and with confidence he took Gerda's hand in his and sang her a song. It was a song that put Gerda's mind and heart at ease.

VIRTUOSO

After the song, an embrace, a kiss, and Gerda laying her head on Manfred's chest, Gerda continued. She decided to truncate the rest of the story.

"Well, I became separated from Uli for an extended period of time after that incident in his office, remaining on and off at my parent's house until we had to flee the house as a family. I moved around with my parents, placed my life in harm's way on numerous occasions, including being imprisoned, thwarting rape attempts against me and escaping being nearly beaten to death, all the time thinking that he would come to me. He never did. He then showed up one day and I followed him to Berlin."

Gerda was anxious to finish the rest of the story. "Uli's family had lost the coal mine as a result of the Russian occupation post-War, but Uli had developed a very comfortable life in East Berlin. It turned out that all of his studying and research in metals made him an expert in metallurgy, and he was sought after by many parties who wished to benefit from his expertise. Among them was the Soviet secret police, the KGB. Later I would learn that they were Uli's employer, but he hid it from me in the beginning."

Gerda paused briefly as she remembered the fear she felt those days. "Once I came to know, I knew that I had to be far more circumspect with him. I regretted going back to him. He was incredibly secretive about how he spent his day and what he was up to. I became distraught living with him as well, as he would spend all evening and night getting drunk in bars with his new Soviet 'friends.'"

"And that was when Kasparov, the one-armed colonel, came into the picture. Uli was always cavorting with him. I would have to call down to the various bars to find out where he was and demand that he come home," Gerda bemoaned. "At home he would espouse communist propaganda. I lived in fear."

"At the time, I didn't know the significance of the name Kasparov," Gerda told Manfred. On May 1, 1949—she'd never forget the date—her husband didn't come home. For three days he did not appear. Gerda was frantic, calling around looking for her husband. On May 4, Heinrich called Gerda.

"Where is Uli, Gerda?" Heinrich implored.

"I have no idea, Heinrich. You know him, he runs off and never tells me anything," Gerda retorted. "He is probably out gallivanting with Kasparov," she added.

"What name did you mention?" Heinrich asked, speaking slowly and deliberately, adding undue weight to each word.

"Kasparov. He's the one that Uli is always drinking late into the night with. He only has one arm," clarified Gerda.

"Gerda, pack whatever you can. I am sending a car. You will leave immediately," Heinrich instructed her. His voice had taken on a force that she rarely heard from her brother.

"But..." she protested.

"You do it now!" Heinrich's voiced bellowed into the phone.

Gerda wanted to voice her confusion again but then she realized why Heinrich was speaking with force, which he rarely did with her—he was attempting to mask his fear. Gerda understood in that instance that she had better follow Heinrich's instructions. She hung up the phone and did as she was told. Twenty minutes later, the car Heinrich sent had arrived. When she got into the car, she saw Herman. Heinrich had located him and solicited his help to get Gerda out.

Gerda's expression of shock in seeing Herman fell to appreciation. "Mother died last year," she said.

"I know," said Herman. "I want to make sure that the same does not happen to you. Kasparov will never leave Heinrich or his family alone."

"What is this issue about Kasparov?" asked Gerda. "Who is he?"

"Heinrich will explain everything. It is best that we get you to safety. The blockade is still in place and we have to be extra careful. The Soviets are thoroughly monitoring all vehicles. As I am a doctor, they will let me through. You must pretend to be my wife."

That was easy, thought Gerda. She had spent most of the last ten years pretending to be a wife. She encouraged Herman to escape as well. He said no, he intended to stay because he had family in Dresden, East Germany, a few hours' drive from Berlin. However, Gerda knew the real reason. If his vehicle did not come back into the East Zone, it would spark a manhunt, which would also threaten the life of Gerda.

Leaving her thoughts behind and coming back to the conversation with Manfred, Gerda relayed, "Later, I would learn that Uli had deserted his post with the Soviet secret police and had returned to work for Krupps in the Western part of Germany. He had abandoned his job and he had abandoned me. After I had gotten to safety, my former neighbor informed me that one hour after I left, the KGB and the Stasi had stormed the apartment, wanting to imprison me."

Gerda became lost in her thoughts again, reliving the fear.

"Maybe they would have kept me hostage. You know, you always have to be careful with these people," Gerda said to Manfred. "How useless it would have been to take me hostage. Uli would have told them to just kill me, that he didn't care." The story of the narrow escape evoked a nervous chuckle from both of them. The chuckle ended with a heavy breath and a deep sigh of relief that she was able to make it out alive.

"I never would have met you if Heinrich hadn't gotten me out," Gerda commented. Manfred pursed his lips and nodded his head gently.

"That was truly the final episode for me. After his affair, it was the end of love. When he abandoned me repeatedly, leaving me to die, it was the end of the marriage," Gerda said.

"And then you came into my life," Gerda repeated to Manfred. She wanted to be sure that he heard her. She wanted to be sure that even though she was talking about other people, and informing him of her ex-husband for the first time, that he was the center of her universe now. *Was it enough that I came all the way from Germany*, she wondered to herself. *I would hate for him to second-guess me.*

Gerda felt suddenly awkward talking about herself for so long. It was not proper etiquette, and it was not natural to her. She was accustomed to making others the focus of attention. She kept trying to re-engage Manfred in the conversation, she realized to herself, because of her discomfort. But there was one part of the story that she had to finish describing.

"And now I must tell you what happened when I went to Father's house and I didn't see you again," Gerda said. "I couldn't tell you why at the time, but Kasparov had re-surfaced. "Remember, he was the officer that Uli kept drinking with," Gerda affirmed for Manfred. He nodded his head. "Somehow Kasparov had come to know about my close relationship to Heinrich. And he came after me. He thought he could hurt Heinrich by making me suffer. After driving Uli away, and I disappeared, Kasparov was intent on going after Father."

"That is why I was hesitant to leave information regarding my father's whereabouts—I'm sorry, even with you, Manfred—for fear that it might aid Kasparov in finding Father." Gerda found that she was speaking quickly again. "I didn't want to involve you in all of this and potentially threaten your life. Kasparov had already chased Uli away. Nobody understood what would make him stop."

"When he saw me with Father, he followed me back to Berlin. He needed an excuse to enter the West-zone, which he eventually found. He put Heinrich's apartment under surveillance. He located Bastian and beat him badly. There was also a violinist from Japan, whom Bastian and Heinrich knew, whom they intimidated for information. He was demanding to know my location," Gerda told Manfred. She could see him cringe.

"Heinrich was concerned for my life, and he knew I wanted to be with you. When we learned through your old cellist roommate friend where you were, Heinrich did what he felt was best to protect me." Gerda turned to Manfred, gazing up at him. "I feel like I will be safe with you," she said.

● ● ●

Ram was able to build another brass idol factory in the new region of the country. His earlier concern about railroad access for raw materials was assuaged by the fact that his brother, who now worked for the rail company, could assist him in procuring product.

It had hurt him tremendously when he had to walk away from his first factory. It went against his constitution. He had to think of it not in terms of walking away but as defending his family. He was right to do that.

● ● ●

Manfred had been listening to Gerda intently, absorbing all that she was telling him. From time to time he would let his thoughts wander, and a smile would start to creep up on his face. He quickly stopped it, realizing that given the subject matter, it was completely inappropriate for him to react as if it was humorous. He had a hard time helping himself though; he was just so happy to be in her presence again.

Manfred also filled Gerda in on what had been going on in his life. He talked about living with his aunt and uncle, about his job as a bartender and about taking classes at night at the university near to where his aunt and uncle lived.

When he began talking, Gerda showed a lot of enthusiasm.

"Tell me about your life! I want to hear everything! Don't leave any details out!"

As he talked, Gerda's reaction became more subdued. *Am I boring her?* After several more minutes, she seemed to look genuinely worried. There began a strain in her voice. Her repeated inquisitive questions, which he now remembered fondly, became more pointed and more exasperated. *She seems to be losing patience as I respond. Is she eager to get this over with?*

"How are your classes—they must be for singing?" Gerda asked.

"Uh, no," Manfred said with hesitation. "I am studying towards my Bachelor's Degree, but not in music."

"Oh," a suddenly quiet Gerda said, "you must be practicing with friends to maintain?"

"No, as I think about it, I haven't really found anyone."

"Do you go to concerts?" Gerda asked in a resigned tone.

"Well, gee, no, come to think of it," Manfred mused, "I haven't had an opportunity to go." It had not even dawned on Manfred that he had been missing out on something that was so important to him. He was a bit shocked. He had been so consumed with establishing his life that he had not been living. He didn't like that as an excuse; he had experienced the same difficulties in Germany, but had not given up on music.

"Where is the music in your life, Manfred?" Gerda challenged.

Manfred thought for a few seconds. "You know," he remarked, "lately, I just haven't found the time. I keep saying that I would like to get to a concert, but I haven't."

"You must maintain music in your life," Gerda pleaded.

"I know," Manfred responded sheepishly. He wished he had a better excuse to give to Gerda. He hated that she might be disappointed in him.

Shortly before they arrived at Chicago's train station, Gerda turned to Manfred. "You know, I dropped my purse intentionally the first night that we met."

Manfred responded with a smile.

CHAPTER XV

When they arrived at Manfred's aunt and uncle's house, his aunt made a declaration. "Gerda can stay with us until the wedding date."

Manfred was taken by surprise. He had not thought about that.

"Well you can't live together without being married—that is completely unacceptable," his aunt insisted.

Manfred felt a little embarrassed. He had not prepared for the situation. Gerda stayed quiet. *I suppose because she is new*, thought Manfred, *she doesn't want to upset my family by saying something wrong. That must be that etiquette again.* He smiled to himself. He felt a little less tense.

Manfred changed the subject. "Maybe Gerda would like to have dinner now, it has been a long journey."

Later that night when they were alone, Manfred turned to Gerda. "Are you okay with this?"

She paused for a few minutes. Manfred worried that she had become overwhelmed with all of her new surroundings, a new family, and a different culture. She must miss home, he thought. He decided that he should just give her some time.

"What, are you kidding me?" came her response.

Both laughed together.

The next day Manfred went to City Hall and obtained a marriage license. The day after that, the two were married. They had a small, simple ceremony in front of a government official. *What a contrast to Gerda's first time*, thought Manfred. Gerda would also wear a somber expression on her face in between her displays of excitement that she would portray to Manfred when engaged in active dialog. *After all that we have been through, a grand ceremony to make up for the devastation may have been nice to have.* On the other hand, thought Manfred, a simple ceremony was befitting in that it signified a new beginning. *This beginning is humble*, thought Manfred.

• • •

Kasparov had heard the news that Gerda was no longer in Germany. "She slipped through my fingers," he said with disgust. He had to make a trip back to Moscow. His mother had indicated that she was not feeling well and had been in the hospital.

"Why did she force me in the military to begin with?" he asked in frustration.

His daughter had just turned three. He was really going to see her for the first time since he had not participated in her birth and had left shortly thereafter. When he saw her, she came running towards him and exclaimed, "Papi!" Kasparov couldn't help but be affected by this. That is what he had called his own father. Kasparov was deeply moved. He extended his stay and began spending more and more time with his daughter.

He found himself doing things that he never imagined he would be doing. He bought her toys. He bought her dresses. One day, he came home with a violin and a bow. His daughter was too young and clumsy to be able to play it. Seeing her hold it, nonetheless, brought Kasparov a great deal of joy.

The little girl showered so much attention on him. On most occasions he didn't know how to respond. He reverted back to the lessons he learned from his own father. He only knew how to be tender towards his daughter. He shocked both his wife and his mother.

Kasparov was promoted to general. In his mind, the promotion confirmed that the doctor who saw him that night had never uttered a word.

• • •

Gerda and Manfred began their lives together in Chicago. Two lovers, overcoming distance and years of separation, were emboldened by overcoming their difficulties from the past. They would find collective strength in the music that filled their lives and the music that they created in their lives.

Gerda had to hang up her tiara—she would no longer be able to lead a life of passive luxury. But those beautiful blue eyes of hers had a steely resolve to them. She would roll up her sleeves and live the exemplary life of royalty—not because it was handed to her, but because she would create it herself. Their lives would be lives of active luxury—working hard to surround themselves with the finest things in life. It would be a life befitting a king and queen, but one that was built from their own sweat, toil and perseverance.

● ● ●

Manfred had become a produce manager in a grocery store—a far cry from his ambitions of being a singer, but it was a necessary adjustment in order to earn a living. Manfred got a job for Gerda as well. Manfred was so pleased that she took to it with alacrity; Manfred knew that it was the first time in her life that she had to work. She took a job at the same grocery chain, but had to work at another location because of a nepotism rule at the company.

Manfred had changed from his earlier job as a bartender. He had experienced a bit of job hazard in performing his duties as a bartender. Having suffered through the war, Manfred did not have it in him to be wasteful. Every time he would mix a cocktail for a bar patron, he faced a conundrum as there would be some leftover mix in the shaker.

"I can't throw this out," he would say to the manager. The manager only laughed.

What do I do? thought Manfred as he held the shaker in his hands. He lightly moved the shaker back and forth in his hand.

"I suppose I could drink it," mumbled Manfred, intentionally soft enough so that the manager could not hear.

"Hmmm, tastes pretty good," he said using the same tone.

I think that is what I better do, you know, so that I won't be wasteful, he said to himself.

This occurred during every instance that he would prepare a drink. By the end of the evening, Manfred had served maybe twenty to thirty drinks. He had to take the train to get to work. Every night on the train ride back to his uncle's place, Manfred would fall asleep. Luckily his was the last stop. The conductor began to recognize him and would always wake him up once his destination had been reached. As he stumbled into the house, he would make a bit of a ruckus. Having a few drinks also made Manfred terribly nostalgic. He couldn't help but sing some of the *Lieder* of his memory.

This, of course, would wake up the household, evoking a visceral reaction from Manfred's aunt.

"What are you doing, Manfred!" his aunt shrieked.

"Helllloooo, Aunt," Manfred would say, slurring his words. "I doon't undherstand. Whhhy are you uuuup so laaaaate?" Manfred asked, barely able to stand.

"Manfred, you got to bed this instant!" his aunt shouted.

"Ohhkay!" Manfred would shout with a salute.

"Man, I doon't knowwww why she isss always ssscreaming at me aaall of the t..time," Manfred said under his breath as he stumbled away.

● ● ●

They lived in a small one-bedroom apartment. Manfred had located it prior to Gerda's arrival. At the time he took it, Manfred's uncle showed a lot of resistance.

"You won't be able to afford it," he insisted.

"Well, Uncle," Manfred started. He didn't feel comfortable being disrespectful, but Manfred knew what he could do and, more importantly, what he wanted to do for Gerda. He thought of explaining to his uncle that Gerda had been used to living in grand homes with many servants.

"I just want Gerda to be comfortable." Manfred settled for that comment with his uncle, hoping to leave it at that.

His uncle kept shaking his head. "This is too lavish."

As much as Manfred had the urge to argue with him, he chose not to.

The apartment was located next to an elevated train station.

VIRTUOSO

When Gerda first saw the place, she commented to Manfred after several seconds, "By a rail station, just like how I grew up!"

Manfred knew she was saying this for his benefit. The myriad of differences in the two settings was beyond words. It was easier to reflect on the solitary similarity—as melancholy and fallacious a comparison as it was.

"Gerda," started Manfred uncomfortably.

"Yes?" she turned to him, maintaining her smile.

I can see right through it, thought Manfred. "I know this isn't what you are accustomed to."

"What, are you kidding me?" asked Gerda. "It's perfect," she said. She extended her arms and twirled around inside the living room.

Oh, thought, Manfred. *How do I explain to her?* "You see…Gerda… the bulk of my salary will have to go towards paying for this apartment."

Gerda listened intently.

"So for us to have money for food and other items," he said, "we will have to rely on your salary."

Gerda shrugged. "That's what it is there for."

"We could move to a smaller place in another area for less," Manfred offered. His voice was timid.

Gerda paused for a second. "No. You chose this place imagining us here, so we have to try to make it work here," Gerda declared.

"I forgot to mention," Manfred said, "I have no money for furniture." He had a grim tone to his voice although he thought to himself, *There is some humor to this situation that I could find.*

Gerda responded, "We'd better get to work."

As they were leaving the apartment after that first visit, Gerda took Manfred's hand in hers.

"Don't worry. Everything will be okay."

Manfred smiled. *I wish I felt re-assured.*

● ● ●

Gerda set herself to the task of furnishing the apartment. A wooden crate from the grocery store covered in fabric and boxes dressed in old pillowcases began new lives as a table and chairs— symbolic of the inhabitants of that apartment. Each fine piece of furniture which eventually filled their lives was a deliberate, conscious decision executed upon only after weeks or months of diligent saving. They would architect perfection around them in their home, but it was done after painstaking effort.

Gerda was able to provide Manfred some solace by getting him to join a choral group. She was thrilled at how this provided him with some much-needed inspiration as well as an outlet for him creatively. Gerda had encouraged him for weeks to join. He was often busy with other pursuits. Finally, Gerda went on her own to the choral group to get the information for Manfred.

"I would like to sign my husband up for the chorus," Gerda said. She thought about the sentence she just uttered. She said it with such nonchalance. *What a dream this is*, thought Gerda. *It is so wonderful to be able to make a statement like that. I have a husband who loves music.* It brought a broad smile to her face.

There was little money available after paying for the apartment and apportioning money for food and transportation to work. They had to maximize their dollars and, Gerda would see to it, maximize their enjoyment of life.

"We will make it work," she insisted.

They began settling into their new lives. They found an authentic German butcher. They made friends with him and with some of the patrons who had also come from Germany that the butcher introduced them to. Manfred also developed some friendships with members of his chorus.

They began hosting dinners and gatherings at their apartment. Most of their peers thought that they lived well; some even accused them of living extravagantly.

One of the first dinners that Gerda and Manfred hosted was for Manfred's aunt and uncle.

VIRTUOSO

"Manfred, are you still working at the grocery store?" asked his uncle.

"Yes."

"How can you afford all of this?"

Manfred gave him a smile.

"Gerda knows how to make the most of our money." He beamed with pride as he made the declaration.

What their critics failed to recognize was the hard work and effort that went into creating a life that Gerda and Manfred wanted to lead. "Most fall short due to laziness or a lack of determination— many in life settle for much less," Gerda told Manfred the following day in the park. "I am not willing to do that," Gerda stated emphatically. She even surprised herself with how forcefully she made the comment. She knew where it came from. After what she had survived, she was determined to make hers a life worth living. Manfred walked ahead to get them some ice cream. She knew Manfred thought similarly. The music they listened to, that kept them going, that kept them alive, gave them hope that there was a perfection in this world that could be attained. They took that perfection from the artistic realm of music and made it a daily reality. "I don't wish to ever stop doing that," Gerda announced. She found that she was speaking aloud again. The trees surrounding her were her only audience.

● ● ●

While Gerda was always tempted to invoke their previous tactics for attending concerts, this was a new country with a lot of unfamiliarity to it. She knew that Manfred would never agree to it. Every week Gerda would save $0.50 from each of their paychecks. Eventually she had enough to buy the two of them tickets to see a concert.

● ● ●

They attended a concert by Fritz Reiner, a Hungarian-born conductor who had just arrived in Chicago in 1953, coinciding with Gerda's arrival. He was the Head Conductor of the Chicago

Symphony Orchestra. They heard a stirring rendition of *Der Heldenleben*—A Hero's Life—composed by Richard Strauss. It was the last of Strauss's famous tone poems. He composed them so that the music would tell the story. The blaring trumpets of the first section evoked something in Manfred. It was as if he were waking up from a slumber. He felt a rush of warmth in his chest. During the third section, entitled 'The Hero's Wife,' he reached for Gerda's hand. As the violin solo of that section continued, Manfred couldn't help but get emotional. With a tear in his eye he turned to Gerda.

"Thank you for bringing music back to my life," proclaimed an elated Manfred.

Gerda held his hand more tightly. As the piece continued, with the percussion signaling the start of battle and the sweet melodies that evoked the sound of victory overlaid with the violin theme indicating the Hero reuniting with his wife, Manfred felt Gerda's hand quiver. Manfred sensed that Gerda must have felt something stir inside her as well.

Manfred's suspicion was confirmed when she turned back to him and said, "Thank you for being the music in my life."

CHAPTER XVI

Late one night in 1955, Gerda answered the telephone. She knew immediately from the static that it was a call from Germany. She was always so excited to be hearing from home.

"Hello, my darling sister!" Heinrich boomed into the phone.

"Hello, hello!" Gerda did her best to remain excited. It was a defense for her. If she didn't keep her emotional energy level up high, she knew she would cry.

"Tell me what is happening," Gerda urged.

"We have a new conductor. He epitomizes the teachings of Father!" Heinrich proclaimed. His voice was a pressure cooker of excitement.

Gerda was so happy for her brother.

Heinrich continued, "His name is Herbert von Karajan. He is Austrian-born, hailing from Salzburg, the birthplace of Mozart. Like Mozart, he showed an aptitude for musical talent at a young age. Karajan even studied for ten years at the Mozarteum, or *Universitat Mozarteum Salzburg*, the University of Music and Dramatic Arts."

"Oh wow," Gerda exclaimed jubilantly. Her eyes were beginning to swell with tears of joy.

"Karajan has a touch of elegance that he applies to the conducting of music. His concerts are so polished. It wasn't easy for him in the beginning. Karajan had to suffer through the scrutiny of the Allied de-Nazification board," Heinrich explained.

Gerda thought back to the drama of the Celibidache concert and the anxiety she felt for her brother at the time.

"They exonerated him. I think it was partially because he was married to a woman of Jewish ancestry for a number of years before the war ended," Heinrich explained.

There was a brief pause. Heinrich exploded again, as if a burst of steam had been allowed to escape from the pressure cooker.

"Gerda! Gerda! You'll never believe it," he began, gasping for air. "Karajan has no music in front of him when he conducts. Most of the time he keeps his eyes closed! He knows whatever work he is conducting so well that you can see from the way he moves his body, his arm and his head, that the music becomes him and he becomes the music." Heinrich emphasized the last sentence to where he was shouting it to Gerda.

Gerda had to pull the phone away from her ear. "I am so excited! He is music personified!"

• • •

As much as Gerda wished to go back to Germany to visit her family, it was out of the question at that point. They couldn't afford to pay for the journey. Gerda and Manfred stayed in touch with family in Germany through letters and occasional phone calls. Heinrich frequently sent care packages filled with goodies from home that Gerda and Manfred were not able to find in Chicago. Sylvester always enquired about how Gerda and Manfred were coming along, and he would speak of the time when he might be able to pay a visit himself to the US.

"Thank goodness you sent the package with the sausages," Manfred said to Heinrich, when he spoke with him over the phone.

"It was my pleasure."

"I thought that I had found those sausages at a butcher shop here," Manfred explained. "When Gerda tasted them after she cooked them," he continued, "she shouted out a number of expletives—words I didn't even know she knew—and she threw out not only the sausages but the frying pan as well!"

Heinrich laughed. Gerda had told him about that.

"I think she is terribly homesick," Manfred said to Heinrich.

"She most definitely is," Heinrich said. "She cries to me over the phone about it."

"What? She never told me that!"

"No and my sister won't ever tell you that."

Gerda missed home the most when the news from her family

was negative. She felt so helpless. She wanted little more than to be there with them to suffer through the hardships together.

The family clearly suffered from the loss of Christina. Sylvester made do with his life, although it was clear to Gerda he was lonely. He insisted on living on his own, declaring that each of the children needed to have their own lives. He did, however, take advantage of visiting with his children as often as he could.

"Father, what did you do today?" Gerda asked when she called him.

"Oh," Sylvester said, "I listened to a number of recordings."

When Gerda heard the list she felt strain in her heart. "I love you," she said to him. It was virtually the same every time she called.

"Father is listening to such sad music these days," she told Manfred.

She would complain about this to Heinrich. "Why don't you go see him," she would challenge Heinrich. Heinrich obliged when he could.

Heinrich's marriage was having difficulties, Gerda was pained to learn. His wife had left him and was trying to keep his daughter, Sabine, away from him. Gerda knew that he did his best to keep his ex-wife and Sabine in Berlin. He set-up a cosmetics and perfume shop for his ex-wife to run so that Sabine would be nearby.

"It is okay if she doesn't want to live with me," he told Gerda at the time, "but at least she can be near to me so that I can see my daughter."

To Gerda's dismay, one day Heinrich went to the store and found it empty. He was able to track down his ex-wife and Sabine in New York with the use of a private detective. Gerda was distraught to hear that he had to be so far away and that Sabine would have so little interaction with him.

Gerda received an impassioned letter from her brother.

My dearest Gerda,

Since birth family has been everything for me. It was the starting point and the goal for all experiences, achievements and disappointments in my life. With whom did I share when I explored the world, who made a fuss of celebrating when I had accomplished something and where did I go when I was in pain? Father did so much to ensure that his children had all the benefits of family available to them. I am not able to do that for my daughter. My dear sister, please help me.

Teardrops sprinkled the page before Gerda could even get to the end of the letter. "Manfred, we are moving," Gerda stated.

● ● ●

In searching for alternatives, Manfred was able to find work in Connecticut in 1958. They would be only a two-and-a-half hour drive from New York. They found a tiny house that they could rent. Manfred began his work, and Gerda began the process of looking for a job.

Manfred found a job working in an industrial products factory. One of his uncle's friends had moved to the East Coast and had established a factory there. Manfred's uncle was able to convince his friend to offer Manfred a job. Manfred felt very much at home in that environment. He started by overseeing production as he had some knowledge and experience with machines. It reminded him of his time at Siemens. He enjoyed it far more than working at a grocery store. It inspired him, and he felt that the change to Connecticut was not that bad.

Manfred rarely called in sick and even on those days when he was not feeling well, he still forced himself to go to work. The day started at eight o'clock in the morning, but he was always there by a quarter past seven. He always arrived before the president.

One day a customer came by the factory. He accosted Manfred.

VIRTUOSO

"Are you the one making this part?" the customer demanded. He held in his hands two halves of a metal cylinder, each five inches long. One side of each was smooth and the other side was jagged, where they had been joined, before the part broke in two.

"Yes," Manfred said, "I recognize that part."

"Why does it keep failing!" The customer was extremely distressed.

Manfred did not know what to say. *I wish he would stop yelling,* thought Manfred. *Are all Americans this uptight? I had officers in the military that could cope better.* By then the owner and president of the company came to Manfred and the customer. Manfred was relieved. *Now I don't have to say anything,* he thought to himself.

"What's the problem?" asked the president.

The customer starting talking before Manfred had a chance. "You make this cylinder for me. It keeps snapping in two. I think there is something wrong with the way you are making this," the customer insisted. "I think he is doing it wrong," he continued while pointing a finger at Manfred.

"Manfred, I want an explanation," the President demanded.

"Well, sir, can I ask what you are using the part for?" Manfred asked the customer. *I guess I have no choice but to talk to him,* Manfred realized.

"Are all of your employees this insolent?" the customer demanded of the President.

"Manfred!" the President cried.

"Sir, I am sorry." He took the part from the customer. He pointed to the fifty or so one-eighth-inch-wide slits that ran around the circumference of the cylinder. This was where the part kept breaking. "Just please explain to me why all of these slits are needed," Manfred pleaded.

The customer succumbed to Manfred's request. "We have a screw that rotates the cylinder. The thread of the screw passes into successive slits, allowing the cylinder to move."

Manfred thought for a moment.

"What if you were to use a screw that had a less deep thread? Then we could alter the design of this where instead of making slits and cutting away the material that makes it weaker, we can just make indents to preserve the material and hence the strength. What do you think?" Manfred asked.

Manfred could tell the president was livid. He also noticed that the president wasn't really paying attention to what Manfred was saying. He was reacting to Manfred's speaking up. Manfred saw he was turning bright red. "Manfred, how dare you!" he bellowed.

"Wait a minute," the customer said. "Your fellow may be on to something here."

The president stepped aside. Manfred made one cylinder with slits and then re-aligned the machine, put a blunted component in it that would not pierce metal, adjusted the depth and produced a cylinder with indents.

"Let me give this a try," the customer said.

The next morning, Manfred was called into the president's office. The president was very agitated, but Manfred couldn't read why. He could have been upset or happy—he just seemed on edge. *Maybe he's constipated*, thought Manfred to make himself chuckle.

"The customer from yesterday called," the president said.

Manfred didn't know what to think. He wondered if he would lose his job. He worried about what his uncle might think.

"He said he is coming by to have you look at another part," the president said.

"Is there another problem?"

"No. Your change from yesterday worked very well. He wants you to look at a part that he is having someone else make that he is having trouble with." He was a bit sheepish in his tone. Manfred could tell he felt bad about his comments from yesterday. *He has too much pride to admit it though*, thought Manfred to himself.

Manfred was relieved. When the customer came by, Manfred was able to present another change that would help with the new part. The president was a part of the meeting.

"Now you get to make this part," said the customer to the president.

The president was very excited. "Thank you so much, sir!" he exclaimed.

Manfred received a promotion on that day. He would now be involved in designing new products for the company.

Manfred was thrilled. "This comes so naturally for me," he told Gerda. "I just see the part, understand its use, and the answer just presents itself."

Business picked up as a result of Manfred's new role. Customers were thrilled with his intuitive understanding of mechanical products and his ability to solve their problems. Manfred learned how to do industrial design as well.

●●●

In looking for a job, Gerda went to a nearby factory after seeing a posting for a dye purchase clerk at the employment office. While there she met a gentleman by the name of Irving Horowitz. His family had been in the textile business for generations. A Star of David hung in his office. They took an immediate liking to each other. He hired her.

"I find your bubbly personality refreshing," Irving commented.

Gerda blushed. "Thank you so much."

In the beginning, Gerda was not happy. She was still becoming accustomed to the concept that she needed to work. It was not easy on her. Gerda made a determination to keep at it. Eventually she found a way to make the environment hers— applying the same principles in her personal life to what she did at work. Over time, she began to look forward to her work. She exuded a boundless energy that inspired awe in some, like Irving, and envy in others. After working all day, she would come home, prepare a meal for herself and Manfred, and then sew herself a new dress for the following day. Her co-workers were amazed and jealous at her ability.

One day, Gerda noticed from a distance that the coloring for one of the products that the factory was manufacturing was inaccurate.

"That color is off," she stated matter-of-factly to the production manager.

The production manager made a "Tsk" sound with his mouth and kept working. He didn't even bother to look at Gerda.

Gerda did not take well to being ignored like that. She tapped him on the shoulder. "Excuse me," she said in an earnest tone.

"Buzz off. I'm busy."

Gerda walked over to the emergency stop button. She pressed it. The noise level died down to just the sound of light steam passing through a small aperture. It whistled almost like a tea kettle. Everyone working on the production line stood around in bewilderment. Gerda saw the goggles, aprons and gloves come off from the workers.

Undaunted, she walked back to the production manager. "Now that you are not busy, I would like to point out to you that the color is off. It is not the right shade of green."

Gerda watched as the man threw his gloves to the floor. She thought his head might shoot off from the rest of his body. The man started arguing with her vehemently. He asked others around them for their opinion. All felt that it was the right color. Gerda stood her ground. She felt relieved when Irving came by.

"Gerda, I appreciate your concern, but I have been in the business for generations, and it looks okay to me," Irving said to her. He didn't seem upset at all in his tone.

Gerda, on the other hand, was becoming upset. "I know what I am talking about."

"Why don't we just analyze which dyes were put in the mix

and compare that to the file of what it is supposed to be," Irving instructed the production manager.

Within five minutes the production manager came out with a sheepish look on his face. Gerda thought she detected a little disbelief in there as well.

"She's right," he mumbled.

"I don't know how you could detect that with your eyes," a disbelieving Irving stated to Gerda.

"My eyes have always been very good for me," Gerda thought back to the compliments she had received in her life because of her eyes, the name of "blue eyes" her cousin gave her, and then having to cover her eyes to protect herself. She was amused that her eyes would now enable her to earn a living.

Irving immediately had Gerda function as the coordinator of all of the dyes. Gerda sometimes amazed herself in her ability to distinguish between very fine shades of color differences. What appeared to others as the same color would be known by Gerda to be off.

From that point, Irving's commissioned dye business took off. People would come to the factory specifically asking them to reproduce a specific color. Gerda was the one who could match it flawlessly. She became famous in the area and soon the region. The company's business boomed as a result. Gerda had developed a fine reputation for herself. Everybody came to know about her in the industry.

Everybody at the company had also become afraid of her. She did not tolerate sub-par performance from anyone, and the skill with which she established perfection in her home translated to her work. She couldn't conceive of shortcuts or the easy way out. There was only one way to perform a task in her mind, and that was to do the best job possible. Anything else didn't make sense to her.

In growing as an expert in color, Gerda amassed a great deal of information about dyes. She stored this information regarding the various dyes and formulations in a series of cabinets. The cabinets were very old. One day, a cabinet door fell off and nearly damaged her foot.

Gerda first went to the purchasing director. "I need you to purchase me some new cabinets. The ones now are old and are falling apart." Gerda thought she was doing a favor in reporting this to him.

"We aren't going to spend money on that," came his response. "Just learn how to be more careful."

Irving was away, so Gerda stormed the finance director's office.

"I almost lost my foot. If I get hurt I won't be able to work here anymore."

She received two brand new cabinet doors with a bow on each of them. Eventually all were replaced.

● ● ●

Ram had been excited about the news he heard. He had read so much about the Berlin Philharmonic and about Karajan and his approach to music. He was excited that Karajan was sought as a guest conductor for so many orchestras.

"Did you know that they played straight through the war and the surrender of Germany?" Ram marveled to Akbar. He had to communicate with his friend on the phone. Akbar had remained in what was now called Pakistan.

Ram had heard the news that Karajan would be traveling with the Vienna Philharmonic as a guest conductor to Asia, including India, in 1959.

"I believe he is doing it because he has a soft spot in his heart for the Vienna Philharmonic, which he had grown up listening to and which had been the first orchestra that he led," Ram explained to his friend.

Ram had become a sponsor for the event, donating money to ensure its successful execution. He did that with a specific purpose in mind.

"I want to meet Karajan," he told Akbar.

VIRTUOSO

After the performance in Bombay, Ram was able to sit next to Karajan at dinner.

"We are graced by your presence. It is rare for us to have a virtuoso of your caliber here," Ram said to Karajan.

"It is a joy to be here," Karajan replied. "We find it thrilling that you enjoy and appreciate our Western musical tradition."

"I am a huge admirer," Ram admitted. "In our Eastern tradition, we have developed string instruments such as the *sitar*, which is not too different from your bass, cello, viola or violin. We also have hand drums such as the *tabla* and the *dholak* which govern the beat like your percussion instruments."

Karajan listened intently.

"These are vastly different approaches, but the similarity of form suggests that the basic human needs for the enjoyment of music are universal," Ram added.

Ram felt that the evening ended abruptly.

"I wish I had more time to spend with you," Karajan acknowledged. "Your experience provides you with such a unique perspective. I would love to continue a dialog with you. Please come visit me in Berlin. There are many people I would like you to meet."

● ● ●

General Kasparov lost his daughter in 1959. She was eleven years old at the time. She had fallen sick with bronchitis and then pneumonia. The little girl had softened Kasparov up. He had become more mellow in his older age as a result of her. She had shown him a tenderness that he had not had the benefit of in many years.

Her funeral was the first time he allowed himself to cry in public. He saw that his wife was in tears as well, but his mother remained stoic. *How I wish it had been you*, he thought to himself.

His daughter's death triggered something in him. Nearly a decade had passed since he had thought about Heinrich Majowski and chasing after him. Suddenly his vendetta was revived. He suddenly felt that Heinrich was responsible for the negative incidents that were occurring in his life. Somebody had to be blamed. He wanted retribution once again.

• • •

Heinrich came to visit Gerda and Heinrich *Manfred* at their new home in Connecticut, unbeknownst to Gerda. The Berlin Philharmonic was doing a tour of the US and had made a stop in New York. Both Gerda and Manfred had to work on the day that Heinrich was able to arrive, but without Gerda knowing, Manfred managed to take a day off. He met up with Heinrich and brought him to their place.

Gerda would cycle to her work as it was not too far a distance for her. On that particular day, Gerda was remembering a cello concerto that Heinrich played before in Berlin. It was actually the last time that Gerda had heard him perform live. The music was in her mind as she cycled home. Suddenly the music playing within her could be heard from the outside. She was shocked. She began peddling faster. She was surrounded by open fields of farmland on both sides of the road. As she approached the tiny house, she stopped pedaling and broke down into tears. There, in the middle of the road, sat Heinrich on his cello case, playing his cello—the last song that Gerda had seen him play. Gerda was pleased to see her brother happy; he looked fit, although the years had added a few wrinkles and taken away a few strands of hair. Or perhaps it was because of the stress he felt in not being able to see his daughter. The two wept together.

• • •

Gerda and Manfred had a difficult time getting access to Sabine. They persisted, however, and were rewarded with being able to see her with increasing regularity. They did all they could to be a part of her life.

Making the move from Chicago to Connecticut was a tough transition for both Gerda and Manfred. They had gone from an urban setting to a rural one. Gerda felt sorry for Manfred. He had to give up being a part of a chorus, because there was no opportunity in that part of Connecticut. Both had to adjust being without city life. Attending concerts could no longer be done spontaneously. They would have to prepare in advance for a one-and-a-half hour drive to Boston or a two-and-a-half hour drive to New York. While Gerda had been in more rural settings, she took pity on Manfred, as it was the first time that he had lived a civilian life outside of a city.

Gerda became a master at developing her home life. And over time, she extended that passion to outside the home. She had always lived among beautiful landscaping. She was determined to create that for herself yet again. Much like how they had built their life, creating a beautiful garden was their way of making the aura and majestic beauty of music into a tangible form and translating it to everyday life. This was a passion that befit her name, "Gerda," which means "of the garden" or "one who gardens."

She was a host of the finest measure. Guests would become spoiled at Gerda's table. She would serve meals finer than the finest restaurants. "Chefs in New York could learn from your style of cooking and hospitality," one neighbor said after a meal.

Guests would also become addicted. "Oh, here they come again," Manfred would say with chagrin. Gerda knew that she could rely on him to play the part of gracious host to support her. *Maybe he gets tired sometime*, Gerda thought. In her heart, Gerda could not deny that she enjoyed these frequent visits that their friends were paying. It was a compliment to her hospitality. *People don't go where they aren't comfortable*, she reasoned.

Gerda knew that she was honoring her family, her mother and father, by preserving the way of life that they had instilled in her since childhood. Several of her closer friends asked her about this.

"Gerda, why do you go through so much trouble? We are perfectly fine with much less effort. We are here to see you, not to be pampered the way you do. You can sit and rest with us."

Gerda always had a terse response for such comments: "I don't know any better." She shot a glance at Manfred as she spoke. By his expression, she could tell that he recalled the first time he had heard that.

Those who were close to her had to accept that the way in which she behaved was her only way. No matter how sick she could get, she wouldn't stop.

After a few years of hard saving, in 1960, Gerda and Manfred were able to buy their home. It was a beautiful little house at the bottom of a hill and walking distance to a lake. In fact the street was appropriately called Lakeview Heights. Before work, Gerda would cycle down to the lake and go for a swim for exercise. They would spend evenings in a boat on that lake. They would also enjoy picnicking in its environs.

The one feature missing from their lives was not being able to have children. They were surrounded by several families that had multiple children, and they would fill that void by spending a lot of time with those neighborhood children. They would throw parties for them throughout the year. They would attend music recitals, plays and take them on outings. They especially loved engendering an interest in music in them.

● ● ●

Manfred never ceased his role as ambassador for the arts. Every year at Christmas he would find something to send to his friends and family—be it copies of a program or the lyrics to an aria. In the later days, it would be tapes of music that he compiled. This became famously known as "The Christmas Tape" and all friends and acquaintances would look forward to receiving it. His outlet for singing, however, would elude him.

● ● ●

Each one of Gerda's siblings and her father came to visit her. While Heinrich's visits to the US would be frequent as he toured with the Berlin Philharmonic, other members of Gerda's and Manfred's families had less of an opportunity to visit and would come less frequently.

Sylvester had a chance to visit Gerda and Manfred once in his lifetime, in 1963. During this visit, he spent his days walking around the city of Tolland, the small town where Gerda and Manfred bought their home. He requested a map from Manfred. With that in hand he roamed the streets. He observed that several people had their family names on their mailboxes. Every time he would see a Polish name, he would knock on the door. He remembered taking the same action at another time on another continent when he was searching for his family. He found friendship at that time; he was out to do it again. Some of the people he would visit would invite him in for food and drink. Gerda would send Manfred out to go and search for her father to bring him home in the evening.

Sylvester spent nine months with them. They drove throughout the Northeast and to other parts of the country together. They spent several days in New York. They showed Sylvester the museums and attended concerts at the Metropolitan Opera and at Carnegie Hall. They also attended concerts in Chicago and Boston. On the drive to Chicago, they heard about Kennedy's assassination.

"He was a good friend to Germany," Sylvester had said.

While Sylvester was with them, they received some tragic news from home. Crystal, Mia's daughter, had committed suicide. Mia's husband had passed away when Crystal was a young girl and she had been hospitalized numerous times for depression. She would typically be admitted to the same hospital where Mia would work as a nurse. Mia felt more comfortable with this arrangement, because she felt that she could keep an eye on her daughter. Unfortunately, there was no way for Mia to keep an eye on her daughter at all times. Within that hospital, while Mia was on her work shift, Crystal took her life.

"Maybe I am here to comfort you," Sylvester reasoned to Gerda.

"Maybe it is the other way around, Father," Gerda retorted. She had a sense that her father was projecting his emotions onto her.

Gerda had to relay bad news to Manfred regarding his brother Horst. While in the garden, Horst experienced a bee sting.

He went upstairs to his room and lay on the bed because he was feeling very dizzy. While he lay on the bed, life departed his body. The doctor had informed his wife that had he lived, within one year, his legs would have been amputated because he had been suffering from severe diabetes. He was only thirty-three years old.

Gerda worried about how Manfred would cope.

"The only solace I have comes from the fact that like my father, my brother was kept from facing further suffering and hardship that his medical condition would inevitably have forced him to grapple with," Manfred concluded. Gerda was touched with how much strength he was displaying.

Mia came to see them twice. Because of the tragedy that she had just experienced, Manfred and Gerda spent time mourning with her, but then worked aggressively at trying to make her as happy as possible. She always exhibited a great deal of anxiety, concern and fear. In Germany she would refer to it as angst. Gerda and Manfred did all they could to take her around the area, to visit New York and attend concerts of the New York Philharmonic and the Metropolitan Opera as they had done with Father. While they were at home they would surround her with recordings of wonderful music and have her spend time in the garden, surrounded by beautiful flowers. It was a success; her visit was a very festive one.

Despite whatever disputes or discrepancies they had as children, or even if there had been bickering during the trip, at the time of departure, all of those sentiments would become washed away and there was only one emotion felt: sadness for the impending loss.

"Nothing replaces having family nearby," Gerda said to Manfred once Mia boarded the plane.

Even from afar, Gerda's siblings did all they could to brighten Gerda up and try to lessen her sense of feeling homesick. Heinrich continually sent care packages to them, with orchestra programs, recordings and food that they were not able to get in the US. One time, Wilfred sent them a recording of a concert that he had done and broadcasted on radio in Germany. He specifically dedicated it to Gerda and Manfred. He had the orchestra perform with intentional mistakes. Manfred and Gerda were not expecting it. When they listened to it they laughed so intensely.

● ● ●

Gerda and Manfred attempted to get into New York or Boston as much as possible in order to enjoy concerts or the opera, even when family members were not visiting them. The same year they bought the house, they began contributing to the Metropolitan Opera House. They also went into New York to attend concerts of the New York Philharmonic at Carnegie Hall, watching the Orchestra perform under Leonard Bernstein.

Such instances helped ease the pain of being away from home and not being in the center of musical activity. Although tangentially involved, they were still able to feel like they could experience it.

The trips via car to and from New York were always full of engaging conversation related to music. They would often take friends with them so that they could share in the enjoyment with others, taking colleagues or neighbors who expressed an interest.

"Did you know that Bernstein was taught by Fritz Reiner?" Manfred asked.

"Is that so?" Gerda enquired.

"Yes, after Harvard, Bernstein went to the Curtis Institute in Philadelphia where Reiner was teaching," Manfred explained.

"Oh yes, Heinrich was mentioning that. Bernstein was the only one to receive an A in conducting from Reiner."

"That is correct," Manfred remarked.

● ● ●

Although Manfred was now doing something that he was more passionate about and was enjoying it, he was not satisfied with this work alone. He wanted a means to get closer to music. He enrolled in a Bachelor's Degree program at the University of Connecticut. As he had to work during the day, he had to take classes at night. He would fill his schedule every night with classes. The study of music theory and composition was fascinating to him, but what he missed was being actively engaged in it. Unfortunately, there were no convenient outlets for him to achieve that. Manfred never completed his degree, but for years, he enjoyed the thrill of taking classes.

Sometimes he would smoke his pipe on the campus and in the buildings.

Students would greet him with, "Hello, Professor."

While gesturing by taking his pipe out of his mouth, Manfred would respond, "Good evening, good evening."

● ● ●

Manfred had stayed in touch with his hospital-mate Gunther over the years. They corresponded via letters. Gunther had settled in Munich. Over time, Manfred learned that Gunther had developed cancer in his hip. It was linked back to his war injury. It was a lymphoma that had spread beyond the point of being able to cure it. Within a year of his finding out, he had passed away in 1967.

Manfred and Gerda were not able to make it to the funeral. However, they tried their best to stay in touch with Heidi, and began a campaign of phoning her regularly.

CHAPTER XVII

Manfred's good friend Jonathon, who had drawn Manfred singing in front of Carnegie Hall when he departed Berlin, visited Manfred and Gerda in early 1968. He had taken as his profession being a caricaturist for a Berlin newspaper. It was tough for him to get away from his daily job, but he made the effort as often as he could. These were light, jovial visits for Manfred.

"Manfred, you will never believe how I start my day," Jonathon said.

"Well, it is probably like everyone else, right? You get up, freshen up, eat something and go to the office." Manfred guessed.

"That is all true. But once I get to the office, I take a nap," Jonathon declared.

Manfred was startled. "What are you talking about?"

"Yes, it's true, when I get to the office, I take a nap so that I can come up with my caricature concept," Jonathon explained.

With that comment, Jonathon took another shot of his vodka. While taking it, he declared to Manfred, "It's up to you!"

Manfred followed suit. Soon the vodka bottle was empty.

● ● ●

In 1968, Heinrich visited Gerda and wanted to do a concert in her house. Within the family room, Manfred erected an elevated platform for Heinrich. Gerda was so excited that she invited Irving to come to the concert.

"I didn't know you had a famous brother in the Berlin Philharmonic," Irving cried. "I adore the Berlin Philharmonic."

From there the friendship grew. Irving became at first an occasional and then a regular attendee with them as they went to see performances in New York, particularly of the opera. Their day would be well planned out. They would leave in the morning, arrive in time to have a champagne breakfast at The Plaza hotel, watch a matinee opera performance, have dinner, walk around the city, and make it home by night. During the intermission, Gerda would always follow her tradition of having a glass of champagne.

• • •

Heinrich's visits were always regular. Manfred would always go to pick up Heinrich at the train station. On one such occasion, Manfred waited on the platform but did not see him. After twenty minutes of the train leaving the station, Manfred went down to use the phone. He saw a row of telephones. He picked up the phone on the far right end. He dialed home, but the number was engaged. When he turned around to hang up the phone, he saw Heinrich next to him, on the phone, talking to Gerda!

Sometimes Heinrich would bring members of the Orchestra to Gerda and Manfred's home. After a scrumptious meal, they would take out their instruments in the family room and serenade Gerda and Manfred with a live performance. This was a real treat for Gerda and Manfred—a private performance by arguably the greatest group of musicians assembled on the planet at the time.

While visits could only happen on occasion, phone calls were plentiful and frequent. Over time, it became a daily occurrence. Heinrich would often call and play something on his cello for Gerda and Manfred to hear, as if they were all in the same room together. Miles traversed through phone lines, emotions expressed through music.

• • •

Gerda received a call from Sabine one day. "Aunt Gerda! I am a flight attendant with Pan Am!"

Gerda was stunned and didn't know how to respond. At the end, she provided her support. On the inside, she was upset. Gerda recalled how Heinrich had always expressed to her his desire that Sabine pursue something in music. He resented the fact that he could not have been closer to her to try and have that impact on her life that would have inclined her towards music.

• • •

Heinrich was in the main concert hall, the only one in the

chamber, rehearsing a number of pieces of music. Suddenly the door opened. Ram stepped in. Heinrich stopped playing.

"I am sorry to disturb you," Ram said.

Heinrich looked at the man, "May I help you?" he asked.

"I am looking for Mr. Karajan," Ram replied. "Would you know where I can find him?"

"I can show you," Heinrich replied.

When the two reached Karajan's office, he was not there.

"Do you have an appointment with him?" Heinrich asked, slightly annoyed and eager to get back to his rehearsal.

"Not in the strict sense," Ram replied. "Last time we met, I told him I would come to Berlin to see him."

"Oh, was that recently?"

Ram chuckled. "It was eight years ago."

He went on to explain to Heinrich that he had met Karajan in 1959, when the Vienna Philharmonic traveled to Asia and Karajan did his first and only performances in India, one in Bombay and one in New Delhi.

"I went to both," Ram said.

"Wow," Heinrich responded. "You know," he continued, "We have played many times in Japan, and they love our music there. Please tell me how India reacts to our music—there is such a rich tradition in Indian music."

"Why don't you let me buy you a drink and we can chat about it?"

"That sounds like a deal. I am Heinrich Majowski," Heinrich said, extending his hand out.

Ram locked his hand in Heinrich's. "I am Giri," he said, "Ram Sunder Giri."

"Again," Heinrich began, after they had sat down with beers in their hands, "tell me, how is it that there is a following of our music in Asia. India has a rich musical tradition of its own which is very unique compared to European music."

"Heinrich, it is my belief, that all music is universal. Similar to how we Hindus believe that all religions are different paths to the same God, it is my belief that music in whatever form is the same and can be appreciated by all equally. The gift of music is that if you allow it, you can relinquish control of your emotions and allow the music to move you," Ram replied.

"My father has the same belief," an astonished Heinrich said. "He is a very wise man."

● ● ●

Heinrich phoned Ram at his hotel.

"There is someone I would like you to meet," Heinrich said, "I will bring him to the concert tonight and I will leave tickets for you at your hotel."

Ram arrived at the Philharmonic in Berlin and went to his seat. He was greeted by Heinrich and an elderly gentleman.

"Please meet my father," Heinrich said.

It had been Gerda's idea to have them attend the concert together.

Heinrich had expressed his concern. "I don't know how much they will be able to say to each other since they don't have a common language. They may find it boring to have me translate all of the time, but two men such as these should meet."

"Have them enjoy music together. They will bond over that," Gerda suggested.

Both men looked at each other with a smile. Both knew that neither spoke a language that the other could understand. Heinrich had to go as he was performing that evening.

"No intermission tonight as it is a short performance," he said, "I will come up as soon as it is over."

The performance that night was of Tchaikovsky's Piano Concerto Number 1. When the performance was over, Heinrich took some time to arrive.

Ram turned to Sylvester. He made a motion of playing a cello, and he showed a thumbs up. Sylvester nodded. Ram then made a motion of playing a piano and rocked his hand from side to side, indicating so-so. Sylvester smiled and nodded his head in agreement. Sylvester then made a motion of the timpani drummer and showed a thumbs down. Ram laughed and nodded his head in agreement. Ram pointed to his watch and shrugged his shoulders. Sylvester clapped his hands in delight, nodding his head. Sylvester made a circular motion with his finger at the side of his head, to indicate crazy and pointed at his watch. Ram laughed.

Heinrich finally arrived.

He said in German first and then English, "I am sorry it wasn't a better performance, the pianist is under the weather and he was not playing up to his usual standard, and the guy on the timpani drums is not our usual, who called in sick. This new person's timing was way off."

Sylvester and Ram laughed. They both informed him that they had already done the critique

● ● ●

Heinrich shared with Gerda and Manfred how he had become a part of a group called the Twelve Cellists in 1972, a group formed from the members of the Philharmonic. They were doing a number of recordings on their own. Gerda was amazed to hear about this. "Wow twelve cellists playing—there isn't a lot of music available for that, is there?"

Heinrich responded, "We will be playing more modern cello pieces. You are right, there aren't any traditional pieces written for twelve cellos."

Manfred said to Heinrich, "You know, Heinrich, I can not imagine any other single instrument group being able to perform like this. I could not see twelve violins or violas playing in this fashion."

Heinrich confirmed Manfred's thinking. "You are right, Manfred. Only the cello can have the range of tones from the very deep to the higher pitches. Other instruments would not be as pleasing to the ear."

Heinrich paused for a few seconds and then turned to Gerda.

217

"That is why Father emphasized this instrument with me. He understood how key the cello is to the orchestra and how versatile an instrument it can be."

Gerda responded with a knowing smile.

Heinrich then told them the most exciting part of the formation of the group.

"You will never believe how we acquired one of our first pieces." The suddenly jubilant Heinrich's tone recalled the wonder and pure joy of a child excitedly telling a story.

"Rudolf Weinsheimer, my good friend and fellow cellist, was driving in the rain when he saw a young girl on the side of the road looking for a ride. As it was raining heavily he felt badly, so he picked her up and took her to her home. When he arrived at the house, he immediately recognized it as the home of composer Boris Blacher. Rudi had just picked up his fifteen-year old daughter Tatjana." Heinrich barely stopped to breathe in his excitement.

Gerda and Manfred did not have a chance to respond.

"When Blacher asked what can I do to re-pay you, Rudi asked him to compose a piece for twelve cellists!" Heinrich proclaimed.

Gerda and Manfred stared at each other in disbelief.

"Did he do it?" Gerda asked.

"He did," Heinrich replied, "that is how we acquired the Rumba philharmonica!"

"Before that we only had the Hymnus for twelve cellos," Heinrich added after a second's break.

Both pieces were debuted that year at the Easter Festival in Salzburg, the "Oster Festspiele." Gerda and Manfred attended the event with a group of their friends. Heinrich invited Manfred's good friend Jonathon to join them. Sabine also made the trip. They enjoyed the afternoon concert and were relaxing by the lake. Manfred thought it would be funny if everyone behaved in a crazy way for the video camera that Jonathon had. Passersby were there and asked what was going on.

VIRTUOSO

"We are filming Dostoevsky's *The Idiot*," came the response from Manfred.

● ● ●

Heinrich had been in touch with Bastian throughout the years. He had composed a number of songs that were a part of the modern repertory. He also had recorded and preserved a number of traditional folk songs from Russia, Hungary, and Czechoslovakia where he had spent some time.

"Perhaps it was good that I had to be there," Bastian would say with a macabre chuckle, brooding all the while.

Heinrich was intrigued with a collection of Russian folk songs that Bastian had released as an album. He wondered if it could be modified to be played by the Twelve Cellists.

The Twelve Cellists would go on to record numerous other types of works including Beatles hits such as "Yellow Submarine." They eventually released a whole album with Beatles music.

"I have never composed any musical scores," said Bastian. "I really can only write songs."

"Don't worry," Heinrich insisted, "we all have good ears. You come and we will listen to the songs and create versions for Twelve Cellists."

"I am not so sure," Bastian contested. "You know, I am going through a rather painful divorce right now. My wife has disappeared. She has taken our kids."

After hearing this, Heinrich was even more determined to have Bastian attend the sessions with him. Heinrich felt the urge and desire to help Bastian in whatever way he could. He wanted to help Bastian get over the pain of his separation with his family. Heinrich knew that having Bastian throw himself into music would go a long way in aiding him.

"I am sorry to hear about your suffering, Bastian," said Heinrich. "Why didn't you tell me earlier?"

"Well, it is not something that I wanted to advertise," Bastian offered.

"You should just be there to make sure the song sounds the way it should," Heinrich quipped.

Working with Bastian to ensure authenticity, Heinrich and the Twelve Cellists began developing a series of songs from Bastian's albums. They released it first in Germany and then outside of Germany to the rest of the world. It became a huge success, particularly in Russia.

● ● ●

One day, Herman Zschacher, the doctor who had looked after Christina, came to see Heinrich. Heinrich was surprised to see him. Herman accosted him on the street.

"We haven't heard from or seen you in ages," Heinrich exclaimed. "Gerda and I always talk about how our communication has been so limited since the Berlin Wall was erected."

"I am being followed and watched," said Herman. He did not match Heinrich's exuberance at the reunion. "I used my connections as a doctor to come to the West," Herman explained. "But they are watching my whereabouts. I need your help," Herman admitted.

"Herman, you have done so much for my family, whatever I can do to help you, I will happily do."

"Help me get my sister Adelle out," Herman pleaded. "She is a violinist," he explained. "She has been black-balled by the Stasi because of her husband. He used to be an agent for the Stasi, but he abandoned her and defected. She can't get into an orchestra in East Germany anymore."

"No problem, Herman," Heinrich said.

"There's more," Herman said. "I need to get her to America. She has already been in discussions with an orchestra in Boston that is interested in her."

Heinrich looked at Herman. He lost the confidence with which he had been carrying most of the conversation.

"You know how challenging that will be, right? I could keep her here in West Germany, no problem. But get her to the US?"

Heinrich asked. "Do you expect for her to come back?"

"If she can make a life there, she should stay," Herman said. "Her husband is long gone, and she has no children yet."

"Let me see what I can do," Heinrich said.

• • •

After three weeks, Herman approached Heinrich again. By then it was early September of 1972.

Heinrich exhibited a jovial demeanor and a great deal of alacrity when Herman approached him. "Herman! It is so good to see you, my friend!"

Herman looked like he was taken aback by this. "You seem to be in a very good mood," Herman said.

"I am in a very good mood, Herman," Heinrich confirmed. "I want you to come inside and see something in the paper!"

"In the paper?"

"Yes," Heinrich said, "Come and have a look. You'll laugh your head off!"

Heinrich led Herman to the living room and offered him a seat. "I'll be right back," he said to Herman.

When he emerged, Heinrich had a newspaper with him. "I believe you can view a version of this in the library in the East Zone," Heinrich said. "Once the censors are through with it," he added. "You won't be able to take this copy across with you, but I want you to see the caricature that is drawn in the editorial section."

Heinrich showed him a drawing of the Chancellor of Germany, Willy Brandt, being placed into the pocket of American President Richard Nixon.

"Wow," Herman said. "That will probably spark some controversy."

Herman noticed in the corner of the caricature there was the shadowed part of a plant circled. He took the magnifying glass Heinrich had slipped him in front of the paper. Drawn into the straight line marks representing the shadow of the plant, Herman could see the numbers 790022. Without the magnifying glass, it just

221

looked like the shadow. The by-line for the caricature read Jonathon Renstzler.

Heinrich stood over Herman, while Herman was seated, as he reviewed the drawing and took note of the circled numbers. Heinrich raised his eyebrows, opened his eyes wide and nodded his head emphatically once with a big smile.

"Have a drink," Heinrich said.

They passed the next several minutes talking about other social issues and matters of casual importance.

"I should take my leave," Herman said.

On the way back to East Germany, Herman talked out loud in his car. "Heinrich mentioned that I could get the paper in East Germany...Aha!"

A few days later, on September 20, 1972 (09/20/72 or 790022 rescrambled), Herman checked the paper again. There was another caricature there. This time it was of Schubert at his piano with a quill in hand and a beautiful woman in the background saying, "Come to bed, Franz, you can finish that symphony later!" The joke was that Schubert became famous for having an "Unfinished Symphony." Herman noticed in the same corner as the numbers before, the number 49. He didn't know what to make of it.

The next day, he looked again. He saw the letters "CD". Over the next week, he had all of the letters: "CDRHIFIER." When he re-jumbled them, he got the word "Friedrich". He knew there to be a street the Berlin Wall traversed called Friedrich Strasse. The Wall had split the street in two.

The following day, there were the numbers 5100. Herman re-worked that to be 10/05 or October 5th. The day after that, he saw the number 22.

On October 5th, at 10 pm (22:00 hours), Herman brought his sister Adelle to where 49 Friedrich Strasse would have been. It was the thinnest part of the wall, and there was a river several meters away so that small noise was washed away by the flow of the water. There came the sound of a voice. "Go Under!" it said in a strained whisper.

There was a tunnel entrance there. Adelle said goodbye to Herman and made her way through the entrance. A man inside grabbed her hand and guided her through the tunnel. On the other side, was a car waiting with Heinrich inside.

Herman later learned that Jonathon kept putting numbers and letters in his caricatures for a few months. One time he got sloppy and accidentally made the marks too large. His editor in West Berlin asked what it was for. He had a response at the ready: "It is how I catalog them. I have been a caricaturist for so many years now, I must have some way to keep track of it all."

Adelle made it safely to the US, and with Gerda and Manfred's help, she was able to get herself situated in her newly adopted country. She was able to join the orchestra in Boston.

●●●

Manfred's mother paid a visit to them at the end of 1972. "Since I arrived, Muti, I have been attempting to save money to bring you to visit us here," Manfred would say.

On the occasion of Manfred's birthday, Muti announced what she wanted to prepare.

Gerda protested, "I already have something in mind."

Manfred's head began to spin. *Oh how I wish they weren't so damn similar*.

Gerda graciously backed down from her position. *I think she sees how I am disturbed by this*, thought Manfred.

One evening, Muti pulled out the earring that Manfred had given her when he visited Berlin from the hospital. Gerda immediately recognized it.

In the midst of Manfred asking, "How come you didn't make it into two earrings or...." Gerda blurted out, "How in the world did you get that?"

When the story was revealed about the similar steam engines, all were dumbstruck.

"I am without words," said Manfred.

"You'd better sing something," said Gerda.

● ● ●

Manfred and Gerda received another visit from Jonathon. Jonathon arrived at six o'clock in the morning in New York. It was nine o'clock in the morning by the time they got back to the house. They immediately started with the vodka. By noon, the bottle was finished. Jonathon excused himself. After several minutes, he had not come back. Manfred was worried. He went and found him asleep in bed.

"I would like to meet Herman's sister," Jonathon declared when he woke up.

Arrangements were made to meet Adelle. She was so grateful to him for saving her. She was able to get free tickets for them to see the Boston Orchestra perform. It was very special in that she was able to secure box seats.

It was a stirring performance. She performed Beethoven's Violin Concerto.

"It is a very technically challenging piece. She played it with such sweetness of melody," Manfred observed to Jonathon.

"She really is a superb violinist," Jonathon added.

"Good thing you got her out," Manfred said.

CHAPTER XVIII

Late one night in 1973, Gerda received a phone call from her father. She had been in a dour mood most of the evening, and she suddenly became scared when she heard her father's voice. "I am dying, you come to me now."

Gerda wept. He hadn't even fallen ill.

Sylvester made the same proclamation to all of his children. He waited until each one arrived to him. When he was surrounded by all of his children, he said the following last words to them: "All humans craft a vision of the life that they wish to lead. It is grounded in what moves them and what makes them passionate. It gives them purpose when they wake up in the morning. It is fighting for a cause. The obstacles that are faced in attaining that dream and making that vision a reality can often be daunting and are truly unique to each individual. For some, the greatest obstacle can be circumstance and life itself that gets in the way. You must not falter in your pursuit. Always remember the Berlin Philharmonic during the war—they never stopped performing. Orchestrating the symphony of life is your greatest responsibility."

Gerda knew that he was reflecting on not only his own life experiences but that of all his children as well. It gave them peace. It was the best way to say goodbye.

Sylvester then peacefully left this world. He had lived ninety-six eventful years of life. Gerda was so proud of her father. The iron-will and determination with which he had met life, he held true until his natural death. He would decide when life would leave him naturally. He determined when it was time to stop and when he did, life left him. Gerda was in awe.

Gerda was also devastated, but she was at peace with herself. Her father was an important foundation for her. In many ways, she was an anchor for him. That the two shared the most kindred of spirits of any other combination in the family was not lost on any of the siblings. When they hugged each other, all hugged Gerda deliberately longer than any of the other sisters or brothers. Heinrich inherited the intellect, Gerda the spirit.

After Sylvester's funeral, Gerda and Manfred stayed in Berlin for a few weeks. Manfred and Heinrich's wife did all they could to console Gerda and Heinrich. The brother and sister mostly favored sitting in the living room together, listening to old recordings, remembering happier times when their father conducted his own orchestra in that town square in Dorsten.

"Sometimes it is better to let the music do the talking," Heinrich stated.

Gerda didn't need to respond. Heinrich was speaking for both of them.

Although they allowed themselves time to mourn, they never abandoned the ideals of living that their father and mother espoused. They did everything as per usual—they continued with their lives despite the shock and dismay of their father passing. All of the children were realists—they were aware of his age. All had reached the rational conclusion that his time with them was limited and could come to an abrupt end at any moment. Parting, nonetheless, was emotional and difficult.

"I was so used to him being so strong willed. It was as if he had a constitution of iron," Gerda would comment.

Heinrich would add, "He was never sick. We never saw him weak. He was a natural fighter. He made it seem as if he was omnipotent."

"No mortal is omnipotent, but he did seem to be omniscient. He knew the precise time that he would leave us," Gerda said.

"Maybe he even planned it to be this way."

Gerda finally managed a smile. "It would be just like him to do that."

Heinrich continued to perform in the orchestra. In the very next performance that Heinrich was a part of, Karajan made a stirring speech at the beginning of the concert and dedicated the performance to Sylvester. Heinrich was really touched and stood up to say thanks to Karajan. Gerda and Manfred, who were in the audience with legitimate tickets, were also deeply moved.

As the performance started, Gerda kept watching Heinrich. In between movements, she would notice that he was taking out his handkerchief and wiping his cheeks, nose and eyes. It wasn't warm. Gerda tried to make sense of why Heinrich looked so flushed. Towards the end of the performance, Gerda noticed the stream of tears that were rolling down Heinrich's face. She also took note that between the third and the final movements, Heinrich did not put his bow down nor did he look up at Gerda as he traditionally had done. Instead, he closed his eyes and looked down. Gerda could see that tears were continuing to stream. During the last movement, Heinrich was moving his shoulders with much more vigor than he had ever done while performing. Gerda finally detected what he was up to—the exaggerated movements were done to counteract his shoulders' involuntary movements as he sobbed. When the piece was finished, Heinrich no longer had the music to prop him up. He collapsed from his chair in tears—his cello and bow falling with a thud to the stage.

Karajan was the first to get to him to help him up, but Gerda had also rushed to the stage. She held her brother and both wept. The audience cheered and several people in the auditorium stood and applauded for them.

When Gerda got back to the US, she found it hard to adjust to life. Consciously, life was not different for her. Her father had only visited her once, so the normal rhythm of her and Manfred's life went apace, unimpeded. But, subconsciously, something felt terribly wrong for her. She had been gone for so long from Germany that she had felt strangely disconnected and disjointed from the whole series of events. She saw her sister Mia who had worked diligently to look after their father, and Gerda felt a tinge of jealousy. She was naturally pleased that her sister could do that for him, but she wanted to be the person acting as caretaker. It was a role she was comfortable with and that she relished. She felt out of place not having that role for her father, considering how close she was to him. She also felt that she had fulfilled that role for her mother and was not pleased that she could not have been there for her father. She was equally close to both parents, but her father was her kindred spirit. Her mother always tended to dote more on the boys, particularly Heinrich. Gerda would never be able to articulate it well or come to terms with it. It was as if a piece of her was now missing. She had anchored herself in her father's strength—she was the greatest inheritor of it compared to her siblings. It felt like an awesome deficit.

She strived after that day to be even closer to Heinrich. Although it was a challenge at times financially, Gerda and Manfred planned annual pilgrimages back to Germany so that they could be with the family and foster a closer bond. Family was so important to her and Manfred now. Experiencing the loss frightened them into viewing their relationships with their families as precious and dear.

● ● ●

In 1974, Gerda and Manfred went for Heinrich's fiftieth birthday. During that visit, prior to arriving in Berlin, Manfred and Gerda made sure to visit with Heidi, Gunther's widow. They had yet to visit Munich and thought that it would be a good time to do so. Manfred felt a certain level of guilt for not having been able to come for Gunther's funeral.

"I am sorry that it has taken us so long to come to visit you," Manfred said.

"Oh I understand, Manfred," Heidi said.

"Allow me to introduce you to my wife, Gerda," Manfred said.

"It is so nice to meet you," Gerda said.

"It is a pleasure to meet you," Heidi said.

There was an awkward silence. Both Manfred and Gerda wanted to say how sorry they were for the loss of Gunther; they could see that Heidi still wore the sorrow on her face. They felt uncomfortable doing it just yet, however. They thought they should spend their time attempting to cheer her up.

Gerda quickly said, "Thank you so much for taking care of my husband so many years ago. You whipped him back into shape!"

Heidi laughed.

"Your husband was very determined to survive," Heidi said.

After a few more minutes, Manfred decided to broach the subject.

"I am so sorry for your loss," he said. "I was really sad to hear that Gunther had left us."

Heidi began to cry.

"I know how hard it must have been," he added.

He looked pleadingly at Gerda. Gerda stood up and walked to Heidi and gave her a hug.

"What do you do with yourself these days," Gerda asked, trying to change the subject.

"I keep myself busy with our son," Heidi said.

Manfred was stunned. "I didn't know you had a son!"

Heidi called out, "Seth, come here darling!"

In came their son. He looked around ten years old. He had red hair and brown eyes.

Manfred was still getting over the shock that Gunther had never mentioned the son. When he looked at the boy, he wore an expression on his face that showed that he was even more confounded than earlier.

"Hello, my son," Manfred said.

"Come, here, you cute little boy," Gerda said.

Both of them hugged him in turn.

"So your name is Seth," Gerda asked.

The boy nodded his head.

"How old are you, Seth?" Gerda continued.

"I just turned eleven," he said.

Manfred was looking at the boy, still carrying his perplexed look.

"Why don't you give Mommy some time with her friends," Heidi said to Seth.

Seth ran out.

At the doorway he turned around, waved, and said, "Bye!"

Manfred and Gerda couldn't help but laugh.

"He is adorable," they both said in unison.

Manfred looked at Heidi.

"Gunther was never able to have children after his war injury," she said. "We adopted Seth from Russia. His parents died when he was young. He has no surviving family."

"Ah," said Manfred.

Manfred's mind was put more at ease. *This makes more sense*, he thought to himself. *I knew that Gunther had blond hair and I thought he had blue eyes. Obviously Heidi has both. This makes more sense.*

"He was born into a Jewish family," Heidi added. "I want him to be exposed to both Christianity and Judaism"

Gerda was pondering the situation. She saw Heidi's expression.

"It is a shame he won't grow up knowing his father," Gerda said, in an attempt to articulate what she felt was on Heidi's mind.

Heidi smiled at Gerda. Gerda sat next to her and held her hand.

"You are still young and beautiful," Gerda said. "Why don't you get married again?"

"Who me?" Heidi retorted. "Nobody will want me. I am too old."

"Well I think you should try." Manfred spoke up.

Heidi pulled out that very first handbag that Manfred and Gunther had made. *She always was sensitive*, thought Manfred, *I didn't realize she was sentimental as well.*

Later that evening while they were seated at the dinner table, Gerda began asking Seth some questions.

VIRTUOSO

"What are your interests, Seth?" Gerda asked.

"I love music," he declared emphatically.

"Really?" Manfred and Gerda said in unison.

"Oh yes," he added.

"Do you play an instrument?" Gerda asked.

"Yes, I am learning to play the cello, and I am also a member of the choir," Seth responded.

Gerda lit up. She turned to Heidi. "Did you know that my brother is the lead cellist with the Berlin Philharmonic?"

"I didn't know that," Heidi said, her eyes opening wide. "That is really impressive."

"Even I have heard about how great they are," added Seth.

As the meal progressed, a thought occurred to Gerda.

"Why don't you come to Berlin with us," she said to Heidi.

"What?" exclaimed Heidi.

"Yes," Gerda said, "I want you to come to my brother's fiftieth birthday celebration. It will be next Saturday."

"Oh, I don't know." Heidi resisted.

"Oh, come on," Gerda insisted.

"What will I do with Seth?" Heidi asked.

"What, are you kidding me?" Gerda asked.

As soon as Manfred heard it, he thought to himself, *Oh boy, I hope Heidi isn't too soft for Gerda.*

"You bring him with you! I want Seth to meet my brother. Seth will really enjoy it, and my brother always loves to meet young people who are enthusiastic about music."

Manfred was following the conversation going back and forth.

"You spent a little while in Berlin," he said. "You will love it there when you visit again. You know," Manfred said, "this will be the second time I will be taking you to Berlin."

Manfred thought back to that day.

"However," Manfred added, "this time, I won't have to smuggle you in."

They all laughed.

• • •

Heinrich's birthday celebrations started out with melancholy but ended with joy. All of Heinrich's family and friends were still coping with the loss of Sylvester. It had been too recent an experience for them to neatly tuck away their emotions with respect to it and to be able to move forward with unfaltering devotion to those who remained living around them. They still had to come to terms with it.

All of the Orchestra members came out in support of Heinrich's special day. They took turns playing music for him throughout the evening, soloists performing and forming duets, which grew to quartets and then an octet and then an ensemble. Gerda and Manfred had a hard time deciphering how much of it had been pre-meditated and how much had been impromptu. Heinrich could tell.

"It's a colorful mix," he said. "I am glad that they are choosing to be inventive and just go with the spirit of the event."

Karajan was naturally at the event, and he gave a stirring speech.

The mayor of Berlin also attended the event. It was a proud moment for Heinrich.

Manfred and Gerda were able to re-unite with many friends, including Jonathon, Herman, and Bastian. Of course, Heidi and her son Seth were there as well. Ram had made the trip. As had Hogitaro.

Bastian had composed a song for the event. He had arranged to have a singer perform the piece. Bastian stood up in front of everyone and gave a stirring speech.

"I was an only child growing up," Bastian started. "I never had a brother until I met Heinrich and his family. We were on opposing sides during the war, yet our families found a way to help each other out. While neither of us survived that tragedy without a great deal of suffering, we have been able to come through it together."

Gerda and Heinrich were in tears. Bastian was doing an impressive job of keeping his emotions in check, thought Gerda.

"I thank God for giving me the pleasure of knowing you, Heinrich," Bastian concluded. "May you have a wondrous birthday with many more such celebrations to come."

Heinrich went up to the stage and embraced Bastian in front of everyone.

Once the song was over, there was a standing ovation.

At that point, a band took over and people began dancing. Bastian took a seat at a table. Heinrich saw that Bastian was sitting. Heinrich went to where Gerda, Manfred and Seth were seated. "Come with me young man," Heinrich told Seth.

"Bastian," said Heinrich, "I want you to meet a very talented young man."

"Hi," Seth said. "My name is Seth."

"Seth, please sit down," Bastian said. Bastian smiled broadly. Heinrich knew his friend. He was sure Bastian had been thinking about his wife and family. His kids were a little bit older than Seth.

"I liked your song," Seth said.

"Well thank you, Seth," Bastian said. "Do you like music?"

"I love music," Seth responded enthusiastically.

"Do you like to sing?"

"I do," Seth responded, his voice getting more excited, "very much. I also play the cello," he added.

"Wow," said Bastian, "You are a multi-talented young man."

Heinrich observed their exchange with joy. He knew Bastian had not been able to get his own children engaged by music. He tried many times to get them to play instruments. They would never take the approach seriously enough. Heinrich blamed Bastian's wife for not being disciplined enough with them. He knew Bastian was resentful towards her that she allowed them to be lazy when they chose.

In the distance, Heinrich heard a voice. "Seth! Seth!"

"I think someone is calling you," Heinrich said to Seth.

"It's probably my mom," Seth said, getting up to leave.

"Well why don't you bring her here?" Bastian offered. "It would be nice to meet her. She must be very proud of you."

"Okay!" Seth beamed and ran towards his mother.

"Mommy, mommy," Seth said. "The nice man that was talking on stage wants to meet you."

Seth was pulling his mother's dress sleeve towards the table where Bastian was sitting.

Bastian stood up as she approached. He opened his eyes wide when he saw her. He smiled a broad smile, the widest he could.

"Hello," he said. "How do you do?"

"Hello," she said.

"Bastian, this is Heidi, Seth's mother," said Heinrich.

"I'm Bastian."

"I know," Heidi said. "That was a very nice speech you gave and an even better song that you wrote."

"Thank you for the compliment," Bastian said.

He looked deep into her eyes. This seemed to make Heidi uncomfortable, as she fidgeted while she stood. She seemed to be excited at the same time, as she kept looking back. After a while, she seemed to find her boldness, and she looked into Bastian's eyes for an extended period of time with a smile. Heinrich enjoyed seeing them interact like teenagers in love.

Bastian was the first to speak. "Your son is very talented. He sings and plays the cello!"

"Well, I think he is trying to develop his talent," Heidi said humbly. "He has a lot of work ahead of him if he wants to be a leading artist such as yourself." She made this last comment with a look at her son, moving her head down and raising an eyebrow.

Heinrich saw Bastian's gaze go to her hands. Heinrich observed what Bastian saw: a wedding ring on her hand. Bastian's shoulders slumped. Heinrich saw that he was not wearing his.

"I'd love to meet Seth's father," he said.

Heidi was quick to respond to Bastian's question. "Seth's father passed away. He is no longer with us." Heinrich thought to clarify, but he decided against it.

Bastian pointed to the ring on her finger. "Have you since re-married?"

"Oh, no," Heidi said, touching the ring. "I just never took it off." She rolled the ring around her finger as she spoke.

"Ah." Bastian wore a perplexed expression on his face. "It must have been recent?"

"It wasn't too long ago," Heidi responded. After a pause she said, "I just got used to having it there."

"You know," Bastian said, "when my wife wanted to separate from me, that was the first thing to go."

He awaited her reaction. She didn't change the expression on her face.

"I just took it right off. I can see how it is different for you. Your spouse was taken from you, mine walked out. You never had to stop loving him."

Heidi smiled her agreement to Bastian.

"Seth is also adopted," Heidi added.

"Oh," Bastian said. Heinrich knew that given Seth's name and red hair, Bastian thought Seth's father had been Jewish.

"Seth developed his admiration for singing from his father," Heidi said.

Heidi moved her hand through her son's hair. Seth got frustrated with that and moved his head away.

"Actually, my father was also a singer," Heidi added.

"Do you sing?" Bastian asked.

"A little," Heidi said.

"Maybe we can get together at my studio and you and Seth can show off your talents," Bastian suggested. *That's a wonderful suggestion,* Heinrich thought to himself. *What a nice birthday gift, if music can bring these people together.*

● ● ●

Heinrich and Seth visited Bastian's studio the very next day.

It was an elaborate location, attached to Bastian's townhome in Berlin. He reserved the top two floors for his studio.

"Wow," Seth said. He was impressed with the surroundings. He had not seen anything like it before.

"Take a look around," Bastian said.

Bastian was noticeably excited by Seth's enthusiasm. Just the other day he had lamented to Heinrich, "My own children seem so uninterested in what I do or how I spend my time. For them, they view it as work. I can't believe I wasn't able to convince any of my children to pursue music as their profession. I would even settle for them being passionate about music, at least pursuing it as a hobby, but I don't even have that to fall back on."

"Hello, Heidi," Bastian said to her.

"Good morning," Heidi said to him.

"I am so glad you could make it," Bastian said.

"Well, you left quite an impression," she said, leaning her head towards her son.

"And what about my impression on you?" Bastian asked.

She responded to him with a glance and a smile. She made her eyes soft as she looked at him. The expression seemed to display the affection that Bastian was looking for. He perked up when she did it. "Heinrich dropped us off. He said he would be here shortly. He said he had to pick something up from Karajan."

Bastian nodded his head and said to her, "You look wonderful today. Even better in the daylight."

Heidi began to blush. "You are very seductive in your choice of words."

"Please excuse me for one minute," Bastian said to both of them. "Make yourselves at home."

"Mommy, this is such a great place," Seth said to his mother.

Heidi smiled at him. "I am glad that you are enjoying it."

236

"Come Seth," Bastian called out to the little boy when he returned to the room.

"Tell me," Bastian asked, "what is your favorite song?"

"I like to sing 'Edelweiss.'"

"The German or the English version?"

"Oh, the German version," Seth said. "My English is not so good."

Bastian worked his machines for a few seconds. The music began playing in the background. Seth began to sing. Heidi had a big smile on her face after seeing Seth be so excited. She looked adoringly at Seth, and after a short pause, she looked adoringly at Bastian as well.

"Can we also sing *Die Wacht am Rhein*?" Seth asked when he had finished with the first song.

"Sure we can," Bastian said. "Maybe your mother will join us as well?"

All three sang together.

"What else would you like to sing," Bastian asked.

Seth exercised his vocal chords some more. He seemed to enjoy it immensely—he didn't want to stop. Heidi's smiling broadly grew to laughing gaily.

Bastian then turned to Seth. "Now," he said, with emphasis, "I am going to teach you one of my songs."

"REALLY?" Seth exclaimed. "Wow!"

Bastian began teaching the lyrics to Seth. Seth practiced several rounds.

"Are you ready to perform the whole song?" Bastian asked.

"I will try," Seth said, unsure of himself.

He made it through the whole song. Bastian made a recording of it.

"Seth, I want you to keep this," Bastian said. "That way you can always remember our time together here today."

Bastian handed Seth the cassette. Just as he did, Heinrich arrived, cello in tow.

"Hello, everyone!" Heinrich said. "How is everyone today?"

"Just great," Heidi said. "Bastian has been showing us a great time."

"Oh good," Heinrich said, "I am glad you have been enjoying yourselves." Heinrich winked at Bastian.

"Hello, Heinrich," Bastian said, giving him a hug. "Seth here has something he would like to share with you."

Seth looked helplessly first at Bastian, then at this mother.

"I-I...don't think I'm r-r-ready." Seth's voice was unsteady.

"Oh sure you are," Heinrich said. "Let us hear the song you have been practicing."

"How did you know I was learning a song?" asked Seth.

"Because I know my friend," Heinrich retorted. "I also know you. You either sing or play the cello. I don't see a cello here except for the one I brought, but we will get to that later."

Seth closed his eyes. The music started. He began to sing. Heinrich was truly impressed.

"You have quite a gift," Heinrich said when Seth was through. "Manfred was right," he added. "You have a voice as sweet as your father's."

All looked at each other with the faint traces of a smile. It seemed like they all understood the irony of what Heinrich was saying.

"Why don't you and I spend some time together, Seth?" Heinrich asked the boy. " That is, if it's okay with your mother."

Heinrich turned to Heidi. "I brought my cello," he said. "I thought I could give the boy a few pointers."

"Well, of course, that would be wonderful," Heidi said, spurting out the words, fusing them together, barely able to get enough oxygen in her lungs because of her excitement to get successive words out.

"Good," Bastian said. "Why don't we leave these two alone then?" He asked the question with a smile on his face. "Let's go down to my residence."

Heidi had a knowing smile on her face. When they reached his living room, Heidi turned to him.

"That was very cunning."

"Why, thank you," Bastian admitted. "I thought you might enjoy that."

Over coffee and biscuits, the two talked up a storm with each other. They shared some life experiences, but talked mostly about music. They agreed to see each other the next day.

The following day, their activities of the prior day were repeated, without the presence of Heinrich. Bastian made Seth repeat the song he had learned from the day prior. They also sang other songs together.

Heidi and Bastian agreed to see each other yet again the following day. This time, Heidi left Seth with Manfred and Gerda. The alone time together was good for them. They were able to continue their conversation from earlier.

Eventually, Heidi needed to make her way back to Munich. Bastian agreed to come visit her.

He arrived in Munich after two weeks. Seth was excited to see him. He brought with him some gifts, which included some albums that he had purchased thinking Seth might enjoy them.

Bastian began regular visits to Munich. After about six months, he was able to convince Heidi to move to Berlin. A few months after that, the two were married.

● ● ●

As a way to say thanks to Bastian for all that he had done for the Twelve Cellists, Heinrich invited Bastian to join the Twelve Cellists for a concert they would have in Tokyo in 1975 as a part of a world tour. Heidi and Seth joined Bastian.

Bastian re-connected with a Japanese friend of his, Hogitaro Fukiori. They stayed at his place. Bastian had met Hogitaro when Hogitaro was studying in Berlin after the war. Hogitaro was a violinist for the NHK Symphony Orchestra in Tokyo. Hogitaro was living with his second wife, Saori, who was twenty years younger than him, and a daughter Miyako. Miyako, aged ten, was being trained on the cello and the piano.

In addition to his serving in the war, Hogitaro also lost his two brothers in the conflict. He also had an aunt an uncle who had migrated to the US in the 1920s. While his cousin served in the war under the US flag, his aunt and uncle were banished to a Japanese internment camp. Hogitaro would recall how his father lamented the situation with his brother, but there was no way to communicate with him, for fear that it might place him in danger.

"Perhaps the two young ones can show us their capabilities with a duet," suggested Hogitaro.

Seth and Miyako looked at each other. Seth was feeling shy, and his face turned red. Miyako giggled.

"I think that is a superb idea," Bastian said.

Heidi added her encouragement. "Absolutely, show us what you can play together."

The two talked for a while. It was the first Miyako had spoken in the trip, except to smile and exchange pleasantries.

They settled on a piece to play that both were familiar with.

Seth began and Miyako accompanied. There were a few missed notes, a few bars when their timing was off—Seth tended to start before Miyako—and one instance when Seth dropped his bow. Seth was nervous, but when he saw his mother smile and Bastian laugh, he laughed too. On the other hand, when Miyako missed her notes, her face became more red, and she felt deeply embarrassed. Hogitaro and Saori would remain silent.

"Take a bow," Bastian encouraged when they had finished.

They both did, feeling shy and awkward, and felt immediately relieved that they were now done.

"Bravo," Hogitaro said. He applauded for both of them.

Bastian added, "Well done, both of you. Keep at it and you both will be superb in no time."

Bastian turned to Seth. "Remember what I taught you?"

Seth thought for two seconds, realized what Bastian was

asking, and nodded with a smile. He then turned to Miyako, bowed and said,

"*Arigato gozaimasu*"—Japanese for 'Thank you.'

Miyako was stunned, and Hogitaro and Saori clapped in applause.

The concert by the Twelve Cellists was wonderfully well received. The Emperor and Empress of Japan were in attendance. The Twelve Cellists were stunned when Empress Michiko accompanied them on the piano. It was a highlight of the trip. Heinrich was elated beyond words. The Empress gifted to each member of the ensemble a rare pearl necklace developed by the Mikimoto company under special direction by her majesty the Empress. She instructed each of them to, "Present them to someone special."

Hogitaro, Saori and Miyako joined Bastian, Heidi and Seth at the concert. All enjoyed it immensely. It was very exciting for Bastian to see Heinrich perform, particularly when the group performed one of Bastian's songs. For Heidi and Seth, there would be an indelible impression left on them. They would always think back to and remember that concert of the Twelve Cellists in Tokyo.

● ● ●

Heinrich presented the pearls to Gerda during his next visit to the US. Gerda was elated. Elation was replaced with dismay, however, as Gerda accidentally lost the pearls in her bathroom sink. Manfred stopped short of tearing the house apart in order to retrieve the necklace. He himself took apart all of the plumbing underneath the sink. It was to no avail; the necklace was gone. Gerda cried so much.

"I feel like it is a bad omen," she said as she sobbed to Manfred.

● ● ●

As a part of the Berlin Philharmonic and the Twelve Cellists, Heinrich toured the world and would frequently respond to invitations to perform. Heinrich received a letter from the Soviet

Union. Just reading the name of the country gave Heinrich a chill down his spine.

A Russian Fine Arts director in Moscow had learned about the Twelve Cellists and the music they were creating with respect to old favorite Russian folk songs. They extended an invitation for the Twelve Cellists to come to Moscow to perform in 1976.

Heinrich had never anticipated this. When he developed the recording of Bastian's songs, he did so thinking about the beauty of the music. Additionally, the Twelve Cellists had done more modern pieces, so he thought it would provide the group with some balance and depth if they had some more traditional pieces they could perform. He never expected to be asked to perform those pieces live in Russia.

Heinrich felt fear gripping him. He had huge misgivings about making the trip, given his history. He couldn't get the incidents about Kasparov out of his mind. He hadn't heard from him or about him in decades, so part of him felt as if he was being irrational to feel scared. Another part of him could not rationalize his emotion. *The war was over, but he still came after me.*

Heinrich wasn't alone in the compunction he felt about the Soviets. Many of the members of the orchestra and the other members of the Twelve Cellists had fears about making the journey. Each had experienced difficulties interacting with the Soviets immediately after the war.

Eventually Heinrich convinced himself to march forward in the name of music. "We can't hold on to this fear. It is irrational. We must spread the joy of music in Russia as we have in all other parts of the world that we have visited," Heinrich stated. Others nodded in agreement. Heinrich detected that some nodded more slowly than others. He could identify with that. A small part of him remained nervous, too.

"You speak for all of us," the other members confirmed, banding together in unison.

"It is such a publicized event, Heinrich," Gerda complained.

VIRTUOSO

"Kasparov probably isn't in Germany anymore. He is likely in Russia. He has free reign over there. What if he learns you are coming and decides to take advantage?"

"It has been decades, Gerda," Heinrich protested. He flinched. He hadn't even been able to convince himself.

In acknowledging his fear, Heinrich intentionally structured the trip to be well regimented. They were attempting to minimize their time in Moscow as much as possible. They would stay only the least number of days required and get to Stockholm as quickly as possible. There would be only one night in a hotel.

After the performance, where the Orchestra performed not only the traditional folk songs, but also paid homage to Russian composer Tchaikovsky, all of the members went back to the hotel. Heinrich was sure to have transportation pre-arranged. He also insisted that everyone move as a group. When he arrived back at the hotel, he felt a sense of relief entering the lobby. He looked at the clock on the wall. Their flight departing Moscow was in eight hours. *I can manage eight hours,* thought Heinrich.

They stayed on the same floor, so all rode the elevator up together. When they reached their respective doors, each turned around to the other, said goodnight and entered. Heinrich was beginning to feel more at ease. He thought about taking a shower and getting a good night's rest.

As Heinrich entered his room, the light turned on without him touching the light switch. There he saw Kasparov.

Heinrich was about to scream out, but lost his voice when Kasparov pointed the gun at him. Heinrich stood still. He feared for his life. He thought about his daughter, his sister and his cello. He thought Kasparov might shoot him immediately. Kasparov closed the door behind Heinrich, all the while keeping the gun pointed at Heinrich's head.

"Do you remember me?" Kasparov demanded.

"Yes," Heinrich admitted. Heinrich had never had a chance to study his features very carefully. This was the closest he had ever

243

stood to Kasparov. The uniform he wore was more decorated than in the past. His face seemed slimmer, his nose sharper, and his eyes more sunken then he had recalled. He also saw Kasparov's hair for the first time. It was now mostly gray.

"Open your cello," Kasparov commanded. "You will play something somber."

Heinrich did as he was instructed. If his colleagues heard anything, they would just assume that he was practicing. Heinrich had the sudden sensation that Kasparov would shoot him while he played, likely in that same right arm that Kasparov had lost. Heinrich suddenly became slower as he lifted his cello and bow up.

"Hurry up," Kasparov directed.

Heinrich closed his eyes and began playing. He thought to himself, *Maybe Kasparov will take my life outright.*

Kasparov began speaking. "Last time you played for me, I was able to join you in a duet."

Heinrich remembered the incident, and his heart started to beat faster. His nervousness made him drop the bow. Heinrich remained stiff.

"Pick it up!" Kasparov screamed.

As he bent down, Heinrich couldn't contain himself any longer.

"I didn't issue the command to have you shot."

"SHUT UP!" Kasparov cried. Heinrich sensed the anxiety and tension in his voice. He didn't hear the steely resolve that he would have expected. This was not the sound of a cold, calculating murderer. Here was the nervousness of a man doing something that was against his constitution or will.

Heinrich felt emboldened and seized upon the opportunity. "No, it is true. It was an accident. The soldier who shot you was not aware of what we were doing. He thought he was protecting me."

"You betrayed the sanctity of music," Kasparov shouted. His tone was slighter lower, spiked with intermittent crackling sounds, highlighting his unease.

"I didn't. I was there in the same fellowship of man that brought you there," Heinrich insisted.

"This is the result of your actions." Kasparov took off his coat, threw it in Heinrich's direction, and showed his stump to Heinrich.

"I am deeply sorry about that. I never wanted you to lose your arm."

"I haven't been able to hold a violin. How do I join you in a duet today?" Kasparov screamed.

"I know," Heinrich said in a resigned tone.

Kasparov lifted the gun towards Heinrich's head again. Heinrich saw how it trembled now.

"My father died in order for me to have that violin," Kasparov informed him. He was becoming emotional. Heinrich detected another series of quivers in his voice. Heinrich thought quickly.

"If you truly are a lover of music, then you won't kill me," Heinrich said.

"Why shouldn't I?" Kasparov's voice was suddenly more firm.

"I can help you," Heinrich's voice was suddenly less firm.

Kasparov didn't seem impressed. He moved closer to Heinrich. Heinrich heard the sound of the gun cock.

"Let me teach you to play an instrument with one hand," Heinrich pleaded.

● ● ●

It was ten o'clock at night when Gerda picked up the phone. Gerda could tell that Heinrich was not well.

"What's wrong? Are you still in Moscow?" Gerda asked him, frantic.

"Get Manfred on the phone right away," Heinrich boomed into the telephone.

Gerda thought to protest and demand that he answer her

245

questions. Confused and worried, she shouted for Manfred.

"Find out what's wrong," Gerda kept saying to Manfred. She was getting increasingly more anxious. Why wouldn't her brother talk to her? He always talked to her. She suddenly feared that maybe there was something he couldn't tell her.

"Find out what's wrong," she told Manfred again. Manfred put his hand up, requesting her to stop.

"I think it is possible," Manfred said into the phone after several minutes. Gerda's head was swimming.

"What is possible?" she asked.

"Let me come up with some designs," Manfred said.

"Designs for what?" Gerda was growing impatient.

"Who will make it?" Manfred enquired. Gerda saw him hold his hand up again to deter her from asking a question.

"Oh, you have the person. I'll just design it then," Manfred said.

After he hung up the phone, Manfred turned to Gerda.

"Heinrich wants me to design a trumpet that can be played with one hand," Manfred stated.

● ● ●

"I don't know if I can do it," Ram said to Heinrich.

"You have the best masters of brass workmanship at your disposal," Heinrich insisted. "I know you can make it."

"What if it doesn't produce the right sound?"

"You leave that to me," said Heinrich. "I will help you tweak it to be sure that it will produce the right sound."

"I just don't want to disappoint you," Ram said, distraught and nervous about taking on the assignment.

"Whether you make idols of gods or musical instruments, aren't both paths to honoring the divine?" Heinrich asked. "Isn't this what Hinduism teaches?"

Ram smiled to himself. He had a very clever friend, he decided. One who was as persuasive as he was intelligent.

● ● ●

VIRTUOSO

Heinrich traveled to Moscow again. He had three cases with him, one for his clothes and the other two for a contraption that had arrived from India a few weeks earlier. He did something he never thought he would do. He invited Kasparov to his hotel room.

Kasparov arrived without his uniform. Kasparov put on a shoulder harness over both shoulders that had small-diameter metal rods emanating from them to hold the trumpet in place. The three fingers of his left hand could manipulate the three valves. The trumpet had also been rigged so that the smallest finger and the thumb could operate buttons that would cause the two outer valves to move up and down.

"Learning how to play this will be an enormous challenge," Heinrich conceded, "but I am convinced that you can do it. I will help you."

"Ten years ago, I would have shot you on sight," Kasparov admitted, a bit of a smirk on his face.

"It is a good thing we never met until we did," Heinrich quipped. He was relieved when Kasparov laughed with him.

"We can call it the Magic Trumpet. Mozart would be proud," Heinrich declared.

● ● ●

Kasparov went to Germany to live for several months that year. He lived with Heinrich.

"After keeping you under surveillance for so many years, Herr Majowski, it is a wonder that we are in the same room together, meeting as friends," Kasparov declared.

"It is the power of music," Heinrich said.

With the help of Heinrich and the trumpet section of the Berlin Philharmonic, Kasparov learned to master the trumpet. Being able to play an instrument again made him feel complete. He was relieved. His daughter's death had made him softer; he no longer had his edge. This display of kindness overwhelmed him.

He felt remorse for taking the doctor's and the nurse's life.

● ● ●

Heinrich sensed Gerda's unease about the arrangement.

"How do you know that he won't still seek his revenge?" Gerda questioned.

"I don't know that," Heinrich responded flippantly.

"That's not funny!" Gerda shouted.

"I know," Heinrich admitted. "But it is the reality."

"I need to do this," Heinrich said, trying to explain to Gerda so that she would understand.

●　●　●

In 1977 when Manfred and Gerda went to Berlin, Heinrich was delayed in making it back to the city after the concerts in Salzburg. He called Manfred.

"I have a friend from India who is visiting his son and newly born grandson," Heinrich said. "He is heading back to India, and I won't have a chance to see him—can you meet him?"

Manfred and Gerda, who were always overjoyed to spend time with children, eagerly met with Ram and Ram's grandson, Aseem. Later that year, the young boy would move with his parents to the US. Amongst the people they knew, they now had a place to visit in Connecticut.

Gerda marveled when she saw the young boy. "Father would have been 100 years old now."

Gerda and Manfred doted on the boy quite a bit. They bought him several toys, books and clothes. The boy was very comfortable in Gerda's arms. Gerda would always comment, "There is something special about the way he is looking at me."

As they were never able to have their own children, Manfred and Gerda would always freely adopt other children.

"There is something very unique about him," Gerda would insist to Manfred.

They extended their stay in Berlin by two weeks. Every day they went to see the boy. They began bringing records of music— mostly Karajan's recordings. They were amazed at how the boy reacted so exuberantly to the music. He was so engaged by it and thrilled to have it playing. He would cry when they left or when the music was turned off. Gerda and Manfred were really taken by the manner in which the boy reacted to music. For them it was a revelation that he could appreciate and be moved by music at such a young age.

CHAPTER XIX

Ram was flying back to Bombay after being in Berlin for a few weeks. He had enjoyed visiting with his son and grandson. As he boarded the aircraft, he noticed an attendant with the last name "Majowski."

"I have a good friend with the last name Majowski," Ram said, "Is it a common name in Germany?"

"Well, actually, the origin is Polish," Sabine replied.

"I didn't know that," Ram said.

"And I actually do not know if it is common or not," Sabine lamented.

"Well, my friend's first name is Heinrich," Ram said.

"You mean, Heinrich Majowski? Of the Berlin Philharmonic?" Sabine asked in an excited tone.

"Why, yes, are you related to him?" Ram asked.

"He is my father!"

"What an amazing coincidence!" Ram said, now becoming equally excited. "I have been meaning to write to Heinrich, but I have not had a chance to," Ram said. "I wasn't able to see him during this visit to Berlin. I did however, meet his sister and brother-in-law, Gerda and Manfred Ziemer."

"That is my aunt and uncle!" Sabine exclaimed. "I could pass a letter on to my father if you would like," she offered.

"That would be wonderful. I shall work on it during the flight."

Ram wrote to Heinrich about his desire to resurrect an opera called Shakuntala. It was based on the story of an Indian princess. Schubert had been working on it prior to his death. Ram's earlier attempts to resurrect it did not work as his friend John Foulds had passed away.

●●●

Seth continued to exchange letters with Miyako. In the early stages, she would rely on the simplest of English, and Seth was required to adhere to that as well, if he wanted Miyako to be able to understand him. Over time, as her command of the language increased, Seth was able to write to her in a manner that he was more accustomed to. She had done well for herself, prospering in her musical career. She had followed in her father's footsteps and was able to join the NHK Symphony Orchestra.

In 1981, Seth began to travel the world as a part of the Bavarian Radio Symphony Orchestra. He was excited when he was able to come to New York. He stayed with Manfred and Gerda at the time.

They were always excited to interact with young people, so they welcomed him with open arms. It was particularly exciting for them that he had developed as a concert cellist.

Seth was really impressed by the US when he visited. After that initial visit, he made numerous attempts to join an orchestra in the US. His efforts were rewarded, and he earned a seat at the New York Philharmonic.

While he was living there, Miyako came to visit him. He accompanied her to California where Miyako met with her father's family who had been in internment camps during the war. The two of them then went to see Gerda and Manfred together.

Miyako fell in love with Manfred and Gerda's garden.

"It is so beautiful," she exclaimed.

"We have many Japanese themes in the garden," Gerda said.

"We have always been fascinated with Japanese gardens," Manfred admitted. "We made this Japanese peasant gate based on a book I bought that had the imperial gardens at Kyoto."

He brought the book out to show Miyako and Seth the pictures that had inspired him.

Gerda showed the four Japanese characters, each representing a season, that they had on display near the sitting bench.

"We received those from our neighbor," Gerda mentioned. "They know how much we appreciate gardening and the Japanese art of gardening."

Seth commented on the Buddha's head in the garden. "There is a strong Asian theme here."

"Did you see the full Buddha statue in the front lawn?" Manfred asked.

They all walked to the front of the house to witness the full Buddha that was seated there.

Seth and Miyako spent four days with Manfred and Gerda. They enjoyed the visit immensely. As a desire to show their appreciation, they played a duet for them. They started with the first duet they had ever played when they first met in Tokyo, over ten years earlier. They then played one of Dvorak's cello concertos, which the two had modified to function as a duet.

● ● ●

Ram's communication with Heinrich continued, as did his conversations with Karajan. Heinrich had informed Ram that he was seeking a copy of the opera Shakuntala. Heinrich was able to learn that Schubert never completed it. He also learned that an Italian composer, Franco Alfano, had written a version of his own which he debuted in 1921 and again in 1952, since the original version had been lost when it was destroyed during bombings by the Allies. The publisher of the piece, a company called Recordi, had all of its records destroyed. He had gone to Italy to see the Alfano version. Feliz Weingarten had also written a version in the late 1800s. Ram was attempting to stage a production of it in India and thought he would solicit the help of his European associates involved with music in order to achieve that vision.

"This would be a great way to introduce the Western tradition of opera in India," Ram mused. He made this an objective of his. He lamented how although there were several Asians who had achieved fame in Western music, Western music did not have much of a following in Asia outside of certain regions.

"Japan has a strong following, no doubt because of Seiji Ozawa and his success," Ram reasoned. "We have had Zubin

Mehta achieve similar prominence," he added, "yet few orchestras tour through India. I wish to bring them to Bombay."

The staging of Sakuntala never materialized for him, though, at least not with the assistance of Karajan or Heinrich. He was able to pursue it being performed several times for Italian radio during the 1950s, 1960s and 1970s. It was also performed once in Ireland at the Wexford Opera Festival in 1982.

The original version had been written in the fifth century BC by Kalidas under the name *Abhignanashakuntala*.

Heinrich tried to make some contact with colleagues in Italy. He was not having any success.

He told Gerda of his problem, who shared it with Manfred.

"I wonder if my old friend Torsten can help? I haven't spoken with him in years," Manfred wondered aloud.

● ● ●

The grounds of the company where Gerda worked were always cramped for space. The facility did not have much room available to it. Some in the company wanted to demolish the space where Gerda kept her cabinets of information regarding the various dyes. She told them that if they were to do that, she would leave. The day after Gerda retired, the building came down. They had waited until she left.

Gerda spent thirty years working with them. She worked until she was seventy, during a time when most would retire by sixty-two.

● ● ●

Manfred worked at his initial job for several years. When he was sixty, the company was sold to another group. Manfred did not get along with the new owners. They did not have an appreciation for all that he had done for the company over the years. Other individuals with the company's customers who had loved him in the past had mostly retired, replaced with newer people who were not as familiar with Manfred and what he had done for their businesses as well. The new owners asked Manfred to go. Manfred was crushed by their decision.

"I can't believe they don't see the value I could continue to add," Manfred lamented to Gerda.

Manfred also was not ready to retire. He wanted to keep working. He felt like he needed the income. Sitting at home for him was also a new experience that he had not prepared himself for mentally. He was depressed most of the time. He threw himself back into music, developing his collection and attempting to fill his days by enjoying listening to music. However, it was not enough for him.

Eventually, due to luck and perseverance, Manfred was able to secure a new job with a new company. A local manufacturing plant was seeking someone to manage their tool shed. Based on Manfred's experience, he thought he could manage that well. He thrived in that job.

● ● ●

One day in 1984 Manfred received a note in the mail.

> Manfred, it has been too many a year,
> You had me in a state where I began to fear,
> I thought a final resting spot you had made,
> But your memory for me never did fade.

> I know the performance and I think I can convince my production company to perform it.

> Your good friend, Torsten.

● ● ●

Ram booked his flight to Italy in 1985. He traveled to Milan. It was a stunning performance of Shakuntala. One of many goals articulated in a lifetime had been achieved. He had a thought on his flight home that Milan, which also means "coming together" in Hindi, would have been a nice name for one of his grandsons.

He passed away later that year.

VIRTUOSO

● ● ●

Heinrich stayed in close touch with Sabine who had been living in New York for several years. Sabine reported to him how she enjoyed her time there and met many people from all walks of life. By 1987 she was interested in settling down, but nobody that she met was interested in having a family. On Heinrich's suggestion, she got herself a dog, a tiny dachshund. As she was playing with him in the park, her dog swallowed a tennis ball. She took him to the vet. One of the people helping there was a man by the name of Steve Diller. While surgery was being performed on the dog, Steve comforted Sabine. The surgery lasted a long time. Steve and Sabine talked and talked and talked. After Sabine left with her dog, Steve called and checked in on how the dog was doing. From there began a courtship.

After several months, Sabine called her father. "I've made my decision, I want to spend the rest of my life with him." Heinrich was elated. He couldn't be happier. He thought he deserved credit for it, since it was his suggestion to buy the dog.

Steve was of Jewish descent. His father had actually suffered through the torture of being in a concentration camp. He was receiving reparations from the German government.

When Heinrich heard about what had happened to Steve's father, he was intrigued. When Heinrich came to the US, he brought with him the handkerchief he had received over forty years earlier. When he presented it to David Diller, Steve's father, both stood in silent shock and awe. They then embraced. Now their children would be married to each other. It gave Heinrich hope that eventually the world worked the way it needed to.

The wedding was held in Gerda and Manfred's backyard, where they had established a beautiful garden.

At the wedding, Sabine and her husband Steve presented Gerda and Manfred with two Star of David pendants. They proudly put then on the chains that they wore around their necks.

There was a debate for months about the music that would

be played at the wedding. Everybody had their opinions about how the music portion should be staged and what should be played.

"I want a large orchestra," Heinrich cried. "This is my little girl's wedding!"

"How am I going to fit all of those musicians in my garden!" Gerda retorted.

"Pull out some flowers!" Heinrich insisted, smiling to himself because he knew what kind of response that would evoke out of Gerda.

"Boy, I'll get you!" Gerda shouted.

In the end it was decided to have a string quartet—well suited as this would be a small gathering of the closest family and friends.

Heinrich insisted on meeting with the group of local musicians ahead of time and rehearsing whatever pieces he was going to have them play. They actually benefited tremendously from Heinrich's instruction. Two days before the wedding, however, Heinrich changed his mind.

"It just doesn't feel right," he complained. "They are good, but they are not excellent, like the musicians I know."

Heinrich's solution was to have four musicians whom he considered to be the best in the Berlin Philharmonic fly in from Berlin for the wedding. They arrived at Gerda's house with their instruments. Unfortunately, they had none of their baggage. Their luggage had not made the flight. They had taken their instruments on the flight with them, so they had those.

Heinrich shared the story with the wedding attendees. All had a good laugh and enjoyed the irony of having some of the world's best musicians perform at a wedding wearing informal attire.

"Ultimately, it is about the music," Heinrich declared.

All in attendance agreed.

● ● ●

Within two years of Sabine getting married, Heinrich's lifelong confidante, Herbert von Karajan, passed away in July 1989.

VIRTUOSO

He died within months of retiring from the orchestra. Everyone knew that had he left the orchestra any time sooner, he would have gone earlier. It was his lifeblood. It kept him going.

Within months, the Berlin Wall came crumbling down; a united Germany was around the corner.

Immediately following the fall of the wall, Daniel Barenboim led a concert of the Berlin Philharmonic. Beethoven was chosen to commemorate the event. It was billed as a welcome to the visitors from East Germany. Beethoven's Piano Concerto Number 1 and his Seventh Symphony were performed. It was a bittersweet moment for most of the orchestra, as they had just said goodbye to Karajan a few months earlier.

"How he would have loved to lead such a seminal event," the orchestra stated.

Instead of Karajan leading another set of celebrations, the pinnacle of the festivities, on December 25, 1989, Leonard Bernstein had to lead an Orchestra that performed Beethoven's Ninth Symphony. Instead of the words "Joy (*Freude*)" from "Ode to Joy," the word "Freedom *(Freiheit)*" was used.

The Orchestra was comprised of leading musicians throughout Europe. Seth performed as well. Bernstein asked him to join. He was able to see his mother, Heidi.

Gerda and Manfred traveled to Berlin for the event. They ceremoniously stood at the Brandenburg Gate in Berlin on the Westside. They had pre-arranged to meet their long-lost good friend. As they stood there in anticipation, they watched as Herman appeared from the other side. They were overjoyed to see him.

A person walked through the Brandenburg Gate with Herman. It was a one-armed man. Gerda and Manfred were shocked to learn that it was General Kasparov. "Thank you for an excellent instrument," Kasparov said to Manfred.

"Well, you are most welcome," was all that Manfred could think to say.

Gerda was still not facing him. She did not know what she

could say.

"Perhaps she needs more time," Manfred said.

All focused on the festivities around them. There was so much jubilation and cheer. People were embracing everywhere. In all corners, the story was the same—only the characters were different. Old friends, estranged family members, compatriots, all who had survived the artificial partition placed between them, came together once again.

Politics had succumbed to the human spirit.

There was no better way to commemorate the occasion but through the use of music. Several street performers were present. They played all kinds of music. There were solo violinists, solo cellists. Out of the Hotel Adlon came a piano performance, there were guitarists, there were jazz players. All chose their own means but the spirit was universal.

The highlight of the festivities, of course, was the Bernstein event. At the concert both Manfred and Gerda reflected on the fact that it had been forty years earlier when they had seen Celibidache perform in a soul-healing performance. Now, Bernstein led an orchestra with the same piece of music that was a celebration of unity. They had come full circle.

Gerda felt the time had come. She turned to Kasparov.

"I can't understand why you pursued my brother, my father, and me the way that you did. How could you hate that much? What was your motivation?" she demanded.

"Imagine where you would be without music," was Kasparov's reply.

Gerda had a flashback, from over forty years earlier, walking through the streets of Berlin and asking herself that same question.

She understood.

● ● ●

At the time of Karajan's death, Heinrich spoke to Gerda on the telephone.

"Something is on your mind, you are not yourself," Gerda

said.

"I want you to listen to something," requested Heinrich.

Heinrich positioned the phone close to the cello. He played a very somber, sad tune.

When he was done he picked up the phone and said to Gerda, "When you leave music, you leave life."

Gerda thought about how Heinrich had announced his retirement several months before Karajan retired. Gerda knew what her brother was thinking.

"You haven't left music, Heinrich, you will continue to play," Gerda pleaded.

He ended the conversation with a pithy comment. "I am next, my dear sister."

Gerda shuddered at the thought, but not as violently as she shuddered nine months later when Heinrich's prophecy proved to be true. Heinrich was gone.

Gerda's devastation could not be measured in words. She had difficulty speaking of it. She mostly cried. When people asked, she would open her mouth and try to talk. She would fumble through some words and then finally admit defeat. "I can't find the words!"

Of those surviving siblings, all were aware just how badly Gerda would take the news. She could not function for days. All hugged her closely when they were with her. When she got back to the US she would play recordings from her brother and sit in a quiet room and listen. She would recall his comment at the time of Father's passing. She would turn to Manfred and say, "Sometimes it is better to let the music do the talking."

Every year on his birthday, Gerda would make a tradition of watching the video of his last performance. Over the years she had collected each one of the published recordings available of her brother. Her life from then on would always be devoted in part to honoring him. When guests would come, they would watch a performance, and she would beam with pride when she identified the cellist that was her brother.

Heinrich's view about life and music would be proven true yet again. Bernstein would also not survive much longer. He would pass away in October 1990, five days after retiring himself.

"Within a short period of time, three of the brightest lights of classical music have left us," Manfred commented to Gerda.

"We are in the dark ages again," responded Gerda. "Thankfully the tradition will live on, largely because of their efforts to portray and preserve for the world's benefit the glory and the gift that is music," Gerda said. "We shall miss them terribly."

While composing a musical work for all those who had passed away would have been an ideal dream for Gerda, she realized her ambition in another way—she planted a pine tree in her backyard for each member of the family and for each musician, conductor or composer who had touched her life who was no longer with her.

"Now they are all with me," Gerda said as she looked out over her garden. She found herself talking to trees again.

CHAPTER XX

After Heinrich's passing, Gerda began to experience a precipitous decline in her health and physical well-being. Wilfred and Sylva had passed away years before Heinrich. It was only her, Mia and Ernest.

Mia and Gerda began in earnest to build on the bond they had forged early on in their lives to try to assist each other and be supportive of each other. Mia grew even closer to Gerda and Manfred during that time. Mia had been lonely for several years. After her daughter's death and her husband passing away, Mia had few people with whom she interacted. She would live for the daily phone calls to Gerda and Manfred and wait patiently for their visits to her. It became hard for her to travel, so she was not able to come to the US. She was earning a generous pension, much more than what she needed to sustain her life, so she ended up saving most of it. She tried to help out with Manfred and Gerda on the costs of their visiting her, since she was not able to visit them.

During the last several years of Mia's life, Gerda and Manfred made an annual pilgrimage to visit with Mia in the Black Forrest. They would spend two to three months with her and then come back to the US. Both sides looked forward to the visits. Gerda and Manfred were also able to visit with Ernest while there, as he lived within a five-minute walk to Mia's house.

They spoke with her on a daily basis. Ending the phone conversation took several minutes as neither side wished to hang up. Both would continue to express their love and concern for the other. It was a volley of well-wishing that became a chorus. It didn't matter which side would start; the other would be sure to reciprocate.

"Love You!" one side would say.

"Bye!" the other would say.

"Talk to you soon!" came the response.

"Sleep well, my little darling!" was the retort.

"Bye!" was repeated.

"We look forward to seeing you!" was offered.

This went on for several minutes at a time. There was no desire to end the conversation. There only existed the realization that the conversation could not continue forever and they eventually had to succumb to hanging up.

Over time, Ernest's son Klaus re-entered Mia's life. She had taken pains in her younger years to have influence on this young man and be pro-active in raising him. She even assisted him by loaning him one hundred thousand deutschemarks to finance the building of a gas station. Unfortunately, he had chosen unwisely the location of the gas station, and it did not last. Mia attempted to go after him with a lawsuit, but she was never able to retrieve any of the money. It was under the pretenses of the earlier relationship and bond that he became close to her again with his family. He cried out for her, calling her "Mother!" Witnesses sensed that it was a case of manipulation, but they never spoke out against it. Mia was old at the time of their re-connection, and most people were pleased that she would have some people with whom she could interact on a regular basis. He even convinced her to move in with him and his family.

Initially, Gerda and Manfred hailed this as a triumph. Gerda was so happy for her sister that she had some life surrounding her rather than her being all by herself.

After she moved in with them, however, she became more frail and began falling ill more frequently. Gerda called her often, but she noticed a strange strain in her voice.

"Will you ever forgive me?" Mia asked.

Gerda was confused. "What are you talking about?"

"Just answer me, will you forgive me?" Mia pleaded.

"Of course," said Gerda, desiring only to placate her sister and to calm her.

At the time of Mia's passing, it became clear why she had been asking Gerda such strange questions. Gerda and Manfred, whom Mia had always told would have whatever money she had saved, had been excluded from Mia's will, and all the money had been taken by the nephew.

Gerda and Manfred ceased speaking with Klaus. Shortly after this incident Ernest, Klaus's father, passed away. Ernest had been close to Gerda, but was always absorbed and engaged with his work. He traveled throughout the world as a visiting composer and professor. He composed numerous works that had more of a modern feel to the music.

Distress came to Gerda and Manfred later as well. In conversations with Mia's friends who lived near to her and in conversations with Mia's doctor, they came to learn that Mia had not in fact looked forward to seeing them every year. Gerda was deeply troubled to learn this. For well over a decade, she had sacrificed her own health to be with her sister. Gerda could only reason through it that Mia held a resentment from youth that Gerda was the natural caretaker in the family. She had been there for Mother and wanted to be there for Father. Now Mia saw Gerda taking on that same caretaker role with her, and she did not like it.

● ● ●

The eyes that had helped woo her husband, that presented to the world her fighter's temperament, and that had made her indispensable at her work, were now half functioning.

Manfred broke the news to her. "It's your eyes, Gerda. You are going blind in one of them."

Other parts of her body had begun to malfunction. She had been fighting a multi-year battle with rheumatoid arthritis. Her joints were buckling, and her hands had lost their natural shape. She also needed to have a pacemaker installed. All of those close to her knew that she would not have made it if it were not for the strength of her mental resolve to get through whatever life threw at her. That and music. Others would have given up much sooner. She fought on.

It was the same for Manfred. He fought on as well. He had

a bout with prostate cancer, but made it through that. He suffered with his hands, but had procedures to fix that. His back was beginning to give way, and it was hard for him to walk without stooping.

In recalling events together, they would begin to remember events in their lives based on its temporal relationship to a concert. Some birthday party was a month before Bernstein performed Mahler's Ninth Symphony, some visit by a family member was days after Boulez presented Shostakovich, and someone had a child during Mehta's rendition of Ravel's Bolero. Markers for their memory became the concerts that filled their lives.

Because of their affiliation with Heinrich, they were able to get personal access to the likes of Bernstein and John Levine, the musical director at the Metropolitan Opera. All they had to do was mention the word Majowski, and they were instantly given the red carpet treatment. They also became close to individual performers in the music world: Anna-Sophie Mutter, a violinist, Sherrill Milnes, a tenor, Isaac Stern, another violinist, and several others. These artists would begin to contact them directly whenever they were in New York to ensure that Manfred and Gerda were able to make it to see them.

The Berlin Philharmonic had reached its zenith during the Sixties, Seventies and Eighties, under the leadership of Herbert von Karajan. There were numerous recordings for audio and video that were done at the time. The Orchestra was also touring around the world frequently. This made the Berlin Philharmonic famous the world over.

"At least I can still hear," Gerda would tell her friends.

"Without music…" Gerda's voice trailed off. She couldn't finish the sentence.

● ● ●

Ram's grandson lived first in New York and then in Los Angeles. He visited Gerda and Manfred quite often and they became very close. Every time they got together, they would have extensive discussions on music. Like his grandfather Ram, Aseem was a huge fan of classical music. Gerda and Manfred helped expand that love and recognition.

After Aseem and his family moved to the US, Gerda and Manfred interacted with him often. The parents would drive to Gerda and Manfred's home, and Gerda and Manfred would also make trips to see Aseem. It was because of them that later in life Aseem would take on the violin and the clarinet as musical instruments. And it was because of them that Aseem would fantasize about becoming a conductor. It would never come to pass that he would lead an orchestra, but there never was a better opportunity for him to develop the exposure to music than through Gerda and Manfred. They both assumed personal responsibility for his musical education. They continuously sent musical instruments and sponsored musical lessons for him, as he lived too far away for them to provide it directly. When they got together there would be ample sharing about their joy and love of music. When Aseem grew old enough, he would bring works of his own interest to their attention. Pieces that they had not considered before were brought to their attention.

"If we had a son, we'd like him to be just like you," said Gerda and Manfred to Aseem one day. And so it became that they had their son.

Their son had a daughter. At the time, Gerda was suffering immensely with her eyes. Aseem gave his daughter the name Naina, which means 'eyes' in Sanskrit, the predecessor language of Hindi.

With frail, disfigured hands, Gerda would hold her granddaughter. "There is something unique about her eyes and the way she is looking at me," Gerda would say.

Sometimes perfect vision is not needed to see beauty.

Naina would hold her close. She would dance and frolic about to the music that Gerda had playing. Barely a year old, she not only walked, but she had the intuition to hold her arms up to the sky and twirl herself around.

Gerda attempted to feed her some food.

Naina resisted.

Gerda persisted.

Naina resisted.

Gerda persisted.

Naina grabbed the bowl and turned it upside down over Gerda's head.

Gerda's first reaction was indignation. *Oh no*, thought Manfred. *She is going to spank that child. Where is Aseem?* thought Manfred.

When Gerda saw Naina, with her arm extended and index finger pointed straight at her in a scolding motion, she laughed heartily. She wouldn't stop after several seconds had passed.

Manfred became concerned, "Gerda, are you alright?"

"She is just like me."